"An absolutely gorgeous novel, taut as a thriller, lovely as a watercolor, poetically incisive and wry. I devoured this book and was heartbroken when it was over. Ledia Xhoga is a great and visionary writer whose career I will follow eagerly in decades to come." —JENNIFER CROFT, author of *The Extinction of Irena Rey*

"Ledia Xhoga is a superb chronicler of post-national existence, of a narrator shifting between disparate views of reality depending on what language she's speaking and with whom. Deft and insightful, *Misinterpretation* reveals the disorienting process of making choices in one language and then questioning them in another. This is a moving, exceptional first novel." —IDRA NOVEY, author of *Take What You Need*

"Ledia Xhoga's novel about a woman whose life is on the brink of unraveling because of her good intentions explores the complexity of translating our own trauma, even to the people we love. With lyrical prose and a propulsive plot, Xhoga delves deep into the shadows of the human psyche, challenging readers to confront the darker legacies of the past while pondering the delicate balance between empathy and self-preservation. Ledia Xhoga has crafted a literary masterpiece that is as profound as it is unforgettable, solidifying her place as a talent to watch in the world of contemporary fiction." —MAISY CARD, author of *These Ghosts Are Family*

"Ledia Xhoga casts a riveting spell in this novel of an Albanian interpreter whose own shifting reality is as subject to misinterpretation as the words of her clients. A stunning debut."

—ELIZABETH GAFFNEY,
author of *When the World Was Young*

"If in the twenty-first-century Kafka had moved from Prague to Brooklyn, *Misinterpretation* is the novel I believe he would have written. Instead, Ledia Xhoga wrote it. She captures a corollary world to the one Josef K. inhabits in *The Castle*, but rather than not being able to reach the castle, Xhoga's nameless protagonist finds herself living in the castle, a polyglot culture in which everyone misinterprets what everyone else says and does; some residents even misinterpret their own emotions. Xhoga interprets our brave, new multicultural world with a sly, benign wit. Read her novel. You'll be glad you did."

—TOM GRIMES,
author of *Mentor*

# MISINTERPRETATION

# MISINTERPRETATION

A NOVEL

## LEDIA XHOGA

TIN HOUSE
PORTLAND, OREGON

First US Edition 2024
Printed in the United States of America

Manufacturing by Sheridan
Interior design by Beth Steidle

Library of Congress Cataloging-in-Publication Data

Names: Xhoga, Ledia, author.
Title: Misinterpretation : a novel / Ledia Xhoga.
Description: First US edition. | Portland, Oregon : Tin House, 2024.
Identifiers: LCCN 2024014812 | ISBN 9781959030805 (paperback) |
ISBN 9781959030881 (ebook)
Subjects: LCGFT: Psychological fiction. | Novels.
Classification: LCC PS3624.H64 M57 2024 | DDC 813/.6—dc23/eng/20240402
LC record available at https://lccn.loc.gov/2024014812

Tin House
2617 NW Thurman Street, Portland, OR 97210
www.tinhouse.com

DISTRIBUTED BY W. W. NORTON & COMPANY

1 2 3 4 5 6 7 8 9 0

*For A. and M.*

*Not for ourselves alone are we born.*

—CICERO

# MISINTERPRETATION

# 1.

I WAS FIFTEEN MINUTES LATE AND HIS PHONE NUMBER was out of service.

Even in late January, Washington Square Park pulsed with the energy of summer. The chess players were fretting over their moves to the sound of Gershwin. The saxophonist's Great Dane was pining for the dog run. It was Alfred who had suggested meeting here, next to the statute of Garibaldi, a name that brought to mind fragmented pieces of Italy glued together. It was an old mnemonic from high school; Garibaldi was responsible for Italy's unification.

But Alfred was nowhere to be seen. Two men on a nearby bench didn't match his description. He'd be alone. The agency sent photo attachments, which I rarely bothered opening. It was easy to recognize my clients from the look of expectancy, the humble bearing, the wear and tear that showed on their faces and bodies. That his phone was out of service was odd. Had they sent me the wrong phone number? The sound of footsteps. A toddler with squeaky shoes bumped into me, followed by her father and an excessive apology. Two boys holding a minidrone scurried toward the empty fountain. An elderly man was checking his watch. Could he be Alfred? He was far from the statue. Had he given up on waiting for me at our meeting spot? The man looked in his sixties. According to his file, Alfred was only in his early forties, just a few years older than me. Was it his preoccupation with his watch that made him look older? He hunched over it the same way my grandfather used to while winding up his Volna, a watch he'd bought in Moscow in the fifties. I walked toward him. Where was his phone, anyway?

"Alfred?" I said, relieved that I managed to put the accent on the second vowel, the Albanian way. "I'm sorry for being late."

He straightened his back and waved his arm forgivingly. He did look younger from up close. His face seemed stuck in between expressions. It reminded me of an unfinished Rubik's Cube we kept around the house, which I could never resist trying to solve.

"I was worried you were waiting somewhere else," he said, rubbing his sunken eyes. "I saw another woman over there and thought it was you."

"Is your phone out of service?"

"It stopped working this morning. I don't know why."

"Is your dentist around here? Shouldn't we get going?"

His answer sounded muddled. The translation agency that employed me had been sending Kosovar Albanians my way. Their accent was different from mine. It took me a few seconds to get used to it, for me to understand the words immediately. We walked under the Arch and headed toward the street. I was hoping the dentist would still be willing to see him—we were late for our 6:00 PM appointment. While looking for their number on my phone, I felt a tug on my arm. Alfred was holding on to my elbow.

"Be careful."

An SUV had run a red light. It was speeding away now, only a few steps from us. That he was a survivor of torture flashed in my mind again. I didn't know what kind of torture it had been and was not allowed to ask for details. When his hand slid down my arm, the goose bumps surprised me.

The dentist was only a ten-minute walk from the park. We walked there silently and at some distance from each other, like a couple who had just quarreled. In no time at all, we were filling out paperwork. *On a scale of 1 to 10, with 10 being the highest rating, how would you rate your dental health? On a scale of 1 to 10, with 10 being the highest rating, where would you like your dental health to be?* The questions struck Alfred as ridiculous. He opened his eyes incredulously and shook his head in disbelief. He then jutted his chin toward the papers, giving me full power of attorney over his dental history. Judging from his reaction, I opted for the lower numbers. He nodded in approval. Still hoping that some questions might resonate with him, I kept reading aloud.

"Do you brush your teeth in the morning or at night? Or both?"

He was indifferent, eager to dismiss such useless formalities to deal with a toothache that had kept him up all night. He gave a deep sigh as if to say, *It's true that my dental hygiene and genetics have contributed to the state of my teeth, but do they need every single detail?* Realizing there were many more pages to go through—the pile on my lap did look intimidating—he glanced around with doubt. What kind of dentist would make us do all this?

"What would you change about your smile?" I asked.

The answer consisted of several options. I had trouble interpreting the last one. *Smile makeover.*

"Smile transformation," I fumbled. "Changing your smile completely."

"Pick that one," Alfred said without hesitation.

It was the only answer that he chose on his own. Afterward, he smiled, which frightened me. His features widened but didn't soften, as if he were smiling against his will. He had chosen the right option after all.

"Are you ready, lovebirds?" said the receptionist, who looked tired and was massaging her shoulder.

When we stood up, she smiled in a forced way, like Alfred had earlier. *Show less gum,* one of the options from before, sprang to mind. She didn't ask about insurance or payment information. We were an after-hours charity case. She led him to the back, ignoring me. She didn't find me necessary now. The dentist would have his answers by looking at Alfred's teeth, presumably, or at the paperwork I had completed. Waiting around random offices was the least favorite part of my assignments. Not knowing what to do, I sat back down. In the aquarium tank to my left there were no fish but several odd creatures; they were translucent with a hint of hazy gray, and long antennas.

"They're ghost shrimp," said a young woman sitting on the other side of the aquarium. I hadn't noticed her till she spoke. "When they're about to die, they turn white."

She pressed her finger to the glass, pointing at a half-white creature. "He's on his way out."

She wore soft curls under an olive beret and a velveteen cape jacket in chartreuse. A long skirt of a faded material hid her knees and feet. Her appearance clashed with the bland surroundings. I had the impression that, in some mix-up of fact and fiction, she had stepped out of one of those thirties films my husband was always watching. Finding the office underwhelming, she had then zeroed in on the underwater world of the aquarium.

"It's kind of creepy," she said and pouted.

The receptionist tapped me on the shoulder.

"Your husband wants to see you."

"He's not my husband," I said quickly. "I'm only his interpreter."

"Oh, sorry. Could you come in the back?"

The back room was small and crowded with gleaming white machines, rather enormous for repairing such small objects as teeth. Alfred and the dentist were standing motionless to the side of the chair. The dentist looked like a late teen, but she had to be older—she was a practicing graduate student. She kept her hands in her scrubs' pockets and threw puzzled glances at the patient whose language she didn't understand.

"He doesn't want to sit," she told me, her face taut. "Can you please tell him to sit in Armenian?"

"Albanian."

"Yeah."

"What's going on, Alfred?"

"I've never liked these machines."

"It won't last long."

"These machines scare me. My father used to have to force me to sit."

"Look, they'll numb you. It won't hurt."

He didn't move.

"I promise," I said. "They do the work, but you won't feel it. It's amazing."

It took a few seconds, but Alfred did sit down in the end.

"If he's in any pain," said the dentist, "tell him to raise his hand. I will numb him soon."

I explained that to him, but when the drilling started, Alfred did nothing, even though his left hand kept trembling.

In Tirana, when I was a kid, they used to do our fillings and root canals without numbing. The dental office was inside our elementary school. The school dentists were two attractive women, who, in my memories, didn't wear scrubs but blue, flowing dresses. They'd pop in and out of our classroom, calling out our names like Odysseus's mermaids, charming us into an adventure, away from our tedious lessons. It was only later, when the drill touched a nerve and my screams echoed through the school's hallways, that their appeal waned. Despite all that, I had never feared the dentist. Among all types of pain, physical pain was the easiest to forget.

"I'm sorry," said the dental student to Alfred. "I touched a nerve."

Alfred's body slithered on the chair, but he didn't make a peep. Then he sort of shriveled, reminding me of an Albanian expression I hadn't thought of in some time—U bë sa një grusht—*He became small as a fist.*

THERE WAS, AT TIMES, an unnatural intimacy that developed between myself and some of the people I interpreted for. Disclosing personal and confidential information in front of someone played a trick on the brain, making us both believe we were more than acquaintances. But the amount of time we knew each other, and the context of our meeting, didn't justify such closeness. When Alfred's filling was over and we were walking toward the reception desk, he reached for and held my hand. It was an ordinary gesture, a substitute for saying *thank you*, or *thank God, it's finally over.* His hand was chilly. I warmed it with mine. Holding hands with my clients wasn't allowed. Still, when it came to most rules, one had to use judgment.

The vintage girl was still in the reception area. I admired her meticulous makeup, her hairstyle, her unique clothes. How long did it take her to transform herself into a movie star from the thirties? I, too, often longed to escape my ordinary look, to disguise myself behind a colorful façade, or to try out a personality. But it was all a fleeting fantasy. I didn't enjoy making a fuss over my appearance, not even occasionally. I took less time than my husband to get ready. People assumed I was athletic, an erroneous impression suggested by the sporty, no-fuss clothes I preferred. The girl sighed in an exaggerated manner, then twirled her hair. She really did resemble one of the stars in the movies my husband watched.

"Do you speak any English?" I said to Alfred when we were outside.

"Where would I learn it? Everyone around me in the Bronx is Albanian."

We walked back toward Washington Square Park, now at the mercy of a cutting wind. Even from a distance, I could make out the green benches under the hooded lanterns, where Billy and I used to sit many years ago. I hadn't been in that park in years, since we first started dating. As Alfred and I passed the old Hangman's Elm, my younger self flitted away to an alley on Crosby Street, ending at a bar with latticed windows and flickering candles. There used to be a French singer inside, wearing an off-the-shoulder evening gown with a daring front slit. She sang melancholy songs and played an old-school accordion. The most unusual aspect of her attire was a headlight hat she shone over the audience. Was she still there? Was the bar?

"I need an interpreter for my visits at the psychiatrist," Alfred said. "I haven't found anyone I trust."

I hesitated. Sitting through his therapy sessions wouldn't be easy.

"I know we just met," he went on. "But I trust you. I don't trust many people."

Alfred had brown eyes. They were comforting and kind. I had never, till my husband, dated anyone with light eyes. Billy's eyes were green. They could be clear, as a flowing river. At times they were turbulent, with darker shades of hazel.

"I need to talk to someone. I haven't been well."

"I'll do it," I said.

He flashed his smile again. His face was an acquired taste, and I was getting used to it.

"Do you want to get a beer? I know a good place in the Bronx."

It had been a long time since I'd been out alone with a man who wasn't my husband or even with one who was. The past was suddenly at an arm's reach—a casual invitation followed by a feeling of lightness, curiosity.

"I should go home."

Then Alfred shook my hand, thanked me, and left. What would his night be like? He'd take the stairs up to his silent apartment. Open the door in the darkness. Cut vegetables on a wooden board before sliding them into a boiling pot. I saw myself sitting at his table, as his guest. He put on some music. Focused as he was on cooking, he ignored me for a while. He then turned around, refilling my wineglass while fixing me with his gaze.

I walked toward the subway, only then realizing we were going in the same direction. He was a few steps ahead of me. My feet halted, if only momentarily, on his elongated shadow.

OUR ELDERLY NEIGHBOR HELEN, who lived across the hall, entered the elevator barefoot, standing on her tiptoes. For the duration of the ride, she kept one hand on a wooden wall panel and the other on a straw hat topped with a peacock feather. Helen always wore ridiculous hats. It wasn't entirely her fault, for our neighbors humored her by complimenting them. *Cool hat, Helen. Truly unusual.* But what could they do? She'd tell anyone who'd listen that she decorated them herself. Her stance was making me nervous. Standing on her toes while leaning on the wall was an unnatural pose. Would her body crack and break in front of me? We reached the fifth floor without incident. Displaying extraordinary balance, she scampered toward her apartment. But she didn't go in. She waited for me on her doorstep. Then she handed me a flyer from a pile she was carrying. She was inviting me to a Draw and Sip party. The $20 fee included the materials and a cup of wine.

"How was your day?" she asked, her eyes glistening. There was a strange intensity in our simple greetings.

I answered politely and even asked her back the same but didn't stop. Our interactions were unsettling. I didn't know much about her at all, except what other neighbors had told me. She used to be a soap opera actress in the eighties, a fact that had impressed me, even though the writers had killed off her character by the time the show became popular in Albania.

It turned out Billy was home. The hallway was dark, but there were no scattered and mismatched shoes on the floor, a dead giveaway of his presence. He couldn't help picking up my shoes and slippers and tucking them away. My tendency to drop things anywhere except where they belonged had at first startled, then annoyed, then amused him. He still cleaned up after me without complaints, joking at times that growing up in Albania must have conditioned me to get by without household conveniences. It was mostly a matter of temperament.

He was sitting on the sofa in the darkness, watching a black-and-white movie projected onto our wall. A cool white light had spilled onto his face and shoulder, leaving the rest of him in the shadows. The project he was working on, a book of essays about book-to-film adaptations, was giving him an excuse to indulge in the films he loved. He was a film professor at NYU.

It was *Love Affair* he was watching, a 1939 romance film with Irene Dunne and Charles Boyer. The couple were sitting at a bar, aboard a transatlantic ocean liner. In gem-studded jewelry and a black coat dress, Dunne was raising her glass toward the ever-dapper Boyer. They sipped on pink champagne.

Dead people, running around playing house, we had once joked.

"I didn't know you'd be back," I said.

"I texted you in the morning."

I tapped on my inbox. There was his message, saying he was on his way home.

He pressed *forward* until Boyer appeared on the screen alone. In a dark suit, holding his fedora hat, his coat hanging over his arm, he was wandering around an apartment. Then he froze in place. The camera panned to the left, across a mirror showing a painting, then back at his face.

"Look at his reaction," Billy said. "He's realizing she's the woman who bought the painting."

His willingness to pay attention to the unspoken had always impressed me. He was fond of discussing at length the implications of a gesture or the meaning of a smile.

He flipped on the light switch. To our left, the slab of dark walnut that was our dinner table appeared, along with a forgotten plate, and two murky glasses. Behind his curls hovered a Polish circus poster featuring a cartoonish lion soaring through flames.

"Blue suits you," he said, pointing at my blouse. He said that about every color I wore. "Did you work today?"

"I interpreted for a Kosovar Albanian. Took him to the dentist."

He paused the movie. He took off his glasses and cleaned them with his T-shirt. His eyes seemed smaller, but shinier, two pieces of cut green marble.

"Was it a one-time thing?"

"Yes. A one-time thing."

"That's good," he said, nodding. "I'm glad."

He worried needlessly, fearing that my interpreting sessions would wear me out. I turned toward the wall. Dunne and Boyer were silent. I remembered that Terry, the character played by Dunne, would later conceal the truth about her accident and that she was in a wheelchair.

"That woman's kid drew on our hallway wall," he said with a hint of annoyance. It took me a second to realize that he was now talking about an Albanian family who had stayed with us that past weekend. "And her husband was so loud on the phone. He never knocked. He'd call our names at the same time he barged into the room."

"Knocking is sort of an American thing."

"Since when?"

"He considered us like family, so he felt close enough to do that. Take it as a compliment."

"I just don't like strangers using my bathroom. Or, say, what if I walk around in my underwear?"

"It was only for a weekend. And you never walk around in your underwear."

He sighed, but a smile spread over his face.

He was softer than he let on. His eyes would often tear up during an emotional scene in a movie or some argument we'd have. He even balked at killing a cockroach, clenching his jaw as it crawled over our kitchen counter. All I felt, while pressing on a cockroach with a paper towel, was a dim discomfort at my power over its existence.

IT WAS BILLY WHO suggested I should attend the poetry reading in Manhattan. He frequently forwarded literary events to me, hoping they'd be helpful for networking and finding translation work. He believed that the quiet company of dictionaries would be better for my mental health.

The invite had a creative subject—*A Kurd, an Albanian, and a Bulgarian walk into a bar.*

I got there late. The Albanian and the Bulgarian had already done their readings. A waifish brunette stood behind a wooden podium in the corner, reading plaintive poems in a trembling voice. The poems revealed glimpses of a fragmented life— she had lived in Italy and France before coming to the US.

Honey-bursting grapes, cracked wooden cradles, red blots on the snow—the images flowed in quick succession, then hovered over the gleaming candles on the tables, the beer dispenser, the tip-counting bartender. Other phrases, like *dressed in sorrow*, or *suffused with the smell of blood*, heavily alliterated, took a nosedive into the beer-soaked floor. Then they lay there, as if wounded.

I had always enjoyed readings in the red room of the KGB bar, awash in Soviet memorabilia. There was a Lenin poster on the wall, a photograph of the famous cosmonaut Valentina Tereshkova, a draping hammer-and-sickle banner, period art from World War II and the Cold War. Despite the theme, the atmosphere felt decadent, a hangout for aristocrats.

The Kurdish woman's voice was making me lightheaded. She talked of ugly and repulsive things in such a gentle, almost hypnotic manner. Feeling dizzy, I had to lean back against the bar. Sometimes words affected me physically, causing as much nausea as motion sickness. If it happened while I was interpreting, I held tightly to the chair or pressed my feet on the floor. Repeating some quote from Buddha or Thich Nhat Hanh, or simply counting, usually helped.

Leyla, the Kurdish woman, thanked everyone, gathered her papers, and bowed to the long applause. There was a confessional quality to her writing. As she sauntered around the bar, many were friendly to her, believing, perhaps erroneously, that they already knew her. She had opened a curtain, and we couldn't help but peek inside. The reading's emcee offered to buy her a drink. I complimented her work, joining a group of people who had circled her.

We talked about her poetry. Some asked her questions about her life and how she came to New York City. She had hinted at domestic abuse in her poems. She had described her terror when a man had followed her in the streets and underground. But while her poetry had been fluid and revelatory, she spoke little about her circumstances. The conversation soon swerved toward the most recent election. Months had passed since November, but people still wallowed in indignation. Leyla didn't seem perturbed in the least by the exasperation around us. She must have been tested, I thought, by worse disasters.

"What do you do for money?" she asked me.

"I'm an interpreter and translator," I said. "I speak Russian, Spanish, and Italian. And Albanian, of course."

"I've been looking for work everywhere—in restaurants, babysitting, anything. Maybe I can do translating also. I'm fluent in Italian and French, well, besides Kurdish and English."

"Do you have a green card?"

"I'm waiting for my political asylum papers to come through. I'm applying as a domestic abuse case."

"They might no longer approve them."

"I know."

She then told us she was working on a book of poetry but wasn't making as much progress as she wanted. She shared a studio with four other women in Crown Heights.

"It's a tiny space. The TV is constantly blaring. I walk around the city for hours, not wanting to go home."

I left the bar with Leyla and Sanaz, a friend of hers who was visiting from out of town. As we walked toward the train, Leyla kept looking behind us. We were almost at the station when she swerved us toward a side street.

"It's less windy this way," she said. It was obviously an excuse, for the gusts continued to bite our faces just the same.

"I don't see anyone behind us," Sanaz said with a hint of defiance. "Nobody is following us."

Leyla pretended not to hear her. Her habit of looking back was contagious. I started glancing behind us also, remembering her poems and their atmospheric dread. But besides an overfed rat playing behind the recycling bins, the narrow side road we were in was deserted. On that cold night, most people kept to the main street, the shortest way to the subway.

We made it to the station. Leyla didn't come down to the platform.

"I'll go home later," she said, pushing down her woolen hat. "After my roommates go to sleep."

She wound her shawl around her neck, getting ready for another walk in that thirty-degree weather.

"You two go home," she said. "I'll be fine."

I remembered that Billy would be in LA that upcoming weekend for a friend's book party.

"Do you want to come for dinner to my place next Friday?" I asked them. "You can even spend the weekend. My husband won't be home."

"You don't have to do that."

"Why not? It will be fun."

"I'll bring wine," said Sanaz.

"I'll make byrek," I said.

"I love byrek," said Leyla.

On my way home, I wondered if Billy would mind going to LA alone. He wanted us to attend his friend's book launch party together. I wasn't going but hadn't told him yet. His friends and acquaintances on the West Coast were pleasant and buoyant, but their attention was spread thin. They thought of me as some kind of obscure Eastern European character, drawing on whatever *that* meant to them. Used to classifying people, they treated me as peripheral. Billy contradicted my impressions, calling them self-involved extroverts, saying they were like that with all new people, nice enough, but hard to get to know. Still, I often left the parties in a strange mood, with a vague discomfort in my chest. I'd comb over various encounters, linger on some word or remark, telling myself that forgetting that evening was the best thing to do. They lived so far away that we barely saw them. The only friend of Billy's I truly liked was Anna Cruz, a violinist who lived in Brooklyn, but who traveled all over the world to give concerts. We had been friendly from the start, and met up for drinks whenever she was in town.

"Would it be okay if I don't go to LA?" I asked Billy when I got home.

"I get it," he said. "A six-hour flight, and for only two days. We can use my companion pass another time. Maybe for a short vacation?"

"I wish Miles great success with his novel," I said, even though Miles's fiction had always given me the sensation of walking through kelp.

"He really likes you," Billy said, bringing me close. "He does."

Miles came from a wealthy family but had no compunction about acting penniless on social media. When he wanted to attend some writing residency in Paris or on a Greek island, he'd set up a GoFundMe campaign in which he portrayed himself as a starving artist.

*Don't your parents own a house in Tuscany?* I wrote under one such post on Facebook, a comment for which he never forgave me, though he humored it with a laughing emoji and, outwardly, was much nicer to me. Still, Miles did love Billy, I knew that. They'd known each other since childhood.

"He called me a week ago," Billy said. "Asked me to go to Thailand for a full moon party. He even had miles."

"Miles had miles. Ha!"

"By the way," he said, in a lower voice, his eyes burrowing into mine. "What happened with that guy you took to the dentist? The one from Kosovo."

The doorbell rang twice. It sounded more jarring than usual. All that could be seen at first through the peephole was a felt cowboy hat. Some dried herbs (basil, thyme?) stuck up from a red hatband. Helen's face, confined by a tight chin strap, appeared next. She had painted her cheekbones a vibrant lilac. She stared straight at me. Had she heard my footsteps? Did she know I was there, watching her?

She waited for a while, then took a step back. She adjusted her hat with her bony hands, like some paparazzi was about to take her picture. She rang the bell again. There was no reason not to open the door; she was my neighbor. But she'd never visited me before. Her look of expectancy made me uneasy. She had the same flyers with her, the invitation to the draw and sip party. I tiptoed back to the living room hoping she wouldn't hear the creaking floor.

"It was Helen," I told Billy. "From across the hall."

"You know who she reminds me of?" he said. "Norma Desmond, from *Sunset Boulevard*. The way she sashays around the hallways in those hats and long dresses. Didn't she used to be an actor?"

"In a soap opera."

Like Norma Desmond, Helen had probably made a fortune in her youth. She now spent her days in idleness, chatting up neighbors and drawing.

"So, the guy you took to the dentist," Billy said. "What happened to him?"

"I never heard from him again."

"Just checking," he said.

He left the room, but a mild apprehension stayed behind. He thought of me as more fragile than I was. Had he seen through me earlier? It was true that I hadn't talked to Alfred since that night. He could have already found someone else to interpret for him.

# 2.

ALFRED REACHED OUT VIA EMAIL.

*My psychiatrist said that your psychological training for interpreters is about to expire. You need to take a refresher course, she says. An imposition on your time, clearly. Will you do it? You are someone I trust. Isn't it funny how it goes? You can spend years with someone but never trust them. Or you can, in a second. They are strict about rules in America. Too many people here. Do you remember how the dentist wouldn't even look at my teeth without having us sign a hundred pages? Another thing is that I'm married. My wife's name is Vilma, a woman from Tirana, like you. Our baby, a girl, will be born in one month.*

*I used to be afraid of my father. Children know everything. He loved me, he did, but things never worked out for him. I had vowed never to be a father. Yet, here I am. Vilma, my wife, can't wait for the baby. The psychiatrist says that having my wife interpret during the therapy sessions is not an option. Relatives are not allowed. The training is only forty hours. Would you prefer to take it all in one week or in two weeks? Here's a link to the registration. Can you go ahead and register?*

*If you can, for which I'll be grateful, I'll need you to sign some paperwork. You will need to scan and email it to the organization that sponsored my recovery. Can I stop by your office tomorrow?*

*Thank you!*

*A.*

The nondescript, rectangular construction in Gowanus was built especially, it seemed, with the intention of splitting it into as many offices as possible. Mine was the smallest division, not much bigger than an average closet outside of New York City. There was little room to spare besides a small desk and two chairs.

Alfred was early, but he didn't text to tell me. The door suddenly framed his lone figure, the low-hanging shoulders and gaunt face. When our eyes met, he raised his hand in a greeting.

He had cut his hair and shaved, revealing a crooked mouth that bent further when he smiled. He had just returned from an interview for a security guard position, he explained. In his navy suit and burgundy tie, he looked the part.

"You'll get the job."

"Ishàlla."

He pulled out the paperwork for the training from his backpack. We both signed it. I went to scan it in the copy room. When I returned, he had made himself comfortable in the corner chair, where no one had sat before. He dug through his backpack and handed me a bag of Albanian mountain tea sprigs.

"Vilma's father brought it from Albania."

"Let's have some."

"You can keep the rest. I brought it for you."

He rubbed his hands to warm them up. I turned on the space heater. As I brewed tea in the building's common kitchen,

I tried to picture Alfred's wife. What kind of Albanian woman was this Vilma? Was she beautiful in an uninteresting way, partial to gaudy clothes, and a touch arrogant? Was her life's dream to become a TV presenter, a model, an influencer? There was an easygoing aspect to Alfred, a kind of passivity that certain high-spirited women might grow to despise. Or was Vilma—laid-back, modest, soft-spoken, surprisingly unharmed by the injustices around her—the sort of woman who found purpose in suffering, especially her husband's? All my theories were in vain. Alfred still carried an aura of mystery about him, so how could I speculate about his wife? At first glance, he gave the impression of someone who was used to doing menial jobs, but then the more we talked, the more I got the sense he was well-read, maybe an autodidact of sorts. There was a spiritual side to him, too. It was easy to imagine him as a medieval monk, wearing a long tunic tied by a rope at the waist while assisting the poor. But, no, Alfred wasn't a monk. He hadn't learned to detach and observe; he was still suffering. That night at the park, he had appeared mysterious, but the bright lights of the dentist's office had revealed his terror. He could barely handle a smile, let alone choose a wife. It was much more likely that it was Vilma who had chosen him and not the other way around. Sure, Alfred would have had to propose, but Vilma had pulled the strings.

When I returned with the teacups, the office had turned dark. It was one of those winter days when the night veil descended over the city without warning. The warm air from the heater had fogged up my only window. The distant lights above the barge-mounted excavator near the canal appeared as smudges on the glass. Alfred sat quietly. He hadn't even taken out his phone, like people do. He was staring at my chair, as if he were in the middle of a conversation with another, invisible me. When I turned on the desk lamp, he recoiled. Then he winced, covering his eyes with his palm.

"I don't like bright lights either," I said, attempting to excuse his reaction.

Alfred lowered his hand. Then he looked past me and toward the door. That other me sitting in front of him had just walked out. He continued to sit in silence, glancing at a print of Berat's castle on the wall, then staring at a photograph of my parents. His attention forced me to study my father's eyes, his closely cropped silver hair, then my mother's careless bun, her piercing eyes. The faces stirred a sharp longing I tried to push aside.

"We'll have no trouble sleeping tonight," I said, pointing to the teacups. "This tea is relaxing."

"I'm having trouble with insomnia," he said. "When I sleep, I see terrible images."

I was hesitant to ask about the images, but he told me about them himself. "They're mythical creatures," he said. "But the features are mixed up. I'll see a zebra with a human face, with wings and patches of fur. The weird body parts terrify me. Vilma says I should remember they are not real, but who could get used to such nightmares?"

His most remarkable feature was his eyes, I decided, and that hint of kindness they left behind. It was easy to worry about Alfred once one had made eye contact with him.

"I saw Cerberus yesterday. Do you know it? From Greek mythology?"

"No."

"I used to read Greek mythology when I was younger. He's a three-headed dog that guards the gates of the underworld to prevent the dead from leaving."

"Where are the dead going?"

"To spy on the living."

This was a joke, it turned out. He grimaced, revealing a gap between his teeth where the left canine used to be. It was kind of touching, like spotting the demolished wall of a house. Aware of my glance, he pursed his lips and rested his chin on his palm. Alfred had long eyelashes, whose shadows now reflected on his hollow cheekbones. He was following my movements with his eyes, as I ran my hand over the steam or placed my teacup on some printouts. He rarely blinked. Under the dim light, his bony face reminded me of a clay bust, still rough and unfinished.

"Thank you for doing the training for me," he said. "As I said in the email, it means a lot."

"How's your wife?"

"Impatient."

"Have you decided on a name for the baby?"

"My mother's name. Roza."

"Is your mother back home?"

He nodded.

"I wanted to bring her here," he said.

"Will you?"

"I can't. Since my father's death, she doesn't leave the house. I guess she'll never come."

I became aware of my facial expression, then of the need to shape it into something neutral. But maybe it was the effort that gave me away. Alfred was now studying my face with renewed interest.

"Odd," I said, with barely any emotion. "My mother is the same."

A scenario from my childhood played in my mind. We had made plans to go out of town. She had participated willingly, even excitedly. At the last moment, she announced she wasn't going.

"I'm sorry," Alfred said. "Is she alone?"

"She is. My father passed away."

"My mother is alone also. We pay someone to do her shopping."

He ran his hand over his black hair, which glistened under the light.

"I'm awash in guilt," he said, pointing to his chest. "I'm having a baby. My mother will barely see her. My daughter won't see the worst, thank God, but neither will she know the good things from back home. Do you have children?"

"No."

"Not yet," he corrected me.

I didn't tell him that Billy and I had only discussed the possibility of having children abstractly, that we were both ambivalent about it.

"My father comes to see me sometimes," he said. "Every summer, a moth lands on my hand. For the longest time."

We were alone in my office and perhaps the building; everyone had left for the day. And yet we were whispering, like children who had found a hidden nook to share secrets. His chair was wobbly—it creaked when he leaned back. The space heater hissed, then stopped. A noisy truck outside shook the windows, giving me a jolt.

"So, this therapist," he said, doing his best to smile. "She might help us both."

From some recess of my mind, a sentence awoke. *If the interpreter's circumstances resemble the client's, do not accept the assignment.*

"I don't need any therapy," I said. "We're going there for you."

Alfred nodded. "Yes, of course."

He touched his cheek with his fingers. His skin had warmed and reddened. He held the teacup with his other hand. "I do love this tea," he said, bringing it to his lips.

What he said, about the therapist helping both of us, stayed on my mind. The most prudent thing was to cancel our upcoming appointment. But that meant he would have to postpone his therapy till after the birth of his baby. Becoming a parent opened the doors to the traumas and unresolved issues of childhood. Even he could sense that would be the case.

An Albanian folk song broke the silence. Alfred's phone.

"Excuse me. My wife."

He rose at once and left the room to take the call. He stood outside the glass wall of my office, turning his back on me. It had taken some effort to reconcile that image of him as a solitary figure, waiting for me in the park, with that of Alfred, a husband and father to be. Albanian men typically got married early, giving in to their family's pressure to create a family. Why had I imagined him single?

"I'm sorry I have to leave," he said when he returned. "But maybe I don't have to right away. I'll tell Vilma there was a train delay."

"It's getting late. You should go," I said, not knowing what to make of that unnecessary lie.

"In a few minutes."

We resumed drinking tea in silence.

"Have you been in therapy before?" I asked.

"Once, for a short time. You?"

"No. Never."

Before leaving, he reached for my hands. His palms, calloused in parts, and soft in others, were warmer than mine. I closed my fists inside the cocoon of his knotty fingers. I felt the uneven surfaces, the different textures. Our handholding lasted only a few seconds, but the sensation in my fingers persisted, as if he had left behind some message for me to retrieve later.

"I think I should go," he said and reached for his black coat. "We can walk to the subway together. Are you leaving?"

"Not yet."

Once he left, I turned to the translation of a refrigerator manual into Russian and Italian. *Locking. Unlocking. Auto mode. Fast cooling mode. Fast freezing mode.* It was mind-numbing work. Most people dealt with an appliance for years without knowing what it was truly capable of.

A text message from Alfred. *Sweet dreams.*

I felt the pressure of his hands on mine. Then I heard his voice. *So, this therapist. She might help us both.*

• • •

LEYLA AND SANAZ gave off a heady, flowery scent as they entered my apartment. They also brought with them bottles of Italian wine, high spirits, and stories of a tattoo artist in Union Square who had designed intricate geometric patterns on their arms and wrists. An impromptu stop at Sephora's makeup counter had altered their appearance, making their faces more eye-catching and alike. They both modeled a smoky eye effect, a golden-flecked blue shadow with an elongating line. Their outfits, loose blouses in earth tones, added to their resemblance.

They had walked all over the city, they said, but their tiredness didn't show. They hadn't seen each other in years and couldn't get enough of rehashing old memories. Their conversation reminded me of my long WhatsApp conversations with Alma, my cousin and childhood friend who lived in Athens. She was married, with three children. Despite so many years apart, we were still giddy together. What really mattered in a friendship, and what lasted, was that someone had once seen you completely, as you were. It saddened me to think of Alma, who, although one of the smartest people I knew, had been working as a house cleaner for years. The last time we talked, she'd been upset, having overheard some Albanian relative describe her job as *cleaning the shit of the Greeks.*

I poured wine for them and checked on the byrek, already in the oven. Leyla and Sanaz skittered around the apartment. I could hear their voices in the living room, admiring the view of the Manhattan skyline from our windows, as the aroma of baked phyllo and cheese permeated the apartment. I wished Billy were home that evening. He might complain about our visitors, who took over his study occasionally, but I was sure he'd enjoy the company of the Kurdish women. He was probably on the plane now, but I pictured him listening to Miles's reading, fidgeting in his chair, although pretending to be wholly engrossed. Would I mention the women to him later on, when we talked on the phone? I had gone to that literary reading intending to get away from refugees, to retreat into literature and languages, but had instead brought these women home.

In the living room, Leyla and Sanaz were arguing in Kurdish. Leyla sounded emotional, on the brink of tears. Sanaz appeared calmer, but she was talking fast, as if attempting to reason with Leyla. I recalled that prior evening when we'd scurried down that side street for no obvious reason. Immersed in their conversation, they didn't even see me standing there at first.

"Sorry," Leyla then said, switching to English. "I've had this issue lately. My ex-husband is following me."

"Is your ex living here?"

"No, he's back home. He has asked a relative to follow me. I saw him standing outside Sephora today."

"I didn't see him," said Sanaz. "I even looked where you pointed."

"It doesn't mean he wasn't there."

"I didn't say he wasn't. I just didn't see him. And I didn't see him yesterday either. What do you want me to say?"

"Nobody believes me. I feel it in my body whenever he follows and take pictures of me," Leyla said.

"Takes pictures of you?" I asked. "What for?"

"To send to my ex-husband. He wants to know how I'm doing."

She started rummaging through her backpack. She pulled out a bag of clothes, two books. She flipped through a notebook. She turned her backpack inside out, then started looking through the pockets.

"Is he tracking me?" she said. "How does he know where I am? How is he doing it?"

Sanaz glanced at me. She seemed both puzzled and worried. Leyla interpreted her expression as I did, an insinuation that the story of this relative who stalked her was either nonsense or an obsessive paranoia.

"Why do you make that face?" she said to Sanaz.

"What face?" said Sanaz. "I didn't make a face."

"I saw it."

"Let's take your things," I said quickly, heading to Billy's office. "You can sleep in here tonight."

When we returned to the living room, everything seemed fine.

"Cheers," said Sanaz. "To Leyla."

"To poetry," said Leyla. "And to new, wonderful friends. You have no idea what this means to me. Having a room of my own, even for a night."

"This smell is amazing," said Sanaz. "Is the byrek ready yet?"

"Just a few more minutes."

"I'll tell you about the Albanian I dated in Italy," Leyla said laughing. Her effervescent mood struck me as remarkable considering that just seconds ago she had seemed so angry. Maybe she was hiding her weariness, but her high spirits brought back more questions about her stalker. Had anyone else seen him, besides her? I tried to focus on the story she was telling now. It was amusing, if ordinary, a man overpromising, engaging in false advertising, making plans he had no intention of following through. She described him as friendly, a macho type, the Albanian owner of a pizzeria in a small Italian town. He had wooed her, flooded her with phone calls, sent her flowers, gifts, talked about vacationing together to Albania. Then he'd gone back home.

"When he came back to Italy, radio silence," she said. "A week later I went to the restaurant. Honestly, it crossed my mind he might be dead. A new woman was working there. It was his Albanian wife. He'd been married for years."

She then talked to us about her time in Rome. She had gone to university there for three years. A professor had urged her to apply for a scholarship at an American university—he had connections at Fordham—but she had given in to her family's pressure and returned to Erbil to get married.

"Who would have thought your husband would turn out like that?" said Sanaz. "He's an engineer, from a good family, soft-spoken. Who would have thought that he'd force the hair dryer into your hand while you were bathing and ask you to kill yourself? Or that he'd hand you a knife and tell you to cut your throat?"

"Is that what he did?"

"That and more," said Sanaz. "Better not to think about it. It's hot in here, isn't it?"

During the winter, when it got cold outside, our heater went on overdrive.

"Where can I change? Would you mind if I take a shower before dinner?"

"Go ahead. There are extra towels in the cupboard."

Sanaz left the room. Leyla followed her. I then heard the sound of the keys in the lock, then Billy's footsteps and his voice calling my name. Why was he back in the apartment? Perhaps he had forgotten something. Or had he changed his mind about going to LA? He would enjoy that evening with us, I thought at once. Leyla would talk about her poetry. Sanaz about the documentary film she'd been shooting with her husband, featuring two Yazidi women who had survived a massacre.

"It's such a beautiful apartment," Leyla was saying to him in the hallway. "Thank you for letting me stay here this weekend."

All I heard was silence. Why wasn't he responding?

"Why are you back?" I asked when he came into the living room.

"Miles got food poisoning in Thailand. He's still there apparently. Who's the woman?"

"And nobody told you he was still in Thailand?"

"I only read the email once I got to JFK. Who is she?"

"She's a Kurdish poet. I met her at that poetry reading you told me about."

"Is she staying here?" He didn't wait for my answer. "Of course, she is. There's a bag in my office."

"Just for the weekend. She lives in Crown Heights at the moment. It's kind of complicated. I'll explain everything later."

Sanaz popped her head into the living room.

"I'm having a hard time with the shower," she said. "Am I doing something wrong or is there no hot water?" Then she turned to Billy. "Oh, sorry, hi there. You have a beautiful apartment. Thank you for having us."

Billy turned to me.

"Wait, is she another one?"

His confusion, of course, related to the fact that Sanaz and Leyla had changed the shapes of their features at the makeup counter, making them appear similar.

"You have to wait for the hot water," I told her, pretending he hadn't spoken. She threw a puzzled glance at me, then looked around for Leyla. I tried to steer him toward our bedroom, where we could talk alone. He wouldn't budge.

"A lot of people might need to use my office more than me, but that doesn't mean that they *can* use it," he said.

"They're only here for the weekend. Leyla is sharing a tiny studio with four other women in Crown Heights. Sanaz lives in Chicago."

"What if I brought random people from outside to spend the weekend, how would you feel?"

"I haven't stopped you. You don't bring them in because you don't want to."

A vein in his neck flickered. The Kurdish women were standing in the hallway, darting glances at each other.

"Sanaz," I said, "go take the shower."

She opened her eyes widely, as if to say, *Are you joking?* Maybe she was right—it was an absurd thing to say.

"You said you'd never bring anyone else home," he said. "We've talked about this."

What was he talking about? Had we? Leyla, who was standing behind Sanaz, headed to the office. She was barefoot. Her small feet pattered on the wooden floor. I ran behind her.

"My husband is not feeling well," I said. "He's never like this."

She kept tossing clothes into her backpack.

"Don't worry," she said. "We'll have dinner out. Thank you for inviting us anyway."

"But the byrek is ready. There is no reason for you to leave. It's my apartment, too."

Leyla picked up her scarf. She rested it on her shoulders but didn't twirl it around her neck, as I imagined she would while wandering the city alone, her solitude sharpened by the humiliation of that evening. Billy was in the hallway, clinging to an injured expression. But it wouldn't last long. As Leyla braved that winter night, he'd sprawl into his ratty heirloom chair with a glass of wine. As she let trains go by, he'd be drowsy, scrolling down his phone until his eyes closed.

"They're not leaving," I told him. "You go, if you want."

He seemed about to say something but didn't. Tiny flames leapt up in his eyes. He turned his back on me and walked toward the apartment door. A second later, I heard the banging. It took me a moment to understand what was happening.

He was slamming the door into the wall. Leyla and Sanaz already had their shoes on but didn't dare leave. He was standing in their way. He took a break at some point to ask me a question.

"Is that why you didn't come to LA?"

A part of me wanted to reach toward him, to calm him down. My body wouldn't obey. I felt an irrational fear that I might bump into our hallway furniture and fall in front of everyone. I didn't move.

"I would like to leave," Leyla finally said.

"They want to leave," I repeated.

He didn't seem to hear us. He slammed the door against the wall one more time. For a few seconds he remained motionless, waiting for his anger to leave his body. It felt like the silence after an accident. He appeared deflated. His shoulders stooping, he stomped on the chunks of wall splattered all over, turning them into powder. He stared down, reading a pattern amid the dust.

The women used the opportunity to tiptoe out, walking sideways along the wall of our narrow hallway so as not to touch him. Once outside the apartment, they ran toward the stairs and didn't wait for the elevator. Helen had opened the door just enough to peep. Another neighbor's yapping dog, about to go for a walk, dashed toward our apartment. Billy shut the door hard, right in front of the dog's face. The fire alarm in the kitchen went off. The byrek was burning. Overestimating the strength of my wrist, I pulled out the glass dish only to have it slip from my hand. I tried to hold on to it with my other hand, burning my fingers in the process. I let the dish go at once, breaking it in pieces. Tiptoeing among the chunks of hot spinach, burnt pastry, and shards of glass, I made it to a chair and sat. Billy walked into the kitchen with a tube of aloe vera.

He applied the green gel onto my fingers. Under the fluorescent light, amber flecks and gold ripples appeared in his eyes.

"I feel like a terrible person," he said. "But am I? I've had a shitty day, then there's all these strangers in our home again."

"It was a dinner party. For three."

"It doesn't matter what it was."

"Only one of them was staying for the weekend. She's a victim of domestic abuse. Her husband has people following her."

"You've fallen into a quicksand," he said. "I can't pull you out."

He went to our bedroom and packed a backpack with his clothes. He walked down the hallway toward the door. Before leaving, he cleaned up the dust on the floor. He straightened a rumpled rug with his feet. He put my shoes back on the rack. He closed the door behind him softly. Where was he going at this time of night? The apartment, which moments before had been full of voices, was now quiet as a tomb.

I texted Leyla, explaining that my husband's behavior wasn't typical. I wanted her to understand that Billy wasn't like her ex. Maybe I also wanted to remind myself of that. He was not and would never be a violent man. He wasn't rude. He wasn't mean. He had helped someone who had stayed with us in the past find employment. He even bought extra catch-and-release mousetraps and gave them to the neighbors.

I wrote many texts to Leyla that night saying all that, apologizing, asking if we could reschedule. She never responded.

# 3.

BILLY CAME BACK HOME IN THE MORNING. HIS SHIRT was skipping a button. He kept his left hand behind his neck. While deep in thought or spacing out, he was in the habit of fingering a tiny curl under his hairline. He must have only grabbed snatches of sleep the night before for his stare was blank. I rushed to hug him. He hugged me back. Then we remembered and moved apart, our arms falling to the sides.

"I was at Anna's," he said, attempting to fix the shirt, which was billowing unevenly over his trousers. When our eyes met, he avoided contact.

Anna's house was just a few blocks away. She had left a spare key with us. We'd feed her cats, and water her moth orchids and lucky bamboos, when she was on tour. I had pictured him in a stark room of some distant, cheap motel, while he had been basking in her sumptuous apartment.

"Where is she this time?"

"In Zagreb. For a concert."

It had been months since I'd last seen her. She stepped into and out of my purview so frequently that she had never become a necessity. But she was the sort of friend whom I always wanted to see, whose presence had a way of lightening my mood.

"You'll need to call the super."

"The super?"

"To fix the wall. That's a big hole you made."

"Let me take a shower first."

I waited for him in the living room.

*You said you'd never bring anyone else home.* The sentence had repeated in my mind throughout the night. Had I ever promised him that? When? While we were dating, we had bonded over how society was arranged, had puzzled over the fact that countless rooms, pools, fitness centers, in so many hotels, stayed empty for days at a time. At how some people owned houses they even forgot about, while others spent chilly nights on sidewalks. Now I looked at our old conversations with suspicion.

To my surprise, he didn't come to the living room after his shower. He withdrew into his office. Would he say nothing about the Kurdish women? Would he not lament my devotion to strangers, my obliviousness? Would he not offer an apology? I stared at the ratty chair next to the bookcase. It had belonged to his family for years. He had called Housing Works about it several times, only to change his mind at the last moment and cancel, since he couldn't stand to part with it. I called them again and scheduled a pickup appointment. Imagining his face upon noticing the missing chair made me feel a dim excitement, as if his loss would now be my gain.

The silence between us started that same night. The following day, he spent most of his time in his office and came to bed long after midnight. He woke up later than me in the morning. It was possible to avoid someone completely, even if you lived in the same apartment.

ON A CONSOLE TABLE next to the shoe rack lay a bouquet of hyacinths. The yellows and purples were rich, but it was a gentle beauty, like the unexpected sighting of a deer. The soft petals seemed fragile, easy to bruise. *We'll make it work*, I thought, even though being around Billy still reminded me of a car I once owned whose check engine light stayed on. I looked for a note. He used to send me the sweetest notes with flowers, lines of poetry, love quotes. But this time the note had only my name on it. There was also an envelope nearby, on which Lina, my Albanian cousin who had won the green card lottery and now lived in Bay Ridge, had scribbled, *Do you have a secret admirer, Clara?* After winning the lottery, Lina had stayed with us for a few months. She had her own apartment now but came over occasionally to pick up her mail.

I laughed. Calling me Clara was an old family joke.

But why would Lina wonder if I had a secret admirer? Did she not think the flowers were from Billy? I prepared myself that the bouquet might not be from him, which seemed absurd. We had sent each other many bouquets over the years. After all, it was flowers that brought us together. We met seven years ago, during an evening continuing education course he taught at NYU. I had taken the class on a whim, wanting to break the monotony of my job at the UN. Billy had come in as a substitute, halfway through the semester. The actual professor, who was semiretired, had gotten sick unexpectedly. Billy had added new films to the curriculum. They were all foreign and low-budget, each one bringing attention to some social issue. He showed us a documentary about a child bride in Syria who, despite having a job, was sold to a man by her family; then a short about a young woman in Iraq, sexually assaulted by an older male relative; then a musical film about some gifted Roma children in Bulgaria. The stories were all poignant, but he also made us pay attention to things I didn't normally think about, like the music, the framing, the lighting. He was just as capable of looking at reality in the face, I had thought, as of losing himself in an arty discussion.

When the course was over, I sent him anonymous red roses. The delivery guy handed the bouquet to a janitor who was friendly with Billy. The janitor took the flowers straight to his classroom, in the middle of a lecture. All the students had tittered. Since then, every Valentine's Day, he'd send me red roses in public places.

"Who could have sent this?" I asked. "It doesn't say."

He seemed perplexed. "I don't know. Could it be for your cousin?"

"They're addressed to me," I said, unable to hide a hint of disappointment at his assumption.

"Why did Lina call you Clara? On that note?"

"I've told you about the Bulgarian who was in love with my mother."

"You haven't."

Billy loved Eastern Europe. During college, he'd gone backpacking through Romania and Bulgaria, a trip he told me about during our first date. I still believed his earlier attraction to me related to my accent, which reminded him of his short-lived romance with an older Romanian woman, the owner of the hostel where he had once stayed.

The story about my mother sounded fictional. The woman I was talking about, the one who had traveled through the Balkans as a gymnast, who had tightrope walked in Sofia, inciting the advances of the circus piano player, didn't sound like my mother at all. But it had been her, years and years ago, I thought, trying to placate a sneaky suspicion that it was a made-up story, something I'd concocted to make her life more bearable in my eyes.

"The pianist's favorite composer was Clara Schumann. He'd write letters to her, daydreaming about them getting married, a daughter named Clara."

"Romantic," Billy said loftily.

An uncomfortable silence followed, disrupted, eventually, by a flash of color. Cary Grant graced our wall in a waist shot. It was the same scene as in the film Billy had been watching the other night, except in color. Like Boyer, Grant was in a black suit, held a fedora in his hand, and was on the lookout for the painting. Upon noticing it, he shut his eyes and leaned back.

"Boyer's reaction is more powerful," Billy said. "Don't you think? This is more surface."

"Is this a remake?"

"Yes. Leo McCarey remade it in color. And with different actors."

I found a glass vase for the flowers. Liberated from the string, they loosened up in their new space. I touched the fleshy petals, the sumptuous green leaves. I googled *purple hyacinth*, then scouted through various online forums where people discussed flowers. Some said hyacinths meant regret.

It still seemed odd that Billy hadn't sent me the flowers. Who else could have sent them?

On our wall, bright, saturated images of luxurious ship interiors, elegant women, the blue of the Mediterranean, the charming Villefranche-sur-Mer village, all flashed by in quick procession.

I WAS IN THE TRAINING ROOM, sitting by a long table, next to other interpreters who were typing or scribbling in notebooks.

"Remember this," the instructor said. "If the client's trauma mirrors in any way the interpreter's experience, the interpreter should let the therapist know and have them find a replacement."

I glanced outside, hoping for a glimpse of sky and some clarity of mind. The weather had rendered the window useless. Tiny streamlets disrupted the layer of condensation, but nothing could be gleaned. The same question kept repeating in my mind. Should

I interpret for Alfred? I had never been through any physical torture. Nobody in my immediate family had been killed.

There was a Polaroid picture of a chubby infant next to the instructor, who had just become a grandmother. Her face beaming, she had shown it to us earlier, extolling the baby's apparent intelligence. We had all cooed in unison. But her lightheartedness had long dissipated. A grave expression had settled on her face.

She made eye contact with each of us as she talked.

"Interpreting for a family member is not recommended. Patients are likely to hide painful information from relatives."

Alfred's wife had wanted to interpret for him. Curious about what she looked like, I quickly googled her with my phone, under the table, while the instructor was talking. Nothing came up. Perhaps she didn't use Alfred's last name.

"An interpreter should only disclose things about themselves that are in the best interest of the client."

Images of Alfred flashed in my mind. He was glancing impatiently at his watch. Shutting his eyes against the light. Twisting his loose lips into a smile.

On the other hand, wouldn't my presence be comforting to him? During therapy, he'd have my complete attention.

"Any questions?"

"But wouldn't it be helpful," I asked, "for a survivor of torture to know that an interpreter has been through some rough times also?"

"A client is not a sounding board. That kind of connection is not called for."

"What about touch?" someone else asked.

"Physical interaction should be limited to a handshake or a high five."

Were all aspects of physical interaction classifiable? A hand-shake could be defiant, reverent, seductive. Even a *good morning* had shades of meaning. The average human ear could distinguish over a thousand differences in tone. A person had only to traipse through Manhattan for half an hour to experience the aggressivity gradient of an *excuse me*.

"Half an hour break," the instructor said. "Feel free to grab some lunch."

The training was in a low-ceilinged office inside a shabby Manhattan tower. The elevator was narrow. Mirrors covered the walls and the ceiling. Five of us interpreters had to stand intolerably close as it went down. Craning our necks to avoid breathing into each other's faces, we endured the experience in silence. When the ride was over, we sighed with relief.

The building's lobby was undergoing renovations. Large sections were cordoned off with yellow tape. Floor tiles had been removed. A construction worker was staring at a deep and narrow pit. Beyond the glass doors, a monsoon was in session. All morning, the rain had paused for brief periods, then returned with a vengeance. Those who had left home earlier that morning had gotten caught in it. Drenched employees now hurried through the doors shaking off their umbrellas. The wide sidewalk outside the glass doors was covered in water.

The somberness of my instructor had been contagious. Billy's voice now echoed in my mind. *You've fallen into a quicksand.* But it wasn't true. I could back out. Of course, I could. I knew of other interpreters. I'd find someone good. Alfred might argue about the replacement, but I would try to convince him.

The woman who picked up his phone spoke loudly.

"Vilma speaking. Who's this?" Whatever qualities Vilma possessed, shyness wasn't one of them.

"I'm Alfred's interpreter. Can I speak to him?"

She launched into a spiel. "He went for a walk, thank God. Didn't feel well. I'm happy he's going to that therapist next week. I've been worried about those creatures. Is he going mad, you think? Someone needs to see him. And see him soon. We have a baby coming, did he tell you? I've been feeling lousy. Anxious. Headaches. He doesn't trust many people, you know? But he trusts you."

"I know," I said, quicker than I intended, feeling a touch of pride.

"Wait a moment. He's come back. Why so early, Alfred?"

"Forgot my keys."

"Right. Of course, you did."

She put him on the phone. He didn't speak right away.

"Alfred, are you there?"

"Sorry. Was waiting for Vilma to leave the room."

"Why?"

"I wanted to talk to you in private."

"But she knows everything, doesn't she?"

"Those creatures have started to ask me questions. They didn't used to speak before. But they are speaking now. Why did you call?"

A siren blasted in the street. The construction guy climbed into and disappeared inside the floor opening. A foolish panic seized me. Where had he gone? Was he all right? I caught a glimpse of his hard hat. A security guard stomped into the lobby. He was soaked from the knees down.

"Stepped into a puddle," he said. "Didn't know it was that deep. It was deceiving."

Another security guard handed him some paper towels. He tried to pat himself dry. "I need to change my pants," he said. But his shift had started, so he sat down anyway.

The silence didn't sit well with Alfred.

"Don't back out."

He knew why I had called. The construction worker underground was now waving his arms above his head. Another worker approached the hole. Realizing the man in the pit had no way of climbing out, he burst into laughter before dropping down a metal ladder.

"Just wanted to confirm our appointment," I said.

"It's next Thursday at five."

"Okay, Alfred, see you then."

We stayed on the phone for a few more seconds but remained silent.

"Thank you," Alfred said finally. "I won't forget it."

The construction worker was out of the pit now. I took the elevator up. The instructor talked some more about her granddaughter. During the lecture, the rain lightened up. The clouds cracked unexpectedly; some sun leaked through.

A friend from my coworking place sent me a picture of a flower bouquet. Purple hyacinths. *For you*, she wrote. Was there a message with them? *No, only your name.*

The clump of hyacinths resembled the ones at home. Since they were sent to my coworking space in Gowanus, which not many people knew, the sender had to be a friend or acquaintance. But a simple Google search revealed that it was possible, even for a complete stranger, to find out my work location. My online translation profile included a mailing address where inquiries could be sent.

• • •

SINCE BILLY PURPORTED TO BE a connoisseur of fine dining, he was usually the one who chose the restaurants for our special occasions. When we first started dating, after some exorbitantly priced dinner, he'd ramble on about the flavor combinations, the sundry textures in the appetizers, the lavender aftertaste of dessert. Fine dining was a baffling diversion that hardly satisfied me. It seemed like the best kind of scam, for calling it that would be inappropriate.

The ceiling lights shifted from a buttery yellow to a pale mauve, tinting the long curtains that separated the tables. The colored lights suffused the restaurant with a romantic glow. The ever-shifting scheme prompted some expectancy, as if a surprise show were about to start at any minute. The bossa nova acoustics had a way of blurring the low murmurs and other sounds, but Billy looked up the moment I entered. He was in a beige shirt that absorbed the play of lights, his body becoming a dizzying surface.

"Red looks great on you," he said.

"New blouse."

"I ordered two of these," he said, after kissing me on the cheek. He pushed a flight of sake in my direction. "The white sake is not pure; you can tell by the rice grains. Which one do you like?"

"I like the impure sake better," I said after trying them both.

"Yeah? Me, too."

A short essay under each item in the menu went to great lengths to inform about every ingredient and the cooking process. A waiter appeared out of nowhere, like a spectral figure. Billy asked specific questions about each dish, which he followed with an inquiry about the waiter's own preference. None of the waiter's eager suggestions, however, were heeded. Billy simply liked engaging the waiters, getting his money's worth. We ordered pasta made out of mung beans, served with chunks of mock duck, then the chilled miso eggplant, and a risotto with truffles. Behind the sheer, vibrant drapes sat other couples, some on a first date, shy and hesitant. And others, so used to being part of a set that the commotion over togetherness confounded them. A man gave his partner roses. He pulled them from under the table as if he were doing a magic trick.

"I received anonymous flowers again," I said. "Forgot to tell you. They came to my office last week."

Billy focused on applying French almond butter to a paper-thin Italian toast. Maybe he considered it a small matter, not worth discussing. His earlier conviction that the flowers couldn't possibly be for me seemed compatible with his lack of jealousy.

"Of course, they could have been for Lina," I said. The waiter brought several bowls and small plates, with an artistically arranged dollop of food at the bottom of each.

"I didn't get you flowers today," he said. "But I did get you a gift. It's for both of us."

"What is it?"

"I've booked a trip. To Dominica. It's all refundable within twenty-four hours, so we should decide soon. We'll be in a resort, but it's not cheesy or anything."

He made deep eye contact before handing me his phone, on which was a low-angle photo of a whitewashed building amid vast sand and scattered beach umbrellas. The resort looked stunning.

"When did you book it for?"

"We leave on Thursday morning. For four days."

The medley of shifting lights on his shirt made me dizzy for a second. I made some effort to focus on his face.

"I lied to you about Alfred," I blurted. "He didn't just need me for the dentist."

He stared at me for a few seconds. He had forgotten who Alfred was.

"Oh, Alfred, right. The root canal."

"He needs my help. At the therapist. I've been taking a training course to get ready for it. Mine was expired. His sessions start on Thursday. So I can't go."

He adjusted his glasses. Their blue contour sharpened as the lights changed. He continued drinking sake in silence. I felt curiously detached from his disappointment.

"If you read Alfred's email, you'll understand," I went on. "His mother suffers from agoraphobia. She hasn't left the apartment in a long time."

He almost smiled, but not quite.

"She what? Isn't that like . . . a conflict?"

"He's seeing strange creatures, hallucinations. They were quiet before, but now they're talking to him."

"I asked you twice about it," he said slowly. "Twice."

In Billy's world, the smallest lie was an unforgivable sin. But a knack for honesty or lack of it was shaped by one's experience. His life had been like a basic grid with well-defined paths. Mine was a defective labyrinth in which going straight made it hard to reach the destination.

"You can't stop yourself," he told me. "I know you can't."

Of course, I could stop myself. But who was to say that restraint and distance was the best course for everyone? Maybe it was better to blunder, to bump into things, to make ridiculous mistakes, if that brought you closer to yourself and others. It wasn't the right time and place for an argument, so I swallowed my objections.

"I can give a call to my old therapist. You need someone to talk to."

"No."

"Why not?"

It was difficult to say. I used to make fun of Billy when he took Tylenol for the smallest headache, or when he applied a bandage to the smallest scrape. But maybe these actions pointed to a deeper difference between us.

We ate in silence for some time, listening to the music and snippets of conversation from the other tables. One couple kept FaceTiming with their children, who were home with a grand-parent. They no longer knew how to be alone together or didn't want to.

"How sweet," Billy said. I couldn't tell if he was being sarcastic.

"A bottomless pit of need," I said, parroting what a translator friend had once said about his children. Billy almost smiled again.

"Would you two consider dessert?" asked the waitress.

We said no in unison. Even without dessert, the bill was astro-nomical. Maybe a childhood of abundance stays with you, as much as one of deprivation. No matter what dire circumstances Billy had found himself in during adulthood (he sometimes went on and on about that one week he'd been penniless in Paris and eaten baguettes for every meal), he would never feel guilty for spending hundreds of dollars on a dinner. And no matter how rich I became, spending much more than necessary on a meal would always give me a bit of panic.

We were standing outside, waiting for our car. Billy's glances and movements were diffident, uneasy.

A black Toyota pulled up next to us.

"Can you play some music?" I asked the driver, who was blond with blue eyes and looked like a Brazilian surfer. Looking at his name on the back of his seat, I realized, to my surprise, that he was Albanian.

"Something is wrong with the audio. Sorry."

The rain had settled on a moderate rhythm, but it was enough to bring the traffic to a halt. At times a cab would stop abruptly, the doors would open, and a flustered couple would emerge, having decided to take the subway after all.

"Valentine's Day," the driver said coolly, tapping on the steering wheel.

Billy kept busy with his phone. He was deciding which podcast to listen to. A text message popped on his screen. He opened a video of some people slow dancing. He leaned toward me.

"Nick just sent me this," he said. "I guess the *Dirty Dancing* films are over."

"What *Dirty Dancing* films?"

"I emailed you about it. I asked if you wanted to check it out after our dinner?"

I reached for my phone. There was his email. He had sent it two days ago.

"How did I miss it?"

"My friend Nick from the media department, remember him? You met him once. His wife owns a restaurant on the Lower East Side. For Valentine's Day they're screening two movies simultaneously. The American *Dirty Dancing* and the Indian *Dirty Dancing*, which is a scene-by-scene copy of the American version."

"You sent the email two days ago. And I didn't see it."

"Anyway," Billy said, somewhat impatiently. "Apparently some Bollywood directors copy American movies verbatim. Nick wrote a piece about it in the *Times*."

"I love *Dirty Dancing*."

"I thought you might."

"Why did you think I might?"

"You like big-budget movies, don't you?"

That my choice of movies was often based on my favorite actors, not directors, had once floored him.

"'I've Had the Time of My Life' used to be a popular song in Albania in the nineties," I said.

"It's actually a popular song for funerals," said Billy, whose knowledge of random things often surprised me.

The video reminded me of college parties, where the desire to make out trumped inhibitions. Some of his colleagues were trying out their own version of dirty dancing, rubbing against each other, forgetting their PhDs and that they'd see each other at the next faculty meeting. Their dancing reminded me of late evenings at a bar, long after the excitement had fizzled out, when the stench of beer that had been there all along suddenly seemed sickening, and those earlier expectations of a great time misguided. But it was easier to stick around, hoping there was still a chance the situation might turn around. So one stayed and had one more drink until they ended up in someone else's video.

"Nick said he wants to translate some Italian poets. Maybe you and he should have coffee or something?"

Billy wanting to involve me in his colleagues' projects had made for some awkward situations in the past. He once introduced me to every faculty member in the languages department, praising my language skills.

I pretended not to hear him and occupied myself with my phone.

"But you'll be busy with Alfred," he said. "Or with the Kurdish women."

An image of him stomping on the wall chunks struck me.

"Do you remember," I said, looking straight at the driver as my voice boomed in the quiet car, "that when we last went to Albania, you said that everyone there was a good-hearted ignorant?"

Billy turned instantly toward the driver's seat. He read his badge. Without glancing at me, he looked outside. I expected him to say something in his defense, which should have been easy to do. Out of context, Billy's remark sounded more obnoxious than it had been. We were having dinner in the south of Albania, visiting some of my relatives, who were telling him that he ought to eat meat since his face looked sickly. *He doesn't look well*, they kept saying. *He has no color in his face. What did you marry a vegetarian for? What if he dies young? You'll be a widow. You don't even have any children; you'll be sorrowful and alone in old age.* I didn't want to translate their prediction about my doomed future, but he insisted I should, then got upset when I did, calling everyone there a good-hearted ignorant. Fortunately, nobody understood what he was saying.

He didn't dispute it. He nodded, turned his face away from me, and lowered his window. A cold stream of air entered the car.

"I think of all the opportunities you had growing up," I went on, unable to stop myself. "Your parents paid thousands of dollars for your schooling since you were three. And that's the only reason why you're not a good-hearted ignorant, Billy."

When we left the car, the driver said good night in Albanian, wanting to let us know he'd been listening. In the elevator, a glimpse at Billy's face startled me. He'd been crying. He wiped off his cheek as soon as he saw me looking. For the rest of the elevator ride, my hands were shaking.

In the living room, the heirloom chair was missing. Housing Works had come to pick it up earlier. There were round stabs on the carpet where the chair used to be. I had given it away, hoping he'd be disappointed, but something about his sad face distressed me.

"I called them," I said, sounding more apologetic than I intended. "They came and picked it up."

He pulled out a chair from the dining table. On the bookcase, there was a framed picture of him and his mother sitting on the old chair. He must have been five or six in the picture. Had he nursed some longing of sitting there with his child?

"You know Helen from across the hall?" he said. "She got evicted."

"Evicted?"

"She hadn't paid the maintenance fee in months. She was sleeping in the kitchen and was trying to rent out her living room and bedroom to some students."

Helen's eager face, partially shaded by her homespun straw hats, turned toward me slowly. While strutting around the hallways, she'd struck me as eccentric, lonely maybe, but never poor. She hadn't been sheltered and idle, as I had thought. She'd been braving a brutal storm, all on her own.

"So Helen was poor," I said.

"I guess so," said Billy, raising his brows. "But how would we have known that?"

But maybe she had tried to tell me. She'd been waiting on her doorstep that evening, her moist eyes fluttering while staring at me, the cords on her neck tense. She had handed me that flyer, the invitation to a drawing party. Had she wanted to connect, to break the ice, before telling me about her situation? Not knowing what to make of the flyer, I had dropped it in the recycling bin. Then she'd come knocking on our door, in that cowboy hat adorned with dry plants. Had she heard my footsteps running away from her?

I put my arms around Billy. My body needed some contact, or just a long, hard embrace. He lowered my arms slowly, as if I were a mannequin. "Should go to bed," he said and brushed past me to the bedroom.

Perhaps it was his earlier crying or the news about Helen, but a bout of sadness caught up with me at once. Even after it died, my hands felt restless. On the living room table, the first hyacinths had dried up and were drooping. Before removing them from the vase, I touched one of the petals, but it disintegrated into my fingers.

# 4.

ALFRED WAS WAITING FOR ME AT HIS PSYCHIATRIST'S office. He was standing in the lobby, staring absentmindedly at the street. When the revolving doors spit me out, he turned around and hurried toward the elevator.

"Were you trying to avoid me in the lobby?" I asked him upstairs.

"Of course not," he said, unconvincingly. "I just didn't see you."

We entered a dimly lit, stagnant room. There was a worn-out futon in a corner and two folding chairs. The blinds were half-open, letting in the glare of the cars outside.

"There you are," Alfred's therapist said as she came in, before closing the blinds and turning on a ceiling light. It exposed the cobwebs in the corners and a grimy trash can under her desk. "Please take a seat."

I'd been to see Zinovia before with another client. She was kind and took many pro-bono clients, or at most charged a ridiculously low fee. She spoke with an Eastern European accent that sounded even heavier, since she took pleasure in each syllable, stretching some words to astonishing lengths. Her clothes had echoes of the eighties. She wore double-breasted blazers and neon tights that flaunted her full-figured calves. Her oversized glasses brought to mind a math teacher from elementary school whom we all used to fear.

"I suffer from eczema," she said to us, pointing to a Cetaphil bottle on her desk. "The itching worsens from stress. I apply it to my hands sometimes, during the sessions."

As she lathered the lotion on her fingers, it seemed to me that Zinovia might fall apart at any moment, the same way my old math teacher had once collapsed on the floor during a lecture, her pitch-black hair spreading on the maroon tiles like a mop. We had all stared at the unfinished equation on the blackboard, and a cold fear had sneaked into the room, a shadow of our own catastrophes from some distant future. A vision of Zinovia furiously scratching her arms and face until her blotched skin bled played out in my mind. It continued even as she placed her lotion aside and nodded calmly, her skin perfectly smooth. But everything was fine. Zinovia was fine. The lotion had done its job. There was Alfred sitting next to her, a sheepish look on his face, his back straight, giving the impression of a child who had done something wrong and knew that the grownups were about to discuss it.

Before we started, Zinovia dusted her desk. She worked without rushing.

"I feel better now," she finally said, still eyeing the desk. "Sorry about that. I have to use my colleague's office today, unfortunately. He never cleans."

"You sound just like my wife," said Alfred. "Vilma cleans all the time."

"How was your day today?" she said to Alfred. "What did you do?"

Alfred responded in a barely audible voice. I felt motherly, wanting to brush his bangs to the side with my hand, mouthing, *He's shy* to Zinovia.

"Can you speak louder, please?" I said.

"Nothing exciting," he said. "I fought with Vilma as usual. Then she went to work, while I stayed home and watched TV. I like soccer. I watch it for hours."

"What was your argument about?"

"Vilma gets annoyed if I leave dishes in the sink or make crumbs, that sort of thing. She's eight months pregnant. She gets upset at everything now. This morning, she lost it after I talked to my mother. I become sad after talking to her, she said. And Vilma doesn't want to be around sadness. On top of everything else."

"Does your mother live in New York?"

"No. My mother is back home. My phone calls to her are excessive, Vilma says. But she is all alone. How can I not call her all the time?"

"How often do you talk to your mother?"

I turned toward Alfred, awaiting his response, but I only saw my own mother, sitting on her bed, the inflatable cuff of her blood pressure monitor around her arm. She was dressed in her best clothes, a black silk blouse and skirt I had bought for her. We were about to go out to lunch for my thirty-fifth birthday.

"You'll like this restaurant. The food is good and it's by the lake."

"How are we getting there?"

"I booked a cab."

She had done her makeup, applying a rosy tint to her lips. It enlivened her pale face. Her uneven hair was combed and swept to the side. The henna hadn't worked on all the white. I used to love standing next to her when I was little, looking up, watching her comb her blonde tresses. What had happened to my fantastic adoration?

"I'm feeling off. I need to measure my blood pressure."

She was sitting now, squinting at the numbers on the mercury manometer. This was nothing unusual. She measured her blood pressure several times a day, as soon as she woke up, and at other random times. It had been that way for as long as I remembered. When she was done, she pressed her toes on the heels of her shoes, letting them drop to the floor with a somber sound. I expected she'd feel better, that she'd put her shoes back on and wear the jacket I had bought her, the one she had tried on a million times in front of the mirror.

"Maybe we could go out for dinner instead," she said.

I called the cab driver to reschedule.

"What time?" he said.

I told him I'd call him back. She stayed in her room and never mentioned our dinner again. Later that evening, a neighborhood friend brought me a bouquet of mixed flowers, roses and carnations. I put them in water and placed the glass vase on a small table in the living room. The next morning, the flowers were nowhere to be found.

"Where are my flowers?" I asked her.

"I don't know," she answered.

*Either she's mad or I am*, I thought. It had happened years ago, but my body still stiffened at the memory.

"I often think about the luggage belt at the airport," Alfred was saying. "The way it's always moving around, full of people's possessions, never stopping."

"How many years did you work at the airport?"

"Fifteen years. Since when I left Kosovo for Germany in 1999. I worked at night, collecting luggage, making sure it went to the right aircraft or arrival area. I also helped clean and de-ice the aircrafts. I lived alone for years. I kind of prefer it, to be honest."

"Where did you meet Vilma?"

"At the airport, where else?"

For fifteen years, Alfred had led a solitary life, a life of periphery he called it. He rented a small cottage on a flower farm, on the periphery of an airport town, itself on the periphery of a big city. His nocturnal schedule made it easy for him to stay on the periphery of all relationships. As he told his story, montages of Alfred's bygone years, in the style of a moody, low-budget Eastern European film, flickered by. Alfred rode his bicycle through the daffodils, and then alongside the highway, until he arrived at a bus stop, where he embarked on his daily long ride to the airport. The airport always hurt his eyes with the bright aisles and legions of faces. But the sight of suitcases was comforting. Handling them structured his days in manageable ways, keeping his thoughts at bay.

"It was mutual love, between me and the suitcases," he joked. "Even when I left the airport, they followed me."

He closed his eyes as he described them to us, rectangles in cobalt blue, teal, matte black, and their fast double-spinner wheels. His life went like that for all those years, a sort of functional hibernation, until he entered an airport bakery at 5:00 AM one morning and saw Vilma behind the counter.

"It wasn't her curls, or even her curves, that made me look up," he said, "But that, when handing me a *Brötchen* with chocolate, she said my name the right way, putting the accent on the *e*."

Realizing she was Albanian also, he had chatted with her, discovering that they had opposite schedules. The only way for them to meet was for him to leave the house earlier on his way to work, so he could catch her at the end of her shift.

"She told me from the start that she was in Germany temporarily while waiting for her US immigration papers. Her father lived in America."

"So you thought your relationship would be short-lived?"

"Yes. Her papers got approved before mine. She considered leaving, but then she changed her mind. She waited for me."

"Did you want her to do that? To wait?"

"I enjoyed my alone time, to be honest. And I liked living alone in Germany, on the outskirts. But then she said she was staying. We were meant to be, she said."

"Did you feel the same way?" I said in Albanian.

Because I was interested in the answer, I worried for a moment that the question wasn't Zinovia's but my own. It was absurd. Of course, she must have asked it first. I should have left it alone, but the doubt kept gnawing at me. Zinovia would have interrupted. She would have told me it wasn't my place to ask questions. She appeared unflustered. Was that a shade of pink in her finger? She turned her attention to Alfred. I tried to ground myself in the present moment by putting a meditation technique to use. My arms were resting on my sides. My thumb was clicking on a pen. The soles of my shoes were pressing on the ground.

"When Vilma told me she was pregnant, things changed. I felt a weight on my chest. I had nightmares. I'd see wild, disfigured hybrid animals. I kept thinking about my childhood. I wanted to hug my mother. I hoped she'd come here, even though she never leaves the house."

"I have started to go out," my mother once told me over the phone. "I go out with Neta. We go shopping together. We even took the bus once to that new mall."

On the screen, the dark moons under her eyes quivered, threatening to spill over her face.

Zinovia called my name, bringing me back to the room. I turned to Alfred. He was saying something else.

"I zënë ne grack."

I asked him to repeat it. He did.

I stumbled on finding the English equivalent. A brief silence followed. Zinovia coughed, then crossed her legs. Alfred came to my aid.

"Trapped," he said in English. "The word is *trapped*."

"Thank you," I said and turned to Zinovia. "He felt trapped at his wedding."

Why had I tried to interpret it literally? *Trapped*, of course, instead of *caught in a trap*.

"Tell me about another time you felt trapped," said Zinovia.

I reached for my water bottle. My shoulder gave a dull ache.

"Excuse me a second." I took a sip.

Alfred was speaking slower than before.

"April but hot inside. My father was sweating. The bus ride was bumpy. I got carsick. Or maybe I knew what was coming. Now it always seems as if I knew. Trapped."

"It was hot that day."

"They called us outside, my father and me. They asked for money."

"Soldiers."

"My father said no. A mistake. He was like that. Had a thing about bullies."

"Before the bus stopped, he squeezed my hand. He had never been demonstrative with affection. A hug here and there."

"Let's go see what they want."

"Tied to a radiator, when I came to it. Didn't move for a long time, stared at the cracked varnish. It reminded me of a paper crane. I knew I was bleeding but didn't look down."

"I used to fold paper as a kid. The paper crane, you know? Triangle arms. Triangle beak. Triangle tail. In Germany, when a coworker died, they made paper cranes for him. When I saw them in his locker, I remembered the radiator and vomited."

"My father's body? They say I saw him die. I have no memory of it. In a ditch."

"Vilma says I should think of something nice when it happens."

"A picnic we went to. Early nineties? We all sat by a lake, my parents, some family friends. My mother's cooking. The smell of the pines everywhere. You know the smell of pines? It doesn't get better than that. My father loved nature, the sea, music."

*Something nice. Think about something nice.* I was now at the beach, under the pines. I had on my favorite dress, the pale blue one with ruffles up the front. The greenish-blue sea, the timid waves lapping the golden sand. A singer in a lavender dress was crooning in Italian, *Guarda che luna, guarda che mare.* My father was walking toward the ocean, the golden arm of the sun to his left.

I heard Zinovia's voice. "Are you going to interpret what he said? I've been waiting."

What had I missed? What had Alfred's last sentence been?

"My father loved nature, the sea, music," I said.

She glanced at the clock, then she reached for her lotion. She pumped out a generous amount and rubbed both her hands with it. Our eyes met briefly. She had expressive eyes. They showed something new now, not exactly admonishment, disappointment maybe. It reminded me of the way my old math teacher had looked at me once, knowing I was cheating on an exam.

It seemed unlikely that Alfred had talked for a long time before I had interpreted. But Zinovia seemed upset. I looked at Alfred. He had closed his eyes and was taking deep breaths.

"That's enough for today," she said.

I TOOK DEEP GULPS of air when we went outside. The stale air in the office, her pinkish skin, the scent of her lotion, the sight of that filthy trash can, even Alfred's monotone voice had all made me nauseated.

"It's over," I said to Alfred, who was studying the pavement. "It's done."

He didn't look well. His features seemed disjointed, as if someone had taken apart a puzzle of his face and then put it back together in a hurry. Now nothing fit right. This was not unusual. It was common for a patient to feel awful after dredging out their worst memories.

He needed to be alone.

"Was I ever out of line?" I asked. "Did I ask a question out of place?"

"You were fine. I don't think so."

"Did I interpret everything?"

"I wasn't paying that much attention."

"I couldn't recall that word."

"It's all right. Would you like to go for a walk?"

"I should go home. You need to be alone, Alfred."

We were standing on the sidewalk. He pulled me to the side. He was quiet for some time, observing me. "What are we going to do?"

"You should go home. I'll see you next week."

"No, I mean, about this. About us."

"About us?"

"It's always there. It never goes away. Like hair."

Most animals become nervous and flee an area long before a volcanic eruption. But even when Alfred stood there, blushing, and stumbling over what to say, I still had no idea.

"I have feelings," he blurted. "Real feelings."

I was the slow kind of animal, the kind that thought of running only after the ground trembles.

"You just got out of therapy. That was heavy stuff. You need time to process everything you told her."

"I know that we're married to other people. If only Vilma wasn't pregnant . . ."

"Let's go," I said, afraid that Zinovia might come out at any moment and see us there, engaged in an intimate conversation.

"Can we please get away from here?" Alfred stood there staring at me. I grabbed him by the sleeve.

"Let's keep walking."

He dragged his feet behind me.

"You're misinterpreting your emotions. Raw emotions are a good sign. It means that the therapy is working. But they have nothing to do with me. We barely know each other."

I didn't know how long we'd been walking before he stopped me.

"Wait a moment."

He held my hand and brought it to his chest. He pressed it close to his heart.

"Do you feel it?"

I pictured his bloody muscle under my hand, small and quivering like those naked birds who pluck their own feathers out of stress.

"Let's go, Alfred," I said, pulling my hand away.

"I look forward to seeing you all the time. When I saw you in the lobby today, I felt a strange emotion. I had to run away. I'm sorry."

"We need to keep walking," I said, my voice shaking.

We hurried on through the streets of Manhattan. The buildings seemed slightly tilted, the sidewalks crooked. Where were we? There wasn't a subway entrance in sight.

I kept spewing platitudes.

"You will feel better. After some time. You'll see. Everything will come into perspective."

Alfred stopped me again by holding on to my arm.

"I have to ask," he said. "Do you have any feelings for me?"

"We have a friendly connection. We understand each other."

"I knew it as soon as we met," he said, fixing me with his stare. "That we had a connection. I don't know why."

He grabbed my hand and placed it on his chest again. His hand felt wet this time.

"Enough with this nonsense," I said, shaking his damp hand from mine. "What are you, a child?"

He moved his face to the side the way he might have had I slapped him.

"I'm sorry," I said at once.

He stared at me wide-eyed.

A dozen people came out of a movie theater. Winter coats and conversations in French surrounded me.

"*Excusez-moi, mademoiselle!*" someone said. I stopped in place, waiting for everyone to pass. The group of Frenchmen entered a café around the corner.

"We need to find the subway," I said, but I was talking to myself.

Where was Alfred? I scanned the street. Had the earth swallowed him up?

I ended up in Washington Square Park. Exhausted from the walk, I sat on a bench. What had happened at that interpreting session? I'd had trouble concentrating. I had escaped into my own thoughts, memories, daydreams. In front of me, people went back and forth. None of them was Alfred.

There was an email from Zinovia in my inbox. The subject was *Today's Interpreting Session* followed by an exclamation point.

*It is essential in our line of work to keep our clients' best interests in mind, as they are in a vulnerable position. Clearly, without the right interpreter, they wouldn't get the help they need. My instinct, which will have to suffice, tells me that Alfred needs another interpreter for his sessions with me. I don't wish to leave you in the dark. I recommend that you focus more on the words rather than the overall context of the situation. Are you, per chance, identifying with Alfred's circumstances? If you need to talk, or for further clarification, don't hesitate to call me.*

I called my mother. She kept the video off. The moment I heard her voice, I knew I had made a mistake. And yet the instinct to seek comfort was there, as undaunted as when I was a child.

"Did I wake you?"

"I was up. My blood pressure is high. I see trees behind you."

"I'm in the park. I just finished an interpreting assignment. It didn't go well."

"Are you with Billy?"

"No. Alone."

"What are you doing in the park alone? It looks dark. Women go for a run in the park and turn up dead. The news is full of stories like that."

It was a special talent of my mother to turn even the most pleasant circumstances into a horror film.

"It's a busy park," I said. "It's evening time."

"Go home, will you?"

"Have you been going out lately?"

"Yes, I go to the market with Neta every day. We take a stroll in the evenings. Don't worry about me. And thank Billy for me, will you?"

"For what?"

"For paying Neta's hospital bill."

"He what?"

"You didn't know that? He paid Neta's entire hospital bill."

I remembered mentioning to Billy a few weeks ago that Neta, our elderly neighbor in Albania who lived across the road from my mother, had been hospitalized. He had said nothing. I hadn't even been sure he had heard me.

"Good night," she said. "Please go home."

WHEN I GOT HOME, Billy was playing music, one of those indie bands whose sound he never grew tired of. The songs he loved reminded me of a silk scarf I used to own, soft and sooth-ing, and soon enough irritating.

He called to me from the living room. He was sitting by the window. He had opened a bottle of wine and brought out two glasses. Our bordello lamp, purchased as a joke because of its fringes and bright red shade, suffused the living room with a warm glow.

As soon as I came in, he turned off the music and stood up.

"You okay?"

"Sure."

"It doesn't look like it."

I slumped on the sofa. He sat next to me.

"I finished my essay," he said, extending his arm around my shoulders. As he brought me closer, Alfred's face retreated. My shoulders relaxed under his warmth. His familiar scent was soothing, coaxing me to close my eyes. My mother's voice still echoed inside my head. In my mind's eye I saw her face. She multiplied into several people. Then I wasn't sure if they were my mother or Alfred, for they were all grimacing in such a way that implied a lack of control over their faces.

"Have you been drinking alone?" I asked.

"Was waiting for you. I went to see my mother earlier. She sends you her love."

He was always in a good mood after seeing his mother. She offered a listening ear, validation. She didn't correct his every move. She believed that Billy could do no wrong. A twinge of jealousy irritated me.

"I talked to Merita," I said. "She wanted me to thank you for sending money to Neta. You never told me."

"I wanted to send it anonymously, but they messed it up in Albania."

I remembered him sitting next to Neta, who always dressed entirely in black—a black dress, black stockings, that black knitted shawl over her silver hair. They often chatted with me as their interpreter. They had taken to each other right away, hand gesturing, using up the few Albanian words Billy knew, and some English expressions she'd heard. Eventually they asked me to interpret. But how could one translate affection? The way Neta laughed, "Po jo, moj zemër, jo." The way she squeezed his hand before leaving. "Do vij prap." I had tried to make metaphors and idioms resonate, carrying words back and forth, but my efforts had always missed the mark somehow.

"Wine?" Billy said. Alfred's posture appeared in my mind. The way he shrugged, raising one shoulder only, like a frightened child in front of a teacher. "You were working with Alfred, weren't you? You interpreted for him," he said, as if he saw that image also.

"I did. But for the last time. His therapist thought I wasn't up to it."

Billy was deciding what to say, weighing his words carefully.

"Good. Someone else, someone who counts, put an end to it."

I didn't argue. He sipped more wine. It seemed like a mechanical motion, a sign of nervousness, an opportunity for him to occupy himself with something.

"Go out with friends this weekend," he said. "Give Lina a call."

Wishing he'd stop talking, I covered his mouth with my hand. It was a literal gesture, but he took it as flirtatiousness. He removed my hand from his mouth and planted small kisses on my neck. Although I didn't say it, I wanted him to stop. And he did. He leaned back and studied my face. His eyes became observant, like when he studied a movie scene.

"I was working in the garden today at my mother's house and remembered that day we got married."

"It was a beautiful day," I said, remembering the reception his mother had planned, the canopy of flowers and the coral candles, the lemonade fountain, the long table full of Billy's relatives. All Billy had to do was pick up the phone and invite them to his wedding. It was impossible, with all the visas and expenses, to have my relatives there. He hugged me tighter, as if he suspected I was slipping from his grasp.

"It has been a while," he said. "Right?"

The other night, after he told me about Helen's eviction, I'd felt the old spark. Discussing our neighbor's misfortune, picturing her out on the street, had made me crave his touch. But now, while he was drawing nearer, all I could think about was Alfred's inscrutable face.

"I guess it has."

We heard the ring of the intercom.

"Let it ring," he said. "I'm not expecting anyone. Are you?"

"Let's just check. I'll be right back."

Billy followed me. The man outside was looking down, making it impossible for me to see his face. Was he a neighbor who had forgotten his keys? A delivery person? He drew nearer, regaling me with a close-up of a creased forehead. His head moved up. A veiny aquiline nose came closer until it filled up the view.

"I wonder if it's working," a voice behind him said in Albanian.

He made an unexpected movement. The golden cross of a pedant necklace dangled forth, banging on the eye of the camera.

"It's working," he said.

I recognized Zani, a man I had interpreted for some months ago.

Why was he downstairs? I tried to remember the last time I had seen him. He had applied for political asylum and been rejected.

"I know him," I told Billy. "I've interpreted for him before. Let me go downstairs and see what he wants."

"Don't go. Just ask him what he wants from here. Tell him you'll give him a call another day."

"But he's downstairs. I'll be right back."

I let Zani know I was going down.

In the elevator, the specifics of his case came to mind. He had been caught up in a human trafficking case after some criminals had hired him to be their driver. Although he had come clean with the prosecution, and they had promised him asylum, it hadn't worked out as expected. His application was rejected. He had feared for his life after that, worried that his old employers might come after him.

"Hi Zani," I said to him downstairs. "What are you doing here?"

"I couldn't find your number," he said. "But I still had your address."

He was nearly bald, with a ruddy complexion and a suspicious squint that returned unexpectedly during our conversation. There was a flinty, unpredictable edge to him, a feral quality that spoke of his sharp and tested survival skills.

"I'm so glad you're home," a woman's voice said behind him. "I worried we'd come all the way here for nothing."

"I brought my family with me," he said. "They wanted to come."

He introduced me to his much younger wife, a platinum blonde with a penciled beauty mark above her lips, who permitted herself a cynical smile when we shook hands. She was holding a baby, no more than a few months old, in her arms. An older woman who looked like her mother was accompanying them. She didn't say a word, the mother. She looked tired and defeated, as if she had been waiting in line all her life, with little hope her turn would ever come.

"I need to find a new lawyer," he said. "I fired the other guy. Do you know a lawyer who's really good?"

"I do. I have his card upstairs. He's expensive, though."

"It doesn't matter. How good is he?"

"I haven't seen him lose a case yet."

"He's the one I need."

"How come you *all* came to my house?" I asked.

"The baby needed a checkup at the pediatrician. So we thought to stop by after. I'm sorry to bother you."

Wasn't it late for a checkup? Was the baby's pediatrician near my apartment?

"No bother at all," I said quickly, sensing their desperation. "Let's go in. You can sit in the lobby, while I go up to get the lawyer's card."

They followed me inside. On a bulletin board by the door, there were printouts of Helen's furniture. She'd tried to sell everything before her eviction. I felt her gray eyes on me. They still made me uneasy.

The baby started bawling.

"He needs changing," said the wife. "Can I change him here?"

She was pointing at the desk of our doorman, who had stepped out.

"You should have changed him in the bathroom at Starbucks," said Zani. "As I told you a million times."

I thought about inviting them upstairs, but then remembered Billy. What would his face look like if I made an entrance with Zani and his entourage? He had not even wanted me to come downstairs. He wouldn't have done that with any of his friends or colleagues. Was the decision of whom to invite and whom to keep away from our apartment his alone?

"Why don't you all come upstairs?" I told them. "You can change him there."

"It's okay," said Zani. "We'll wait."

"No, I insist," I said. "My husband would love to meet you."

On our way into our apartment, I touched the dusty hole by the door, a memento from the last time we had guests. It crumbled in my fingers. The hallway looked clean and orderly; the house cleaner had been in that afternoon. She had a knack for making all clutter disappear, often by stacking things in unexpected places, making it impossible for us to find anything. But I felt grateful to her now. The Albanian women, finicky about cleanness, looked impressed. They mistook me for a good housewife. I marched to the living room, followed by Zani, his wife, and the mother-in-law holding the crying baby.

Billy was pouring wine into a glass. He took a quick glance at us. He tilted the wineglass sideways. He was studying its surface as if it were a glass ball.

"You can change the baby there," I told Zani's mother-in-law and pointed down the hallway to our bedroom.

Zani walked up to Billy to shake his hand.

"American?" he asked me.

"American," I said.

"Sorry for showing up here," he told Billy in English. "I needed recommendation for lawyer."

Billy nodded but his tired eyes evaded us all, before focusing on me. He looked me up and down, then returned to tilting the wineglass.

"Your wife cares," Zani said.

"Yeah," said Billy. "Definitely."

"I had other interpreters, but it was only job to them. When they reject my asylum application, I was ready to jump off window. It crossed my mind, I promise. She holds my arm, like she's my sister. I don't know if she knows. I never forget. She saved my life."

I hid my eyes from Zani. He insisted on eye contact. I excused myself. In the bathroom, after some deep breathing, the urge to cry fled. Zani's words *saved my life* echoed in my ear. Had I saved his life and didn't know it? Thoughts of Alfred, which I had so far pushed aside, flitted back. I had considered him my friend. How had his attraction gone unnoticed? He had reached for my hands. His needy eyes had burrowed into mine. Why hadn't I canceled our appointment? The situation had turned from bad to worse, and I had done nothing.

Zani was calling to me from the living room.

"Coming!" I shouted. My appointment with Zani from months ago flashed in my mind again. The deathly pallor of his face before the verdict's announcement. The way he had collapsed into his chair after the judge spoke. He'd be deported unless he filed for an appeal.

Zani and Billy were sitting in the living room in silence, not knowing what to say to each other. The mother-in-law came back with the baby, who was now looking at our ceiling fan and making cooing noises, as if asking me to turn it on. He was a gorgeous baby with intelligent dark eyes and chubby hands.

"Your children? Where?" the mother-in-law said upon noticing my smile. She then glanced around the apartment, as if suspecting that we might have hidden our offspring behind the door or under the sofa.

"We don't have any," I said. "No children."

"Why?" she said. "Beautiful children, you two."

Billy laughed as if someone had just told a joke. Zani's wife and his mother-in-law smiled politely, perhaps thinking he must have remembered something amusing. They pretended to play with the baby, keeping their eyes away from the eccentric American. His hilarity struck me as unnerving. What was so funny?

"I hope God bless you with children," Zani said, mistakenly assuming that there was some frustration in Billy's unraveling. "He will. You just have to be patient."

Billy stopped laughing. An uncomfortable silence followed. I looked for the lawyer's card inside a vintage cigar box we kept on our bookshelf.

"Here it is," I told Zani. "Remember, he's expensive. And no one knows how things will go with the new administration."

"This new president is tough one," Zani said. "But he might be good, I think."

Occasionally, I ran into immigrants whose political leanings were inexplicable. It happened so frequently that it had ceased to surprise me.

"Can you interpret for me again?" Zani said.

"I can't. I'm taking a break for the moment."

"Can't you make an exception?"

"Exception?" Billy said. "Why should she?"

"I got it, Billy," I said.

"But is he getting it?" Billy said and pointed at Zani.

"Yes," I said. "He is getting it."

That Billy had gone from ignoring his existence to attacking him startled Zani. He didn't seem intimidated or even dismayed by my husband's irritation.

"She just said no," Billy said to him. "Didn't you hear her?"

Although he said nothing, Zani seemed pleasantly surprised. Billy had defied his expectations. He had seemed quiet, professorial, and standoffish at first glance. But he was making it clear that he could also be boorish and irate. He had suddenly come to life as the kind of man Zani looked up to.

"Would you all like a glass of wine?" I asked the family. Zani's wife was gesturing toward him. She wanted them to leave. The mother-in-law was preoccupied with the baby, but even she took a few steps toward the door.

"Pour me one," said Zani, looking at Billy with renewed interest. "Where in America are you from?"

"I was born in Manhattan. Grew up in Connecticut."

"I've been to Connecticut. For a construction project."

"Okay," Billy said, unsettled by Zani's friendliness.

"You know a town called Darien?"

"I do."

"Very nice, Darien. I will get a house there one day. As soon as I take care of my immigration paperwork."

Billy sipped his wine and looked out the window. I poured Zani a glass of wine.

I offered some to his wife also, but she shook her head.

"We've got to go," she said impatiently. "The baby needs to sleep. Thank you for the wine and for your help. Zani will use another interpreter."

"I can recommend you one," I said. "I know many interpreters."

"Give me your phone number," said Zani.

Intent that they should leave, his wife was now pulling him by the arm. Billy strode past us without saying a word, then went to his office.

I walked Zani and his family to the door.

Zani turned to me and said, "Your husband is tough man. I like that. But, still, you should have married Albanian. We enjoy drinking together. He likes drinking alone. Not good."

"He's not really a drinker."

"Were your parents upset that you didn't marry Albanian? Sure, they were. They can't even talk to son-in-law."

"It's none of your business what her parents think," Zani's wife said in English. "Plus, she's an interpreter. Keep out of it, won't you?"

Once they left, Billy's strange laugh kept replaying in my ears. He had barely managed to keep his rudeness under control. I stopped by his office.

"Are you coming to the living room?" I asked.

My posture, leaning toward him, waiting for an answer, felt unnatural.

"You'll do it, won't you? You'll interpret for him."

"I told him no. Didn't you hear me?"

He avoided eye contact. His prior warmth had disappeared.

"I wrote to Anna earlier," I said. "I'm seeing her and Lina on Monday. Do you want to come?"

He liked it when I hung out with Anna.

"I'm playing squash on Monday." He turned to his computer. "Sorry, but I asked someone for a quote for my book. They have some questions. It might take me a while."

Back in the living room, I poured myself a glass and drank alone. The Empire State Building was wearing its signature white costume that evening. It twinkled unexpectedly, disappearing for seconds at a time, only to emerge again, reclaiming the limelight. My silhouette and the wine bottle reflected on the glass above the skyscrapers. For an instant Billy's image appeared there also. He was bringing his pillow from our bedroom to his office. He was not sleeping in our bedroom that night.

An airplane beam bore a resemblance to a shooting star until it disappeared. The lights in the nearby building were turning off one by one. I sat there until it all went dark.

A low simmering anger prompted me to march to Billy's office. He had no right to treat my friends like that. He hadn't even apologized about that night he struck the wall. The memory still stung. I braced myself for an argument. It was in vain; he had fallen asleep on his futon. His laptop was still open, on the floor. I covered him with a blanket. He grasped my hand. He wasn't awake; he was just reaching for me in his sleep. His face showed a quiet sorrow, a tinge of frailty. It occurred to me that I'd seen that expression earlier when I had come back to the apartment with Zani and his family. He had been pouring wine into my glass. He had been waiting for me, for us to pick up where we left off. I had an urge to crawl into bed and fall asleep next to him. But his grip on my hand relaxed. I turned off the light and left the room.

# 5.

ANNA AND I MET AT A LITTLE ITALIAN PLACE IN SOHO called Piccolo Posto. She often teased me about the kind of places I took her to. Small and dingy, she called them. She did admit she liked the food, and that she even went back on her own. Still, they never became her favorite restaurants. Like Billy, Anna preferred pricier eateries. With its communal tables and wall signs that said, *An entrée entitles you to a seat and half a table for 15 minutes*, Piccolo Posto was not an ideal place for a heart-to-heart. But lack of privacy wouldn't be a problem. Our conversations were hardly titillating.

Anna was especially fond of *have yous*—Have you seen this play at the Public? Have you seen this movie at the Angelika? Have you been to MoMA lately? Ours was a friendship of amusement, not one of disclosure and revelation. We went places together—movies, plays, parties. Going out with her had always been an escape into a different life for me, the life of the affluent searching for entertainment, far from the mind-numbing translations of appliance manuals or poignant stories revealing the worst of human nature.

She had taught me a new model of friendship. We saw each other casually whenever she was in town. Like seaweed, we floated untethered, without the anchor of intimacies. But in every relationship a point of reflection arrives, when closeness, or lack of it, comes under scrutiny. While waiting for Anna at Piccolo Posto, I wondered why our friendship seemed always about to start. Why had we never confided in each other? The only time I'd seen a different Anna was for her forty-fifth birthday, a year ago. She had asked to meet me after a solitary stroll in Central Park. Her eyes had been dreamy. Her manner distant. She had reminded me of other melancholy heroines then, the frail Blanche who preferred to remain in the shadows, or the insecure Laura, forever waiting for a gentleman caller.

But that was not the true Anna. She must have had a bad day. Naturally, she had nothing in common with those Tennessee Williams women, I thought, as she came toward me and kissed my cheek, cheerful and lively, in eclectic clothes she bought in faraway countries and that androgynous fragrance. With her pitch-black hair and red mouth, she looked powerful and in control. Her face showed no trace of that lost woman wanting the company of trees rather than people for her birthday. She was wearing a wool cape coat in bright blue that came to her knees, and glass bead earrings. She gave me a hug. Whenever we met, I reverted to my adolescence, when, while hanging out with someone popular, it seemed like they were doing me a favor. I even felt it now, that ridiculous desire to show her off. She had an ease about her, a certain aura of superiority, that never failed to come through.

"Nice jacket," she said.

"You've seen it before."

"Have I?"

"Last year."

Seeing Anna always reminded me that my clothes were outdated. *I have to go shopping*, I always thought, but then forgot, until I saw her again.

We went to the counter to order. There were no waiters in Piccolo Posto. Customers ordered in the front part of the kitchen and returned to pick up their food when it was ready.

"What are you ordering?"

"Penne with ricotta and spinach. You?"

"Farfalle in pink vodka sauce."

The lunch crowd had already left and it was still early for dinner, so most of the tables were open. A stylish Japanese couple in their twenties were whispering over their spaghetti and meatballs. The Italian guy behind the counter was knocking back house wine and chatting with the Mexican cooks. He spoke in Italian. They responded in Spanish. They were having a good time, joking and chuckling while their pans sizzled.

Anna and I were still talking about the weather, bemoaning how endless this New York winter was.

"I'm ready for a change," she said.

"Penne with spinach and penne with pink sauce," said the Italian guy behind the counter.

I went to pick up our plates and brought them to the table.

Her eyes darted to my plate and then back to hers. "Is there something wrong?"

"I asked for farfalle," she said.

"They made you penne. Take it back."

"No. I don't have much time. I need to be on a plane in a few hours."

"But they do it quickly. Do you want me to tell them?"

"It's fine," she said, holding on to my arm. "I'm pretty hungry, anyway. And they were just making fun of a customer who complained all the time."

"Okay. Where are you off to this time?"

"Seoul. South Korea."

"For how long?"

"A year. The right offer came at the right time. I will be teaching a violin course at a university."

"When did you decide this?"

"Just last week. Isn't it crazy? I've been overwhelmed here. It's not even about the music anymore. Once you reach a certain status, it's all about the looks. Did I tell you I'll be in *Vogue*? Anyway, I cleared out my schedule from all that. No more dieting. After the election, I'm happy to leave this country. I was devastated. I kept crying and crying. How can this happen?"

Anna went on about how fortuitous it was that she would skip living in her Fort Greene brownstone for a year and settle for Gangnam, one of Seoul's poshest neighborhoods. Would she have asked to meet me before leaving town for a year? I wondered. I had reached out to her on a whim after seeing some photos she'd posted online. I had wanted a distraction from my situation with Alfred, from my resentments toward Billy. But instead of providing a distraction, seeing Anna was prompting me to analyze our relationship. Her phone rang. She glanced at it but didn't pick it up. Some detail about her upcoming trip must have weighed on her mind. This aspect of spending time together—her commitments competing for her attention and that feeling of being in her way while she had more important things to do—had slipped my mind. She would not have contacted me, I knew. Had I not texted her the day before, she would have skipped town for a year and not said goodbye.

"Next weekend I'm invited to a wedding in Seoul," she said. "One of my future colleagues at the university is getting married. In South Korea, when a couple gets married, the groom gives his mother-in-law a goose. Geese mate forever, you know?"

"What does she do with it?"

"Puts it on the shelf."

"What shelf?"

"It's not a real goose, silly. I mean it probably was many years ago, but now it's a wooden figurine or something like that."

As Anna went on about the Korean wedding, I remembered seeing pictures of her attending weddings in various countries—Belarus, Germany, Spain. Why did she never mention her love affairs to me? According to social media, hundreds of people were enamored with her.

"What else is new with you?" she said, turning her attention toward me. "Tell me something happy. Or interesting."

"Someone has been sending me flowers," I said. "Purple hyacinths. Two bouquets so far. It doesn't say whom they're from."

"Intriguing. There's no note at all?"

"There's a note with just my name."

"And they're not from Billy?"

"They're not from Billy."

Just then, Lina entered the restaurant. She was half an hour early. I had told her to meet me at the restaurant so we could take the subway together to Williamsburg. She wanted to introduce me to someone she had been dating.

"Hi there!" Lina said. Her bright eyes looked bigger since she had arrived in America. She was still taking everything in. She placed a gaudy handbag embellished with crystals next to me. It was the kind of purse those Russian ladies who lived in Brighton Beach might prefer, clutching them to their sides whenever a stranger sat next to them on the Q. Lina was only twenty-nine, but she had old-fashioned taste.

"I got off work early," she said. "I came straight here. Sorry if I'm a bit early."

"Do you want to order something?" I asked. "A drink?"

"Let's get one in Williamsburg."

"Do you remember Lina?" I told Anna. "I think you two met once in my apartment."

"Yes," Anna said, shaking her hand. "I met you briefly. The cousin who won the green card lottery. I had no idea such a thing existed. A lottery that allows you to live in another country. Did you win the first time you applied?"

"Lina applied for ten years in a row," I said. "She got it this time."

"May I ask why you applied?" Anna said. "Just curious."

"Because I wanted to move to America."

"But why?" Anna said. "Why America? There are so many countries in the world you could have gone to. Closer to home. I think the Czech Republic is much more beautiful, for example. I just spent a month in Prague last year. Amazing."

Lina stared at Anna. I could see her spinning those questions around in her mind. My cousin had considered it common knowledge that one didn't immigrate to a country for its natural or architectural beauty, but for its economic opportunities. She had assumed that anyone would understand why she had wanted to come to America. Nobody moved to the Czech Republic, not unless you were a well-to-do American in search of adventure. But why would Anna understand? How could Anna, who was born and raised in the West Village, whose father was some kind of CEO, understand water or electricity shortages, or helping out aging parents and relatives who had worked all their lives only to end up with a retirement that didn't even cover their basic necessities? No, Anna couldn't understand Lina's reason for moving to another country any more than Lina could understand Anna's.

"Have you ever been to Albania?" Lina asked.

"Not yet," Anna said. "I had a concert scheduled in Zagreb a couple of months ago."

"How did you like it?" Lina asked. "I love Zagreb."

"I didn't get to see it, unfortunately. The concert was canceled. I flew back to New York that night."

Had Anna mentioned Zagreb to me before? Something about it sounded familiar. Had Billy and I talked about Anna going to Zagreb for a concert? Had she posted about it online? A famous allegro from Vivaldi, coming from Anna's phone, interrupted our conversation.

"I should probably head out," she said, putting the rest of the pasta into a to-go box. "I need to pick up my suitcases."

We hugged. "I'll see you all next year," Anna said.

"I remember meeting her at your apartment before," Lina said after Anna walked out. "Friendly woman."

"Yes. She's friendly." I nodded, feeling a knot in my throat.

"I'm being sarcastic," Lina said. "She wasn't friendly at all to me before."

"No?"

"Not at all. I thought that maybe she was jealous or something."

"Jealous?"

"Since you were such good friends already. Maybe she thought that since your cousin moved to New York City, you might spend less time with her. You know how some people can get?"

Had Anna been jealous over me? All the pleasant moments between us gushed back. She would always bring me presents from her travels, a suede shoulder purse once, a sparkling hair clip, a copy of F. Scott Fitzgerald's *Tender Is the Night* in Italian, because I had once mentioned in passing that I liked it more than *The Great Gatsby*. Whenever she'd get free tickets to a concert or play, which happened frequently because of her connections, she'd text me. She never forgot my birthday, no matter what country she was in at the time. Although she was already gone, I caught a drift of sandalwood. That she'd be gone for a year made me sad. I'd miss her alienating exuberance.

"How do you know her again?" Lina asked.

"Billy went to college with her."

"She's as old as Billy? Midforties? I thought she was my age."

"Of course she isn't twenty-nine."

She pulled out her phone and looked at Anna's social media pictures.

"She plays in a real orchestra. I had no idea. Big venues, too."

"She plays for the New York Philharmonic and is part of a small orchestra."

"Let's go," Lina then said. "We're meeting Ben in half an hour."

"Is Ben Albanian, by the way?"

Lina pursed her lips together and tilted her head slightly. It was an Albanian facial expression Billy had once made me aware of. It was like shrugging with your mouth, he had said.

"I want a man who helps out around the house. American men do dishes and cook. I've seen Billy do your laundry."

"Has Ben done your laundry yet?"

She shrugged. "It's still early. But, mainly, I just want something real, like what you have."

"Like what I have?" I laughed.

"That's right. Billy always looks you in the eye."

"He what?"

"When you're in the room, whenever he does or says something, he looks you in the eye."

Was that true? Did Billy aim his devoted green light at me whenever he did or said something? People always looked at each other; they had to, especially if they lived together or were married.

"It doesn't sound that special really. Looks me in the eye?"

"I think it is special," Lina said. "I've seen plenty of married people before."

I HADN'T BEEN BACK to Williamsburg since Billy and I moved in together in Fort Greene seven years ago. While walking around my old neighborhood, all my old apartments came to mind. One moment I'd be excited about a place, the next, there I was, carrying my two suitcases out of it. I hadn't thought of my old roommates in years, their cameo roles inconsequential to my life. But now their faces, voices, and conversations appeared like in a film, and the clarity of the images surprised me. I also remembered the apartments well, the layouts, the furniture, someone's calico cat that kept peeing on my shoes, a brave squirrel that would leap into our kitchen to steal baguettes. The restaurant where we were meeting Ben was facing the apartment I used to share with a French girl, whose name now escaped me.

"I'm going to buy us some drinks," Lina said.

I sat at a table and looked outside. The building had been unimpressive, but my apartment had been lovely. My room had been spacious and bright with three large windows overlooking a café with outdoor seating. The café's name had changed, but everything else looked the same—the bentwood chairs and the round tables outside. There were maroon curtains behind my old window. What twentysomething lived there now? My curtains used to be yellow, reaching right below the wide windowsills. I would sit and stare aimlessly at Bedford Avenue for hours, at friends or couples, never families, going out for the night. It was there where I'd sit and have long phone conversations with my father. Where my mother called to say he was in the hospital, although he had already died. He had been going for a swim, she said. Maybe he was tired, I had thought, that valiant effort to seem happy for her and for me finally catching up with him. Maybe rest had seemed like the only thing he wanted. It was a heart attack, she explained, a clarification that had arrived a second too late, after that awful idea had lodged into my mind. There was no truth to it, but it used to come back to me every evening, as I sat and stared at Bedford Avenue, without him to talk to. For years, I saw him walking into the water, sifting through the gold the sun had spread on the water's surface.

My French roommate had proved a good distraction back then. She was trying to be an actor and practiced her monologues in the living room. Not only was she theatrical by nature, but she also tended to overdo it with the acting. Her shrieks and frowns always made me laugh. *How did I do?* she'd say to me. I'd lie, telling her she did great, after which she'd beam and applaud with excitement. Her obsession with acting had lasted six months before she concluded she wanted to become a painter.

"I used to live in that apartment there," I told Lina.

"I love it here, except it's so expensive. This street reminds me of Tirana."

"Do you ever miss home?"

"Of course. But what's the point of thinking about it? I told myself I'll focus on succeeding, which means making money. I'm not going to end up like Alma, cleaning toilets."

I felt the sting of her words, as if they had been directed at me. Why would she talk that way about her own sister?

"Alma is one of the smartest people I know," I said defensively.

"How can she be smart?" Lina said. "If she ended up that way? You know Fatos is such a loser. She had Bill soon after she got married, and Klinton a year later. Thank God they waited a while to have Klea."

That Alma had named not just one but two of her boys after Bill Clinton had startled us all back then. Apparently, Fatos's family had some vague connections to Kosovo, and he had wanted to express his gratitude for Clinton ending the Kosovo War while he was president. When their daughter came along, we all suspected they might call her Hilari, but it turned out they didn't. Incidentally, Billy didn't find her sons' names half as amusing as her husband's. A twinkle came to his eyes whenever he mentioned his name.

"She had a chance to make something of herself, and she blew it," Lina went on. "It's too late now."

Lina refused to believe that some circumstances could twist in such a way as to trap a person, even a smart one. She preferred to believe that everything had been up to Alma, and she had failed.

"Can I ask you a question?" she said, studying my face. "How much do these translations and interpreting assignments pay? Wouldn't you make more money working for a business or something?"

Lina was younger than me, and our relationship had, so far, gone along the usual cousinship track—we chatted amiably during family gatherings, kept tabs on each other's major life events, and reminisced over the same family jokes. But although I'd known her since she was born, in some ways, I had only begun to get to know her since she had moved to Brooklyn. A new immigrant, her main priority was financial security. In that respect, she found me lacking, distracted, failing to keep my eyes on the prize. I was undermining the importance of her hard efforts toward success.

"There came a point," I said, "when I felt that I was responsible for everyone's well-being."

"What do you mean everyone's well-being, the entire world's well-being?"

"Yes," I said. "The entire world's happiness."

Lina didn't know what to say. She smiled at first, then her amusement turned to laughter. A desire to explain myself died quickly. It was a bit like a choir, I had wanted to tell her, how the smallest and strongest voices are equally responsible for how the sound turns out. But then what did it matter if she knew what I meant or not?

Lina must have perceived that her laughter was unwelcome. She sobered up.

"I've always felt that other people don't matter," she said.

"They don't?"

"I mean my family, sure. But, generally speaking, only my own happiness matters. I'm nicer to other people when I'm happy myself."

"What is it that makes you happy?"

"A good paycheck. No matter how you put it—money wins. It's the way of the world."

"But don't you ever ask yourself," I said, "What are all those hours you spend in front of a computer for, crunching numbers for who knows who? What difference does it make?"

Something about my tone had put her on guard. She leaned back and said nothing. She had always looked up to me—children often look up to older cousins—and I was her only relative in New York. After all, unlike her sister, who cleaned the shit of the Greeks in Athens, I had once worked at the UN. What would she tell the people back home about me now? *She's lost her marbles, like her mother.*

A blondish man with dull features was smiling in our direction from the other side of the road. I thought he was someone who knew me, an old roommate perhaps, a friend I didn't immediately recognize. Then it dawned on me that after all these years most of my friends and acquaintances had moved on from there.

"That's Ben," Lina said, waving at him. "What do you think?"

"He's really cute," I said, thinking that Ben, most decisively, was the dictionary definition of a frat boy.

"I think so, too," Lina said shyly.

"Your face is reminding me of that time I took you to the circus. You were little; you don't remember."

"Do you know what my first memory of you is?" Lina said, forgetting about Ben for a moment. "I must have been around six or something. We were throwing out the trash together one night. A stranger stopped us by the stairs. He noticed a thread in my skirt, that's what he said anyway, and reached for my knee to pull it. You hit him with something. You hit him hard on the head. He bled. And then I hit him, too."

I stared at her. I had no memory of that happening. Was she confusing me with someone else?

# 6.

DEAR INTERPRETER,

*Zinovia has alerted us to your difficulties during your most recent appointment. She has informed us of her decision to terminate your assignment and to find a replacement for you. Can we meet to discuss? Please refrain from scheduling any other interpreting appointments. The mental well-being of the individuals and families we serve is of paramount importance to us.*

I was rereading the email while waiting to meet with the coordinator of the organization that hired me for interpreting work. The lively atmosphere of the hallway offset the email's somber tone. Whitney Houston's "I'm Every Woman," a fusion of languages, a piercing laughter wafted through the open doors of an auditorium across the hall. Awkward teens stood in a circle by the door drinking orange punch and Pepsi from plastic cups. Women in colorful, wraparound cloths, black hijabs, burkas, and others, less conspicuous, in jeans and sweatshirts, huddled near side tables covered with refreshments.

"Hello there," called the coordinator from behind me, opening her door. "Sorry for the wait. Today is our get-together in the auditorium."

"Great turnout."

"You're welcome to stay after. We have some new people. Please introduce yourself. We want them to feel welcomed."

She motioned for me to sit down.

"Give me a second," she said, while searching for something in her computer. Perhaps she wanted to read Zinovia's email once again, refresh her memory about my incompetence. She was young and slight in body, with stringy hair, the sort of busy woman who often forgot about her own appearance. Her no-frills outfit, T-shirt and jeans, resembled my own clothes. While reading, a serious expression took over her face. She seemed merrier in the wall pictures, embracing new refugee arrivals from South Sudan, Liberia, Syria, Iraq. Cascading green foliage circled the frames, crossing over some file cabinets before shooting up the ceiling. Was Zinovia's email about me that long? I went back to studying the room. There was only one window inside, but it was enormous. It faced a building clad in uneven blocks, older than the one we were in, from the turn of the twentieth century or even earlier. Had the architects, after seeing the building, varied the monotony of their job by playing a prank?

*You know what would be great here? A huuuge window.*

Picturing them pointing at the wall made me laugh. The coordinator looked up.

"So, why don't you tell me what happened in your own words?" she said. "Zinovia is adamant that you should no longer interpret for Alfred."

Where would I start? Alfred waiting for me in the park, looking at his watch. The speeding car in front of us, his hand holding me back.

"After we met," I said. "I thought it was important for him to get therapy as soon as possible. He sees visions, creatures that talk to him."

The way her eyes widened reminded me of Billy studying my face the night before. Had they both thought the same, that something was wrong with me?

"He needs therapy, of course. But are you the right person to interpret for him?"

"I'm not."

"Okay. Let's start from the beginning, shall we?"

"Sure. I took him to the dentist. For a root canal. Then he asked if I could interpret for him during his therapy sessions."

"Did you discuss Alfred's situation with him beforehand?"

"We did talk, yes."

"Did he tell you what was troubling him?"

"He told me about the creatures he sees. Hallucinations."

"Did you identify with him in any way?"

"Our mothers' stories are kind of similar. So, yes."

I looked at the window again.

*Is this big enough? No, let's make it even bigger. Let them enjoy it. Why be stingy?*

"Are you smiling because you're nervous?" she said.

I wasn't sure if I felt nervous.

"It's the window. It's huge, but it faces a wall."

She looked me over again. "Yes. Maybe nervousness," I added.

"Are you familiar with compassion fatigue? Inappropriate reactions, detachment from social connections, mood swings—that sort of thing."

"I've heard of it."

She was expecting me to say more. But what?

"Something to look out for?" she finally said.

"I'll look out for it, sure."

"Your identification with Alfred's mother is unfortunate but not uncommon," she said. "I recommend that you take a break of three months from doing other assignments. We'll then meet again to reassess."

"Can I do other kinds of interpreting? Court interpreting?"

"It's better to take a complete break."

"Okay."

"Translations are fine, of course."

She was writing something down, first in a notebook, then on her PC. I followed two of the trailing plants with my eyes. One was hanging over the windowsill, behind her. Another was right above her head. I pictured the plants coiling around her body, tying her arms in place, until she could no longer move. They'd wind around her chest over and over.

"Listen, I'm wondering if you could do me a favor," she said.

"Of course."

"Apparently, Alfred felt comfortable with you as an interpreter. He has cancelled his second appointment. Do you think you could have a talk with him and see if you can convince him to go back to Zinovia?"

Since that day we left Zinovia's office, Alfred and I hadn't seen each other. Some distance was necessary, I had thought.

"I can try," I told her. "I'll give him a call this week."

"He's actually next door, at the get-together. I met him earlier. Can you talk to him now?"

"Of course."

Even after I left the office, the image played out. The plants, coiling around her neck, over and over. Running out of breath, she collapsed on the floor.

The hallway was choked with people. In the auditorium, a Sudanese woman in an orange headscarf wrapped loosely around her head stepped up onto a small stage. Her dress was striking, with huge, orange flowers, matching her headscarf. Unfamiliar languages always put me on the lookout for repeated sound combinations. I then waited and hoped for them to become comprehensible through context. Learning a foreign language wasn't too different from getting to know a new person. Acquaintance was linked to exposure. Familiarity meant understanding patterns.

The Sudanese woman handed the microphone to her interpreter.

"I used to work for UNESCO, protecting women and children," the interpreter said. "Women and children who faced awful choices from a young age. Join a terror group by force or die. Stay in an abusive marriage or get killed. One day strangers broke into my house, tortured me, and set fire to my kitchen. I was afraid for my life. I left my children behind when I escaped my country. I found myself in refugee camps alone, suffering from anxiety and loneliness."

I spotted Alfred a short distance ahead of me.

He was standing next to a pregnant woman fanning herself with a *People* magazine. There she was, Vilma, the pregnant wife, the object of all my speculations. Taller than Alfred, she was bulky and wore a flowery dress too small for her body. Her arms bulged out of her short sleeves. Her brown curls barely covered her low-cut neckline. Whenever she took a breath, her cleavage deepened. At first sight, Vilma reminded me of an Albanian expression my cousin Alma used to be fond of. *She looks like the sort of person*, Alma would say, *you might have a fight with while eating baklava.* Maybe it was that hint of irritation while addressing Alfred, or the way her eyebrow curved when he spoke to her, but the more I studied her, the more volatile she seemed. No stretch of imagination was required to picture Vilma quarreling while relishing a delicious dessert.

I couldn't bring myself to go and greet them. But my new assignment, so to speak, was to convince him to go back to Zinovia and continue therapy. I stood nearby, hoping Alfred would notice and come to talk to me.

I could hear their conversation.

"Alfred, you're going to break your new phone. Is that what you want, huh?"

"It didn't break. Why do you think I would want that, Vilma? Whoever would want that?"

He bent down to pick up his phone, exposing a hairy lower back and a ribbon of white boxers. "Look, it's not broken at all."

He gave Vilma his large Samsung phone, which had slid down his leg. She grabbed it and tossed it inside her red bag.

Under the fluorescent lights and Vilma's imposing presence, Alfred looked miserable. He was no longer the enigmatic man who had been waiting for me at dusk, in Washington Square Park. His marital issues were on display for everyone to see. He seemed anxious, annoyed, but still eager to satisfy Vilma.

Someone tapped me on my shoulder. It was Leyla.

"What are you doing here?" I said, giving her a hug.

"You gave me a card with this organization's number. I called and they said I should come tonight. To meet people."

She looked more worn out than I remembered her, with mauve circles under her eyes and a cold sore on her upper lip. Her voice wasn't exuberant, like before. She sounded sleepy.

"Anything new with your paperwork?" I asked.

"It's not looking good," she said. "They might no longer approve domestic abuse cases. We talked about this already, didn't we?"

"Yes, that night at my apartment. Listen, I don't know if you got my texts, but I'd like to apologize about my husband. He was upset at me. It had nothing to do with you."

"I know. But my ex-husband used to throw things all over the house. He banged the door, too, sometimes. It reminded me of that."

"I'm sorry. I wish he hadn't done that."

She glanced down for a bit.

"Is that something he does a lot? He destroyed your wall."

"No, not at all. We were having some problems and he took it out on the wall."

"Okay. I get it."

She didn't believe me, I could tell. She suspected that I was lying and covering up for Billy. Ahead of us, Alfred offered Vilma an empty chair. She refused to take it. Then he looked straight at me. When our eyes met, he gave a little nod.

"At least he didn't take it out on you physically," Leyla said. "Right?"

"He wouldn't take it out on me."

"I hope so."

"He would not."

She remained unconvinced; I could tell.

"Are your husband's friends still stalking you?"

"Yes. His cousin is here now. The other day I was on the subway. I dozed off. A bright light woke me up. He was taking pictures of me and had forgotten the flash was on. Of course, he got off the train the moment I woke up."

"Do you think he'll ever come here?"

"My husband? No. But he does need to see a doctor. He needs medications. And nobody tells him that."

"Let's get together sometime, get coffee or lunch?"

"I can't afford that kind of thing."

"I'll pay."

"Did you have a chance to look around for an interpreting job for me, as you said you would?"

I paid closer attention to her appearance. She was wearing a pair of denim overalls that crumpled around her plastic boots, and a long cardigan that came to her knees. She had dirt in her nails, like children do after playing outside. She even smelled a bit, like she hadn't showered in a couple of weeks. Why hadn't I noticed it earlier?

As I stumbled for an answer, she stared at my face. I couldn't come up with anything, so we fell into silence. She said she wanted to get some water. She now stood by the cooler while taking short sips from a plastic cup. Would she come back? Was our conversation over? I didn't know what to make of it. She had never responded to any of my messages after Billy's angry rant. How could she expect me to look for a job for her? Then I felt guilty. Looking for a job on her behalf hadn't even crossed my mind, although I had often wondered what had become of her.

A familiar voice in my native language distracted me.

"Greetings. How are we doing tonight?" Alfred was standing next to me, but kept his eyes fixed on a group of people ahead of us. He spoke quietly and with a strange formality, like secret collaborators do in old movies.

"I'm fine," I said. "How about you? How is it going with Zinovia?"

He turned slightly in my direction and took a steadying breath. I worried if his absurd anxiety would make Vilma suspicious about us, for something that wasn't even there. She was nearby, with her back to us, talking to one of the other Albanian interpreters.

"I will not go to Zinovia anymore."

"Why not?"

"You quit. Why did you quit?"

"I wasn't the right person to interpret for you."

"Who decides that?"

"Was Zinovia not able to find anyone else?"

"She did. They were ready to start the training, but I told her not to. I felt terrible after that last session. I didn't want to repeat it."

"But it's normal," I said. "To feel bad after a therapy session."

"I'm not sure if I felt bad because of the therapy or about what happened after."

"Think about your life. Your baby's life."

"Do you think we can meet sometimes so we can talk?" Alfred said. "We can sort this out."

It was important to convince him to go back to therapy, the coordinator had said.

"Yes," I said. "Let's meet up soon."

"When?"

"Whenever you want. Email me."

"But I have your phone number."

"Okay. Text me then."

"Can I? When is a good time? Evening time?"

Vilma turned around and smiled at me. When she drew near, Alfred didn't have to introduce us. She knew who I was.

"Thank you for helping Alfred at the dentist," she said in English. "I was working that night. And for taking him to the psychiatrist. I can't hear about his past in my condition."

She ran her hand over her belly. "You understand?"

"Of course. Congratulations, by the way."

"Thank you. Alfred and I are excited. I'm glad he's getting the help he needs."

Vilma eyed me eagerly. Her hopes, laid bare in front of me, made me conscious of a growing discomfort. I looked at Alfred, but he avoided my gaze and went to talk to someone. He hadn't told her he had quit therapy.

She leaned toward me. "Do you think he'll be all right?"

"I don't know," I said. "Let's hope."

"Does he talk about me during therapy?"

"I can't discuss that."

"It's just that we've been fighting a lot. I worry I'm responsible. For those creatures, you know?"

Maybe, if she wasn't standing so close to me, I would keep feeling sorry for Vilma, who was now holding on to my arm. But her painted mouth was much too close, emitting a warm breath and a strong cheddar-and-sour-cream odor. A tiny potato chip, the size of a sunflower seed, was stuck stubbornly on her upper lip. It kept swinging and sliding like a crowd-pleasing gymnast, holding on for dear life. I feared she'd grab my hand and have me feel her heartbeat the way Alfred had done. *Do you feel it? Do you?* What if *that* was something normal within their family?

I was relieved when Alfred came back. He looked uncomfortable when he saw us standing close to each other.

Vilma took some distance from me.

"I work at a beer garden in the Bronx," she said. "Why don't you come by with your husband sometime?"

Did she really emphasize *your husband,* or did it just seem that way to me? As if I had intended to go there with other people's husbands. How did she know I was married anyway? Had they talked about me at home? *Is your interpreter married?* Vilma must have asked. *She is.* Alfred had said. *I don't hang around with unmarried interpreters, Vilma, what sort of man do you take me for?*

"Where is your husband tonight?" she said. "Why isn't he here?"

"I just stopped by for a work thing."

"Maybe we'll see him next time," she said. "At the beer garden."

Perhaps she was simply being cordial. After all, she was inviting us to a restaurant she worked at.

"It was nice to meet you. And nice to see you again, Alfred," I said.

"Likewise," she said warmly, touching my arm again. Yes, I was imagining things. Vilma was simply grateful that I had been interpreting for Alfred.

THE AIR OUTSIDE WAS CHILLY. Shriveled-up bodies breached the cold air as they rushed toward the subway station. Tiny, twirling clouds fled from everyone's mouths. On the sidewalk opposite me I recognized Leyla's quilted coat, long enough to brush the ground. She was walking at a brisk pace. Was it because of the cold? Or was someone following her?

I had a good view of all the people behind her. Were any of them her husband's cousin, his friends? It didn't look that way. Everyone was minding their own business, hurrying toward the warm underground, which confirmed my earlier suspicions. Nobody was following her. Maybe Leyla suffered from some delusional disorder, some kind of paranoia that muddled her perceptions. Even her friend Sanaz hadn't seemed convinced that someone had been spying on them as they shopped at Sephora.

A gust of wind made me shudder. A boy inside a gyro food truck slammed shut a window. On the other side of the street a man cursed a car that splashed him. It was then that a bright light, a camera flash it turned out, hovered in the air at a short distance from Leyla. A man was pointing his phone toward her. Once the flashlight died, he lowered his arm and took a look at his phone, ensuring the photo was satisfactory. Startled at this turn of events, I crossed the street and followed them both, possessed by a sudden resolve to see everything through.

The man walked briskly, keeping the same distance from Leyla. He looked young from the back, wearing skinny jeans and a hooded puffer jacket. Would he follow her all the way to the subway? Did he intend to take more photos of her? Maybe the photos he'd already taken were enough. While Leyla continued straight, he turned left and disappeared inside a sports goods store. I followed him. It was unbearably bright inside, and loud, the kind of store where music is in the foreground. He paced in front of a rack of Nikes and Adidas, picked up a shoe and studied it, running his fingers over its leather, testing the Velcro strips. I stood nearby, pretending to look at women's shoes.

"Do you need any help?" a salesperson asked him.

"Just looking around," he said. He had dark, wavy hair, but I couldn't see his face.

He took his time examining the shoes. His phone rang, a piercing, unpleasant sound. He let it ring, focused as he was on the shoes. He picked it up after a few seconds, but it was too late. He inserted it into his back pocket.

The salesperson approached me. "The store will close in fifteen minutes. Just letting you know."

The sharpest fluorescent lights flickered a few times before turning off. The music stopped as well.

I walked up behind him.

"Those are nice," I said, breaking the deep silence around us.

He jumped the moment I spoke. "You frightened me," he said, placing his hand on his chest. "Yeah, those are good."

At first his voice was dull, but the more we stood there, picking up various shoes, studying and admiring them, the more comfortable he felt. His voice became bouncier. His chest expanded. He grinned, revealing chipped, yellow teeth. They were in a terrible state—no middle-class American would be caught dead with teeth like that—but otherwise this roguish scoundrel wasn't bad-looking. His yellow-hazel eyes were close together and had a magnetic quality, promising mischief.

"You looking for shoes, too?" He jutted his chin forward, with childlike bravado.

"Yeah."

"Saw a sick pair the other day," he said and pulled up his phone. "But can't find them anywhere in my size."

"What did they look like?"

He started flipping through his photos while looking for a picture of the shoes. There was Leyla walking the streets alone at dusk, her shoulders slouching under the weight of a backpack. Leyla at a park, her face turned toward the sun. Suddenly aware that he was showing me her photos, he tilted his phone toward him. A sudden fear got to me. It wasn't just his presence or his offhand way of glancing at her pictures, but the idea that revolting things that seemed implausible could happen at any time. With so little effort, you could get intolerably close to them.

"Here they are," he said finally, showing me an ugly pair with an orange-and-black nylon upper. "Watchu think?"

"Very cool," I said, "Unique."

He came closer. He smelled of sweat, cigarettes, and a hint of cheap perfume. His proximity was appalling.

He stared at me. I held his gaze. The ceiling lights flashed again, expanding his pupils. His arm brushed mine and leaned on it softly. Confused by the fact that my revulsion wasn't pure, but tainted by something else, I didn't move. It wasn't attraction, exactly, maybe a feeble curiosity, a fleeting desire to encourage his salacious gaze. Whatever it was, it crossed my face and he saw it.

"Sorry, guys," said the salesperson. "But we're about to close."

"Got a number?" he said boldly.

"I don't have a phone," I said foolishly.

"Get out of here. What does that even mean?"

He crossed the sales floor and stopped by the register, where he picked up something, pushing a bunch of flyers onto the floor. He didn't collect them. He was uncouth, like a bear.

"Here then," he said and waved a BIC pen in my face.

He tried writing his number on my hand. It didn't work. He warmed the tip of the pen with his breath and wrote his number on my wrist.

"In case you change your mind," he said, grinning. "Or find your phone."

He nodded in my direction as a type of goodbye and ran out of the store.

Inside the subway station, I was surprised to see that Leyla was still there. She was sitting on a wooden bench on the opposite side of the track. She was looking to her left, at a train approaching the station. The train came and went; she remained on that bench. I crossed to the other side.

"Leyla," I said. "I saw that guy who takes pictures of you."

She showed no surprise to see me there. She seemed to be in some kind of daze.

"Was he outside?"

"Yes. And I got his number. In case you want to report him to the police. You can find him now."

I was still recovering from the shock of what I had done, stalking Leyla's stalker, but she appeared indifferent to my adventure.

"Why did you do that?" she said. "Who told you to do that?"

I had acted on impulse and out of guilt for having accused her, in my mind, of making up the story of being followed. I'd mistaken the day-to-day monotony of my comfortable life for some of kind of natural, universal order.

"I don't know why. I just followed him inside a shoe store. Then we started talking about shoes. Don't you want his number?"

Leyla turned to me. "Why are you here?"

"You can't let them get away with it."

"You're right. I should go to the cops. They'll catch him, and right after they'll deport me. My tourist visa expired last month."

"I didn't know that."

"Why don't you go home? You're afraid of your husband, aren't you?"

Her insistence was infuriating.

"I'm not afraid of my husband. I already told you that."

"So why don't you go home, instead of following that fucker to a shoe store?"

Fortunately, a train approached the station. I got on. It wasn't the train I needed but I wanted to get away from her. From the window, I saw her clutching her backpack to her chest and turning toward the tunnel, waiting for a train she wouldn't take.

SINCE THAT NIGHT when Zani and his family dropped by, Billy had restricted himself to his office and the kitchen. He'd mumble some excuse initially, like he had to work late and didn't want the computer light to bother me, but then he did away with the explanations. He still left my chocolate bars and coffee on the kitchen counter, but that and his other random acts of care smacked of inertia. We had turned into two good-mannered roommates who, having once liked and done nice things for each other, thought it fair to cling to past routines.

As I entered the apartment, I heard his voice coming from his office. He was likely on the phone. His movements were familiar to me. After spending an hour or so hanging on to some heated podcast, he would pace around the room. He'd then scroll through a list of names, deciding whom to call. He was still fuming about the election.

An impulse to have a conversation took hold of me. I wanted to tell him that the silence between us made me sad, that we had to talk about how to fix it. I cleaned up a stain of coffee on the stove and washed two dirty mugs. I filled a glass with water. Perhaps he'd hear the glasses clanking, or the water gurgling, and come out.

I paid attention to the voices coming from his room.

"I feel terrible."

"I know."

He wasn't on the phone. He had a visitor. I recognized Miles's voice. He must have been visiting from LA. What were they talking about? Miles couldn't have been that upset to learn about our marital problems. If anything, he was reminding Billy how fortunate he was that it had happened now, while we didn't have children. We didn't make sense as a couple. We just didn't fit, he was likely saying. Best to pull off the bandage, once and for all.

Billy then came out. He hadn't shaved in days. His upper body looked bulkier—he was wearing two sweaters; the heater had stopped working and we hadn't called the super yet. He now reminded me of his mother, whose full figure had always been his inspiration for hitting the gym.

"Miles is here," he said, matter-of-factly. "In case you wanted to say hi."

"In a bit," I said, feeling an instant reluctance. "I'll come and say hi in a bit."

He waved and went back to his room. An old memory caught up with me. When Billy was teaching the film class, I'd see him occasionally at this café by NYU. The café was always crammed with students, lounging on tattered sofas and sipping on neon bubble teas. He'd notice me and wave from afar. That impersonal greeting, although appropriate, had felt odd. Our class discussions had encouraged intimacy. We had all shared more than we intended to, a credit to his teaching. It seemed to me that we had reverted to those earlier years. We were in the same room, yet he was waving me goodbye from a distance.

While crossing the hallway to the living room, I heard more of their conversation.

"Is she back then?"

"Yes, she's back. They brought her in over the weekend. Her father has a friend who owns a private jet. Her arm was shattered."

"Will she be able to play violin again?"

"Her mother said it's unlikely."

Were they talking about Anna? They had to be.

"The important thing is that she is alive."

"Of course. But violin is her life."

Anna's last performance of Haydn's "Farewell" at Lincoln Center sprang to mind. After the final adagio, the musicians in the orchestra had all left the stage in a dramatic fashion, a tribute to Haydn's last performance for Prince Nikolaus of Hungary centuries ago. Every musician's exit had caused uproarious laughter, except Anna's. Sashaying away in her silk dress, she had left everyone in awe. I replayed her graceful exit in my mind. Anna there. And Anna gone. Anna there. And Anna gone. Anna gone. Anna gone.

I WAS EATING DINNER ALONE in the living room when someone knocked on the door. To my surprise, it was Miles, in his leather aviator jacket, his feathery hair an awning to his eyes. He was smiling at me through the glass door. He was passing through to the bathroom, most likely, and saying hello on his way there. Or maybe he wanted to talk so he could gloat about the fact that Billy and I were living in separate wings of the apartment. He knocked again. I stayed put. He knocked a third time and pointed to the handle. I got up and opened the door.

In the past, Miles would always kiss me on the cheek. Invariably something always went wrong. Our noses would bump into each other, or he'd go for a second kiss when I had only planned on one. Some awkward laughter would follow, some comment about Europeans doing things differently. This time he hugged me, and nothing went wrong.

"I was on my way to London and stopped to see how you guys were doing. Of course, I was devastated about what happened to Anna."

"What happened to Anna?"

"Billy didn't tell you? She got into a car accident in South Korea. She was badly hurt, but she'll be fine."

I pictured her funeral, the men in suit jackets with red roses in their lapels. There'd be articles about her, surely. *World-Renowned Musician Dead in South Korea.* But why was I thinking about Anna's funeral after she had just escaped death?

"Maybe Billy texted me about it. I should check my phone."

I scanned his face looking for signs of what Billy might have told him about us. He had on his spare expression of a tortured, destitute artist. He was glancing down, biting his lower lip. He was thinking about Anna, surely, feeling sorry for her. I didn't feel much for her at all, except a generic sympathy, what you might feel about a story in the news that involves a stranger. This was no reflection of my feelings for her. I typically kept bad news at a distance, allowing it to catch up with me on its own time.

"She won't be able to play violin anymore," he said. "At least that's what her mother said."

"I'm sorry to hear that." I pictured a church full of windows where the sun would come through and shine on her open coffin. As always, she'd be the most beautiful woman in the room, but frozen this time.

Miles studied me for a moment.

"How are you and Billy?"

"I don't know. How are we?"

"Billy and you will be fine."

I didn't know what to say. He patted my arm.

"He'll always choose you," he added, to my surprise.

"What was that?"

"He'll choose you."

Billy used to tell me that Miles liked me. I had never believed it until now. Coming into the living room and checking up on me was a small kindness, but it had exceeded my expectations. I'd never given him a chance, I realized. Maybe geographical distance was to blame for our awkwardness around each other, but it was also true that I'd never made much of an effort to get to know him. He had always seemed ostentatious, inspiring little in me besides a cursory glance. When his name flashed by on social platforms, I read the first few words and scrolled on, assuming he was dispensing one of those revelations calculated to be both showy and self-effacing. But what came to mind now, when he was being so kind, was an old Leonard Cohen song, a verse about shooting at someone who outdrew you.

"Take a seat," I said. "Can I get you a drink or something?"

"Billy already made me coffee."

"A snack?"

"I've got to catch a plane to London. I'll be on a panel for my new novel."

"Oh, right. Congratulations!" I regretted that I had never opened his book after Billy bought it. I wanted to say something nice about it but didn't know what.

"Billy told me that it got a nice review," I finally said.

"And several not-so-nice ones."

"You know what they say. Credit belongs to the man in the arena."

"Thank you for that. You'll be okay, right?"

"I will."

"Sorry I have to run so quickly. But if you need to talk, about anything, you know how to reach me."

He gave me another flawless hug. He then stopped by Billy's office. I heard them say goodbye to each other and the apartment door close. Not a moment had passed before Billy appeared in the doorway. He looked helpless, standing there, with his arms folded. *Why don't you turn on the space heater?* I wanted to say. *Your hands must be freezing.*

"I called Juan," he said. "They're fixing the heater."

"Thank you."

"I'm going away for some time," he said.

"Where are you going?"

"I applied to an artists' residency months ago. I didn't get it, but the guy who got it can't go now, so they gave it to me. His wife got pregnant. I was the second choice. I said yes."

*He'll always choose you*, Miles had said. And I had believed him.

"Is it a writing residency?"

"It's kind of an odd thing. I'll be a bridge guard."

"A what?"

"There's a bridge between Slovakia and Hungary and basically you record or write down whatever you observe around the bridge. It has been destroyed a couple of times throughout history, so the mission of the guard is to protect it against the devastation of human beings. It's mostly a symbolic thing, obviously. The rest of the time you do your own work."

"So you're leaving. To protect a bridge. Between Slovakia and Hungary. From the devastation of human beings."

"As I said, the mission is symbolic."

"What about your classes?"

"One class is mostly online anyway. And Nick said he'll take over the other one."

"How long will you be gone?"

"Six months. I'll be leaving on Saturday."

"But that's in three days. Six months apart?"

"I had this dream the other night," he continued. He spoke slowly while fixing me with his gaze. "We were on a boat and the shore was suddenly in view. But you were not looking at the shore; you were looking back. Maybe you wanted to be on a different boat or something, and I was thinking, in my dream I was thinking, that we might both be happier if that happened."

I had hoped for an uncomfortable conversation, but he had made use of a metaphor, rendering all words pointless. I could see the boat also, leaping up and down among the waves, with a mind of its own, as I stood there stranded, unable to do anything. Aware of my silence and his expectation, I blurted something unrelated.

"I talked to Miles earlier," I said, as if it was possible for either of us to forget what he had just said.

"Yes, he was on his way to London."

"Can I borrow his novel from you?"

"Of course. I'll bring it over right now."

"I'm sorry about Anna. Miles said she got into a car accident." He avoided my eyes. "He said she's home now. Do you think I should go and visit her?"

"Sure. Her mother sent an email to her friends asking people to contact her if they want to pay a visit."

"I guess I wasn't on the list." It was a joke, but it didn't land.

"I haven't managed to go," he said. "I'll text you her mother's number."

His shoulders drooped a little. Something about his face reminded me of an Albanian expression—Një ftyr i ikte, një ftyr i vinte—*A face would leave and a face would come.* He seemed uncertain about something. Was he thinking about his upcoming trip? Was he waiting for me to tell him not to go? I took a step toward him, but he didn't even notice. I had the impression that something else was being said but I wasn't hearing it.

He turned off the hallway light and walked back to his room. Once I was alone, the meaning of his dream sank in. Except it wasn't only a dream. It was our life he had been talking about. From now on, the apartment would be silent and dark every evening. Since we had gotten married, we had never spent more than a few days away from each other. I pictured a hay roof house between two European countries and Billy going for walks by the bridge, taking pictures every day, fulfilling his symbolic mission of protecting it from the devastation of human beings. I turned the phrase *devastation of human beings* in my mind until it felt meaningless.

# 7.

ALFRED COULDN'T MEET UNTIL THAT FRIDAY, THE NIGHT before Billy was to leave for Europe. I agreed to meet him. Staying in the apartment, while Billy prepared his suitcase, didn't sound appealing. Since that night he'd told me he was leaving, we had exchanged a few words and only out of necessity. What would I do while he packed? Hover around him with questions? *Did you pack your pajamas, love? Your allergy pills? Six months is a long time, are you bringing enough?*

It was a warm winter evening. The wind had chased away the clouds. The sky was flaunting a great expanse of blue shades that turned to lavender in the far distance. A plane left behind white scribblings, so intricate that it seemed certain some message or sign could be gleaned from them. I stared at the lines, foolishly hoping for some guidance or reassurance. I sat on a bench and waited for Alfred. Couples and friends were leaving Washington Square and strolling toward the street to restaurants and bars. When would I say goodbye to Billy? His plane didn't leave until 1:00 PM. We'd see each other in the morning, of course. Would we say *I'll miss you* or stick to logistics?

A piano tune drifted through the park. It was a melody of a few notes, but then some techno beats sneaked in unexpectedly, transforming it into a hypnotic groove. I turned to see where it was coming from, but a crowd of people blocked my view. It was then that I noticed Alfred. He was walking hesitantly toward me, tall and thin, in his blue interview suit, holding an orange folder under his arm. The closer he drew, the stranger his face seemed. He was attempting to smile but still managed to look tormented. His face inspired the desire to help him out, even if only so I could teach him how to smile naturally.

"Hi," he said, sitting next to me. "Nice to see you again."

"You're wearing your suit. Did you have another job interview?"

"It's later tonight. The third one so far. Hopefully one of them will work out."

"Of course it will. I wish you good luck."

"I was surprised that you agreed to meet me. I was feeling overwhelmed that day. I said things I shouldn't have said."

He was barely looking at me. He fixed his eyes straight ahead. Something preoccupied him. Did he recognize someone? In the distance, a few men were playing chess. A couple of children were drawing on the ground with chalk.

"You have to go back to therapy," I said. "It would help you."

"Is that why you came to see me?"

"I care for you, Alfred. As a friend."

This time his smile was unexpectedly fresh, revealing his missing teeth.

"Zinovia is good. She'll help you."

"I'm afraid."

"Of what?"

"I don't want to relive everything."

His eyes took on a strange shine.

"Maybe you won't have to."

"Are you sure?"

"No," I said. "But you should still go and see her. She knows what she's doing."

"Will she put me on medication? I don't want to be on drugs while being a father."

"Are you still having those dreams?"

He looked to his left, then looked back at me.

"Still there. My dreams are still there."

"Only when you sleep or even when you're awake?"

"There is a dog to my left," he said. "A border collie. She's a metallic green, like some beetles, you know? She has wings. The wings are transparent, thin, the shape of butterflies' wings. She is sitting on a bench. She has regular legs, like a person. She is wearing a long skirt. Over there."

The children had now climbed onto the bench where he was pointing. They were drawing a lopsided ship on the back planks. He reached forward and held my hand. His palms felt familiar, the softness, the rough surfaces, his knotty fingers. I wanted to embrace him. I wanted to ask him to put his face in the crook of my shoulder. *Close your eyes, Alfred, close your eyes. Let's close them together and forget.*

"You need to go and see Zinovia," I said again. "What if you see *that* while you're taking care of your baby?"

"She doesn't do anything bad," he said. "She just sits there."

"For now. You need to be in therapy for your daughter and for your wife."

"You're right," he said. "Rationally, I know you're right."

"Then do it. Go see her."

"I'll think about it."

"You have to do it."

We were silent after that, holding hands. Alfred kept looking to his left. I got lost in the people—roller skaters, couples, mothers with strollers. What was Billy doing now? I pictured the open suitcase in the center of our bed he hadn't used in days, the clothes and the hangers strewn all over the chairs and the dresser.

Maybe he was deliberating on a sweater, or which jacket to pack. I pictured him looking lost, with his hand behind his neck, playing with the curl under his hairline. I wished to be home.

"Are you okay?" Alfred said.

"My husband is leaving, Alfred," I said. "He's going away for a long time."

I stretched my arm around his back, resting my hand on his shoulder. His back, rigid with tension, slackened from my touch.

"What will you do?" he said, still avoiding looking at my face.

"I'm going back home for a while," I said, a decision I hadn't shared with anyone. "To see my mother."

"I wish I could go home also," he said. "I'm not ready for a baby."

"You'll be a good father, you'll see."

Something cold and red hit me on the face. For a second, I was too stunned to move. Vilma, clutching her red purse, was standing in front of us. Where had she come from? I had been looking around us all along. Had she descended from the skies? It was the middle of winter, but she had taken off her jacket, exposing her fleshy bare arms. A second strike followed, a harder one this time, and on my left shoulder. I got up at once. Raising both her arms, her lips pressed together, she now aimed her purse at Alfred. Her right breast was nearly popping out of her low-cut flowery shirt. She stood in front of us like an Amazon, statuesque, strong, merciless, her curls defiant, her eyes wild. Her lipstick, a bloody red, was the same color as her purse. As she was hitting Alfred, her throat let out a guttural cry. Alfred was so shocked that he, too, sat motionless on the bench a second too long, enduring the beating. After Vilma swung at him again, he stood up and held her wrists, as if he were cuffing her.

"Let me go, Alfred!" she screamed. "Let me go!"

I took a few steps away.

"You're afraid, huh?" she shouted at me. "You have an affair with my husband, and now you're afraid. Come here, you cowardly slut."

Random sentences came to mind, all of them absurd. It was better to say nothing. Vilma was looking at us, awaiting a response.

"It's not like that," Alfred said. "I'm not cheating on you."

"He's not cheating on you," I repeated.

We sounded ridiculous.

"You two think I am stupid. Lying to me about going to some job interview, wearing your best suit, and yet here you are, meeting her in the park, holding hands and kissing. You didn't think I'd find out, did you? I can read you like an open book, Alfred. A book with pictures, if you must know. The words are no use to me when it comes to you."

She paused for a few seconds, breathing heavily, then turned to me.

"Come here. Come here, I said."

I didn't move. She came at me again, one hand under her baby bump, the other clasping the red purse. Alfred rushed behind and restrained her by enfolding her in his arms. The chess players, their attention arrested by the game, didn't look up. The spectators around them, however, all turned eagerly in our direction.

"You're not a translator."

"Hush, Vilma," Alfred said, watching her sternly. "We're not having an affair. We're friends."

"I will divorce you," she shouted back. "You know I will."

"I *am* going to a job interview," Alfred said, bringing the phone close to her nose. "Look at my phone. Here is my appointment. Read it."

Vilma grabbed his phone from his hand and tossed it inside her red purse.

"What? Give me back my phone, Vilma."

"You did lie to me, Alfred," she said, pointing at him. "You know you did."

She turned to me again.

"Are you happy? While I'm like this?" she said, pointing to her belly. "I will contact the organization. I'll tell them everything about you. What kind of translator, are you anyway?"

"Not a good one," I said quickly.

"That's right," she said. "You should be fired."

"I already am," I said, trying to placate her.

My words enraged her even more. Maybe she thought I was making fun of her. She lunged at me again. Had Alfred not come between us, she would have scratched my face with her acrylic nails.

He put his arm around her, pressing his orange folder against her chest, as he veered her toward the street. She shook off Alfred's arms. But she stopped struggling and relaxed. When I looked back at them, he was placing his hand on her bosom and feeling her heart. What did Vilma's heart look like? All I could think about were those slabs of meat hanging at the butcher's. But after he did that, her brave front faded. The anger in her eyes vanished, replaced by a hurt and pleading expression. Her lips trembled as she looked up at his face. "Ashtu?" she was saying. *Is that so?* Her body, no longer stiff, leaned on Alfred's. As they held each other close, her suffering, no longer her weapon, poured out of her. Her silent tears struck a chord within me. I had to look elsewhere.

They walked out of the park, their steps synchronized. I pictured the green hybrid animal stretching her legs toward the ground and smoothing down her skirt, before hobbling after them. The chess enthusiasts had forgotten the game and were staring at me, curious as to what I might do next. It was a three-person show, but the remaining actor was still on the scene. Did they expect me to burst into a song or dance? When I glared back, they turned around at once.

A WAVE OF EXHAUSTION overcame me. I lay down on the bench, the cracked planks scraping against my palms. The myriad sounds of the night echoed inside my mind. I kept my eyes closed. Everything felt weightless: Vilma's jealousy, Alfred's issues, even my arms and legs. I was sure I was floating in the air, just above the bench, my hair blowing in the breeze like in those stage tricks at the circus. Upon opening my eyes, I realized I hadn't moved. But I still felt adrift. It was then that the vintage woman caught my eye. She was a few steps away from me, sitting on another bench. I recognized her at once. She was wearing a magenta velvet jacket that matched her lipstick, a long black skirt, and Mary Jane shoes. Just like at the dentist's office, she reminded me of an old-school movie star suddenly come to life. I sat up. The dentist's office, where Alfred had his root canal, wasn't that far from here. Maybe she lived or worked nearby. She was on the phone. Her right hand moved upward and then down, as if she were holding a baton. What was she talking about? She rose to go and joined a group of people to the right of the Garibaldi statute, where the music was coming from.

I walked over to them, and to my amazement, some of the faces looked familiar. Years ago, my French roommate, the one who had wanted to become an actor, had invited me to some random party held at a woman's loft in Bushwick. It was this same woman that the vintage girl had just hugged before moving on to other friends. The woman's name didn't come to me, but the party had been fantastic, full of quirky people who adored dressing up and dancing. It was that same crowd now, in front of me, swaying and leaping like no one was watching. Their glow-in-the-dark glasses, bunny ears, and mustaches pivoted and twirled to the music. Someone was playing the piano. Where was it coming from? To the left of the fountain, I noticed a grand piano on wheels. I drew closer. The man playing the piano was possibly in his nineties, wearing a white jacket with a red rose in his lapel. He had long white hair reaching his shoulders and played with his eyes closed. How had he brought the piano into the park? Had he pushed it there on his own? Another odd thing was that while it looked like his piano was the only instrument, the music sounded complex, a collage of synthetic sounds.

The woman was smiling at me. "Don't just stand there. Dance. I'm Donna, by the way."

It was the same woman. Of course, she didn't remember me after so many years.

How long had it been since I had danced like that? My body felt light, like in those fun dreams when it's possible to walk on air if you run fast enough. Gleaming, flickering straight lines. Zigzags. Meandering snakes. Everyone moved erratically, as if the adhesive that held their arms and legs together had come loose.

"You know what?" Donna said to someone. "These new shoes are killing my feet. I knew I shouldn't have worn them today."

"I'm getting tired, too," was the response. "A cocktail would be nice."

"I'm seriously thirsty for a real drink," said a man in a top hat who had earlier introduced himself as a nineteenth-century gentleman asking for twenty-first-century reform. "Didn't someone mention a party in the West Village?"

"That would be perfect. Right around here!"

"I know where the party is," someone said. "Who wants to go?"

"Give us the address," Donna said.

In fifteen minutes, we were inside the lobby of an apartment building.

"The party is on the fifth floor," said the doorman.

We all moved toward the elevator. I felt like the heroine of my childhood, the spontaneous Alice who followed the white rabbit down the hole into a subterranean fantasy. Like Alice, I wanted to leave the current world behind, if only for a few hours.

The elevator doors opened into a spacious loft. The first person that caught my eye was a woman who reminded me of Helen. She was dressed in a white nylon dress. Her glamourous hat was embellished with tiny LED lights. She opened her arms in an embrace toward the man in the top hat to whom I had been talking earlier. Every aspect of the party was astonishing—it was like entering a museum of curiosities. A topless woman with a glittering eye mask cackled with laughter, her tremendous teeth hovering dangerously close to someone's ear. Another woman (a duchess?) sat in a corner, wearing a floor-length burgundy gown. She carried a sign saying, *I can read palms*.

I offered her my hand.

"There is nothing you can see that is not a flower," she said. "There is nothing you can think that is not the moon."

"It's so beautiful," I said. "But what does it mean?"

She didn't even consider an answer. She waved me away. Someone else wanted their fortune read after me. Lingering was discouraged.

I made my way through jugglers, people dancing on stilts, a fire eater, hybrid animals, dead celebrities' impersonators. Donna introduced me to one of her friends, an Italian woman with a blue cage that fit on top of her head like a hat. A plastic cardinal was peeking through the unlocked door of the cage, but when she saw me eyeing the bird, she shut the door at once.

"Would you two like a Corpse Reviver?" she asked.

"Absinthe cocktails are our favorites," Donna said.

I wondered why Donna said *our*, considering she barely knew me, but when the birdcage woman handed me a buff-colored cocktail, it didn't matter. The drink was delicious, a bit tart, but effervescent, with a hint of licorice at the end.

"Take it easy," said Donna, when I reached for a second one.

The first drink felt like nothing, except that the conversation around me was sounding familiar. Why was everyone suddenly talking about things I knew?

"It was certainly unusual for a Hollywood film of the fifties," the birdcage woman was saying, "that the director was credited in the film's title. The title card reads 'Leo McCarey's *An Affair to Remember.*'"

"Enough with the movie talk," the duchess called out from the corner while reading someone's palm. "Talk about something real."

"Reality is subject to interpretation. What if the people in the movie are watching us?"

Then someone brought over an enormous chocolate chip cookie. A few people had to hold it up as they munched on it. I helped to carry it also, while trying a bite.

"It's actually a mushroom cookie," Donna was saying. "But it might have walnuts, too. Nut allergies anyone?"

"I'm not allergic to anything," I said.

The cookie didn't taste that great, but I couldn't stop eating it. Reality and fantasy became even more mixed up as the night went along.

"Come to this room," someone said. "Ready for some dirty dancing?"

Donna opened the door to a new room. A dense fog hung above the floor, coming all the way to our waists. The plain walls became luminescent, then images appeared. On the walls facing me and behind, they were showing the American *Dirty Dancing*, while on the walls to my sides, the Bollywood *Dirty Dancing*, a flawless frame-by-frame Indian imitation of the American version, was playing. The American and Indian films were the same, scene for scene. Patrick Swayze caressed Jennifer Grey's arm, and the Indian actor did the same to the Indian actress. Jennifer

Grey's father accused Patrick Swayze of impregnating his dance partner, and so did his Indian counterpart. But the dancing was different. The steamy body contact and pelvic thrusts in the American movie were replaced by the gentle movements of the Indian dancers.

"The American *Dirty Dancing* is way sexier," I told Donna.

But she was no longer around. The woman in an LED hat, the one who looked like Helen, was there.

"You look like my neighbor Helen," I said. "Have you heard that before?"

"I know Helen," she said. "She got evicted."

"Does she have any friends and family? I've been worried about her."

"I don't know," she said. "But she's at another party right now. Across town."

"Another party?"

"Yes. There's always another party."

"Exactly like this?"

"But of course."

"That's amazing."

She turned on all her lights. It occurred to me I was conversing with a chandelier.

"You're distracting me from watching the movie," I told her. "Do you think you could turn off your lights? Or go to another room?"

And where was Billy? I wanted to watch the *Dirty Dancing* films with him. I should have stayed home. He was always uncertain about what to pack. He often relied on my help. I should have been there. *Happiness looks small in your hands until you let it go and then you learn . . .* Where had I read that phrase?

Billy appeared. He was trying on a jacket.

"Look, it's wonderful," I told him. "Two love stories at once."

He took off his jacket. "Maybe it's the sweater that's not working. All along I thought it was the jacket."

"Listen, I thought we'd watch these movies together."

He turned to one of the walls.

"A love story? I don't know about that. It's contrived."

"Lina says you always look me in the eye," I told him. "Is ours a love story?"

Lina then came around, doing a jump-rope workout.

"Is it a love story?" I asked her. "He won't tell me."

"I've always felt," she was saying, while skipping around me, "that other people don't matter. I'm nicer to other people when I'm happy myself."

"Everyone is," Billy said, shrugging. "That's how it works. But which of those sweaters should I pick?"

"Why should I decide everything?" I said. "Why don't you ask someone else? Your mother. Or maybe Anna; that's right, ask Anna."

Billy evaporated into a mist. I found myself in the middle of a summer field. Cumulus clouds, gray, plump, soft, were hanging over my head. Near me, an Indian couple were holding hands.

WAKING UP IN A NEW and unfamiliar location frightened me at first. The first thing I noticed was that the walls weren't a pale gray like in my bedroom at home, but a dirty yellow. I sat up immediately, only to sink much deeper into an air mattress, my legs almost touching the tiled floor. The mattress had deflated overnight, offering a worm's eye view of a sparsely furnished living room immersed in the morning light. To my left, there was a messy kitchen with purple walls and appliances that had been painted in other vivid colors. There was a unicycle hanging from a metal rack, its lemon-colored wheel hovering above my head. The last thing I remembered was that party in Manhattan, somewhere in the West Village, drinking odd-looking cocktails and eating walnut cookies. But the limestone and vinyl-sided town-houses peeping just outside the window frames told me we were in Brooklyn or Queens. The more I looked around, the more familiar the place seemed. Yes, we'd come here the night before from the other party. In a cab or someone's car? Who else was in the car? What had we talked about? Everything seemed vague.

It came to me that this was Donna's place. On the wall behind my head, there was a mural, a New York City map showing attractions of various neighborhoods. The wall to my left was covered entirely by moss, branches, and rocks. The other walls were busy, too, with countless inscriptions, love quotes, and crude drawings—a pierced heart, a mermaid holding a rifle, a skull in headphones. Coincidentally, essential objects, like a sofa, were missing. She didn't even own a dining table and chairs. She sat on tatami mats when she ate, she had told me, like in Japan.

I got up from the bed. Had Billy left already? Had he reached Europe? What time was it? My phone was dead. I didn't see a charger, or a clock. I was still in my clothes from the night before. I heard footsteps. Donna entered the living room, wearing a blue kimono with one huge peacock on each side of her chest, their beaks open upward, as if wanting to bite off her chin. She had short, pasty legs that looked grayish from the knee down; she didn't shave. Party images from the night before flashed in cinematic segments.

"How are you feeling?" she asked.

"Much better. You know, I came to your place before, years ago."

"I know," she said. "We talked about it. With Colette. The French girl."

"We talked about it? We did not."

"You ate a lot of that cookie last night. No wonder you don't remember."

"Did I? Thank you for letting me crash here."

"No problem. Coffee?"

As she prepared the coffees, some of our conversations from the night before came to me. Donna was born and raised in Nashville and had moved to Brooklyn when she was nineteen. She'd been a runaway teen. By the age of forty, she had tried out forty-five professions—she'd been a dog walker, a flight attendant, an interior designer, a pole dancer, a bartender, a house painter, and the list went on.

"You can stay as long as you want," she said. "Until your husband leaves."

Her comment caught me by surprise.

"You talked about him a lot," she said.

"I did? What time is it? Do you have a charger?"

"Would you like to get brunch?" she said. "A new Mediterranean restaurant opened up around the corner."

Perhaps Donna and I would become friends, go to parties, meet new people, have charming, memorable adventures. The prospect was enticing. What was the point of seeing Billy that morning?

"Not today," I said, with a lump in my throat. "Another day."

"Sure. Text me."

She gave me a charger and handed me a coffee.

"It's 10:00 AM."

"I have to go home soon," I said. "I want to say goodbye to Billy. He's leaving town for a few months."

Donna seemed taken aback.

"Excuse me for saying this, but he is a jerk," she said. "The way he behaved with the Kurdish women is unforgivable. He wasn't even supposed to be home that weekend—why couldn't you have friends over? And not only did he cheat, but now he's leaving you to go and photograph a bridge?"

"He didn't cheat," I said. "What are you talking about?"

"You told me that last night," Donna said, her eyes opening wide. "You told me that he left your apartment that night and ended up in Anna's apartment."

"Right. She wasn't home."

"You said she was home," Donna said. "You said her concert in Zagreb was canceled and he didn't tell you about it."

I stared at some objects on a cardboard box in front of me, at a bushy tail squirrel with sparkly eyes holding a fishing pole, an elegant white mouse standing on a tiny barstool, about to ask for a drink. Taxidermy was Donna's new hobby. She engaged in ethical taxidermy, she had insisted, only sourcing animals that had died a natural death. Now I pictured those animals not as they were, well-groomed and adorable, but abandoned on the side of the road, bloody, with their guts hanging out.

"Look, if you didn't mean to tell me that, I'm sorry," Donna said.

"Did I tell you that Anna was in her apartment that night?"

"I assumed she was in her apartment by what you said. You said that her concert in Zagreb was canceled. She told you that herself when you were having lunch."

"Right. She did say that."

"Sorry," Donna said. "At least he could have sent you flowers or something. Even if nothing happened between him and Anna, he should have apologized."

I put down the coffee mug.

"Right," I said, before heading out. "Flowers. He could have done that. Hyacinths, maybe."

I took the subway back home.

MY FATHER HAD LIKED Billy from the start. *Billy is like a well-built house,* he told me once. *There are wildflowers outside but the building itself is sturdy and it will last. You won't have to worry about the foundations. That's where the trouble always is, in the foundations.*

I remembered our wedding. Billy had pulled me aside before the ceremony. The long dinner table was still empty; nobody had arrived yet. A chandelier tied to a tree illuminated the wineglasses and the silverware. "If anything changes, if you don't feel like this anymore, or if you meet someone else, let's talk about it, okay? Only no lies, no hiding, no going behind each other's back. Deal?"

Billy's mother loved telling people a story from his childhood. She was proud of having taught Billy *not to lie, no matter what.* As a child, whenever he did something he wasn't supposed to, and felt the temptation of lying, he would run to his parents and tell them everything at once. Had that story, overheard countless times, created my impression of him as a truth teller?

Helen's *for sale* furniture printouts were no longer on the bulletin board. Someone had torn them off. From now on, there would be no sign at all that she had ever lived in our building.

The first thing I noticed upon entering the living room was a fresh bouquet of hyacinths. The third one.

There was a note this time.

*Waited. Had to run. I love you. B.*

The apartment looked different again, the way it appeared after a long trip, its day-to-day blandness magically evaporated. Every piece of furniture was competing for attention, each color more vibrant than I remembered it. My newly sharpened vision captured things I had forgotten—a turquoise rotary phone that used to belong to Billy's parents but that still worked, a Pinocchio clown wearing a maroon frock my father had bought in Italy for me years ago. I opened the window. The clarity of the horizon also took me by surprise. The sharp corners of the buildings cut into the blue cloth of the sky and into the steel towers behind them. Suspended in the air, the sun hovered above one of those taller towers, spilling light into the city and onto my face.

# 8.

ALTHOUGH I HAD MENTALLY PREPARED MYSELF FOR Billy's leaving, getting used to our silent apartment proved difficult. On my first night alone, falling asleep didn't come easy. I slept in his office, among his sheets, in a T-shirt he had discarded before leaving. I flipped though the Martin Amis novel he had once read to me in bed, each sentence reminding me of his voice. Living alone sharpened my hearing. When our next-door neighbors came home, the jiggling of their keys made me think, if only for a few seconds, that he had returned. The burble of a shower, the drone of a podcast seeped into my sleep. Had he come in late at night? Was he in the other room? I got up and wandered the apartment, realizing I was alone.

I wrote to Leyla, offering her a temporary room in our apartment. She didn't acknowledge my email. It didn't surprise me. Her distaste at being in the position she was in often caused her to act brashly. She couldn't afford niceties. Wanting to give the illusion of control over her situation, she slipped into being contentious, even rude.

She called me the next day.

"Is he really gone?"

"He'll be away for a few months."

"He's not going to make a surprise appearance, is he?"

"He's in Europe."

"And flip out when he sees me, like before?"

"He's gone. And I'll be leaving also, to Albania. You'll have the apartment to yourself for two weeks."

"Okay," she said. "Be there soon."

She came over later that afternoon, dragging behind her a beat-up suitcase and carrying on her shoulders one of those enormous hiking backpacks. She leaned her suitcase against the wall and stooped further. We lowered her backpack to the floor together. As she looked around the apartment, I knew she was thinking about the last time she was there, about Billy blocking the hallway and refusing to move.

"You didn't fix that yet?" she said, pointing to the wall hole. "It looks bad."

"We sort of forgot it."

She took off her quilted jacket and handed it to me. There was a small cut on one of the shoulders and some dark stains on her sleeves. She headed toward the living room, but stopped at once on the threshold, which, like the rest of the living room, was flooded with sunlight. As she stood there, debating whether to go in or not, something about her face didn't look right.

"Take a seat," I said. "Do you want something to drink?"

"No, that's okay. Where is my room?"

She retreated to the darkest corner of the hallway. The suspicion that she didn't want me to look at her face made me focus on it even more. One of her cheeks had lost its luster. It was bruised, I realized.

"This room here," I said, pointing to Billy's office. "You'll sleep here."

"Don't turn on the light," she said when we entered the room, where the blinds had stayed drawn for a week. "I fell down the subway stairs. I don't want you to see my face."

She walked toward the bed to put down her purse, crossing through a shaft of light, courtesy of a twisted slat. There are times when what you don't want to happen does, all at once, irreversibly. Every further pretense becomes futile. The smartest choice, or the one to cause the least embarrassment, is putting all your cards on the table. Leyla turned her head in my direction and toward the sun, exposing the stain of discoloration that spread from her temple to her cheek and chin. Her flesh had turned yellow, olive green, and bluish. Some of the colors had bled into each other. It looked painful. Something came over her soon enough, shame or maybe the memory of what had happened. She tossed her thick black hair to the left, hiding her cheek.

She started to unpack, pulling all her clothes out of the backpack. I told her she could put them in the bottom drawers of Billy's desk which our guests sometimes used as a dresser.

"Do you mind if I take a shower?"

"Go ahead."

While she was in the bathroom, I took out of my closet a new coat. It was a gift from Billy, an impromptu purchase. We'd seen it in a shop window, during a vacation upstate. He had insisted it would look great on me, which it had when I tried it on at the store. But at home, the coat had seemed too ornate, with its faux-fur collar and golden buttons, its coral hue a shade brighter than necessary. Might Leyla be interested in it? I now thought.

She came to the living room later on, her freshly dried hair suffusing the living room with the peppermint scent of my conditioner, which she'd used reluctantly, telling me that she'd soon buy her own. I had left some refreshments for her on the table.

While eating madeleine cookies and sipping lemon tea, she glanced at the titles on my bookcase. Her eyes, used to scanning strangers for signs of danger, looked serene. She reminded me of those wilted flowers that bow away from the sun but straighten shortly after the rain. Making a struggling person happy wasn't hard. But giving was complicated; it required some maneuvering through the piles of misgivings and suspicions. People were afraid of misfortune, thought of it as contagious, airborne, and couldn't help imagining its blue fog choking them. An old friend of mine, who had once won a scholarship at a prestigious European university, would avoid her Albanian compatriots like the plague, especially the struggling ones. *They're sticky*, she'd tell me.

"I'll leave in a few days," I told Leyla. "I'll have to show you the laundry room. There's a gym, too."

She laughed. "I've been losing enough weight as it is wandering the streets. But I will need to do some laundry."

"I have this new coat," I said. "I never wear it. Do you like it?"

Her face fell. *I've offended her*, I thought. When Anna passed on to me some of her impulse purchases with the tags still on, I never thought much of it. But accepting someone's clothes seeking variety didn't dent one's pride like taking them out of necessity. Both Anna and I knew I could afford new clothes if I wanted them.

"You know," Leyla said, after a pause. "Back at home, growing up, I had so many shoes and coats, I didn't know what to do with them. Why, I could have opened a store. My mother is a seamstress. She had her own business in our neighborhood."

"Never mind. I'll just donate it to a thrift store."

"It's a nice coat."

She took another sip of tea and stared at the cup.

"Why do I even pretend to have some pride left?" she said. "Right?"

"Your situation is temporary."

"It's useless to pretend though."

She touched her left cheek with her fingertips.

"I hadn't seen him for some days. But then yesterday there he was. I got mad. I went to grab his phone. It's frustrating that he has all these pictures of me. It makes me sick. It literally does. I wanted to break his phone in pieces."

"Where were you?"

"In a subway station."

"What happened exactly?"

"We struggled. He pushed me toward a wall."

"Was it the same cousin?" I asked. "That young man from the other night?"

"The same. Rakan." She touched her cheek again. "Does it look terrible?"

"It's healing nicely."

I looked down at my wrist. The digits of Rakan's number had faded entirely. But although I'd made no effort to memorize it, his number sprung up in my mind.

"Maybe he'll lose track of me now that I'm here. I still don't understand how he finds me. Anyway, let me try on the coat. I do like the color."

She went to try on the coat in front of the hallway mirror. She moved one shoulder forward and back, brought up the collar, then put it down.

"I like it," she said. "I think I'll keep it."

Someone knocked on the door. We jumped. Billy came to mind. But it was only the doorman, who had left a package. There was a box in front of the apartment next door also. My neighbor opened the door to pick it up. Since she spent the winters in Florida, we barely saw her. Whenever she returned, she'd dress the same as she did in Boca Raton—pink capri pants, floral blouse, flip-flops. She had silver-gray hair and must have been in her sixties, like Helen. In fact, it occurred to me that I'd seen her talking to Helen once or twice.

"Hi there," I said. "Did you hear about Helen down the hall?"

She nodded. "She was evicted. Very unfortunate."

"Do you happen to know if she had any family?"

"She mentioned a sister in Australia. I don't think they were close. There might have been a brother also."

"Do you happen to have her number?"

"I don't."

"Okay, thank you."

I was about to go inside.

"Did she give you one of her flyers for the drawing party?" she asked.

"Yes, she did."

My neighbor put her hand to the side of her cracked lips. "She was a nude model. Did you know that?"

"I didn't," I said, feeling out of breath. "Helen?"

"Yes, she modeled for art schools and such."

My neighbor went on to say that Helen got paid from tips, so she wanted to invite as many people as possible. She had given a flyer to all the neighbors, sometimes slipping one under their door.

"Bertie from the third floor went, you know Bertie, the widower?"

"I've seen him, yes."

"He didn't know Helen would be there in the nude. He had always wanted to draw, he said. Poor man. Can you imagine? At her age? In the nude? Too much skin."

I pictured Helen's white flesh, her torso twisted sideways, her breasts, pubic hair, the defiant stare she would offer to those struggling to capture her on paper.

"I'm not that surprised," my neighbor said, rolling her eyes. "I always had a feeling it wouldn't end well for her."

"I'm not surprised either," I said before taking leave. "She was a good-looking woman."

WE WERE DRIVING UP the West Side Highway on our way to Hamilton Park in New Jersey. Years ago, Billy and I had celebrated a friend's birthday there. We had admired that view of Manhattan, starting from the George Washington Bridge all the way down to One World Trade Center and the Verrazzano Bridge. *A beautiful spot for a first date*, Billy had said. *Isn't it?* We had even planned to take a picnic over there, but it hadn't happened.

"Like them?" Rakan said, lifting his knee and showing me his new sneakers. He was sitting on the passenger's side, making no effort to conceal his lingering gaze at the hint of my cleavage.

"Give me a second," I said. We had to wait until we hit some traffic for me to give them my full attention. The shoes were certainly attention-grabbing—black with neon-auburn flames that reached toward the laces and the back.

"Hot," I said, although *hideous* would have been a more apt one-word description. He gave a nod, agreeing.

"I went to so many stores before I found them," he added, gazing at his shoes as attentively as he had at my cleavage. "Sick, right?"

"Totally sick."

His intense preoccupation with footwear was comical, but it seemed important not to laugh. He struck me as the kind of young man who would not take kindly to being teased. I already had some fixed ideas about our date, having decided in advance where to go and what to do, but it was possible that something unpredictable could happen. So far, he was well-behaved, yet impetuous, like a child who was trying but couldn't sit still. He enjoyed, for example, interspersing his sentences with some kind of physical motion involving me.

"Nice car," he said, jabbing me in the ribs. "Your boyfriend's?"

"My husband's," I said.

He stroked his patchy chin-strap beard and fist-bumped my arm playfully.

"You married? No shit."

"I used to be," I said. "No longer."

"All right, all right. Only God judges."

"Were they expensive?" I said. "I might get a pair."

"Yeah, kind of."

"What do you do, by the way?"

"Lots of things. Random gigs. Here-and-there stuff. Help out my cousin, sometimes."

"With what?"

He made a sweeping arm motion, as if to say it wasn't worth talking about. He was pushing all of that aside. He didn't want to get into it. He was frivolous, fond of short back-and-forth phrases. Since I had picked him up in Chinatown, we had been engaging in mindless banter. It was an unusually empty conversation, almost hypnotic.

"How far is this place?"

"No more than thirty minutes. If there's no traffic."

He opened the glove compartment and looked inside for some CDs.

"You still use those?" he said, before deciding on Bob Marley. "Old-school."

He leaned to my side, much closer than was warranted for inserting a CD. He pressed the *play* button. I could smell the cigarette he had smoked recently, and something else, sweet and pungent—coconut lotion maybe, or some cheap cologne.

He was smelling me, too. "You smell good," he said and leaned for a peck on my cheek. Unlike his dull conversation, his moves were quick.

His face contorted into a grin that lingered. His teeth and gums still exposed, he reached forward and touched my earlobe. He massaged it gently with his thumb and forefinger. That curious gesture made me anxious, but the disquieting discovery was that it was enjoyable. The repulsion I felt for him retreated momentarily. My insides trembled. My hips shifted. I pictured us in the back seat, him parting my legs and reaching for my belt. Just like that day at the store, he could read me with the instinct of an animal. Perhaps he could even see what I had imagined. His facial muscles relaxed. His expression turned serious. He leaned forward and licked behind my ear.

"Easy," I said, unconvincingly. "I'm driving."

"I love America," he said, adjusting himself in his seat. "Things like this never happen in my country. You don't meet beautiful Bulgarian women at a shoe store, and they call you. It just doesn't happen."

I had told him that I was from Albania, but he didn't remember, or rather, as it turned out, he liked pretending I was Bulgarian.

"Bulgarian women are sexy; I dated a Bulgarian once," he said. His voice turned wistful, but he restrained himself from telling me the details. "Anyway."

He was observing me now, barely restraining a smug smile. Perhaps he was curious if he'd made me jealous.

"Your English is great," I said, fighting an urge to laugh. "You have a bit of an accent, but it's perfect otherwise."

This was true. His words were simple but clearly enunciated, with a hint of a British accent.

"I went to London a couple of times to study. My cousin's family is generous. To those who deserve it, of course."

Startled at this revelation, I pressed him further.

"Are there some who don't deserve it?"

He shuffled his feet and turned his entire body toward me. Upon getting into my car earlier he had refused to buckle himself in. *If we die, we die*, he had said.

"He paid for his ex-wife's schooling in Italy. My cousin did."

"Right."

"And what did she do after finishing school? Dump him. Like he was a dog, not a person. Wouldn't you get mad if you paid all that money for someone's school and they dumped you?"

"Yeah," I said. "Of course I would get mad."

"You can't do that to someone. Take their money and run. You just can't."

He raised his voice, wanting to convey his own anger on his cousin's behalf. It sounded fake. The truth was he was turned on, which was the reason for this confession. A noticeable transformation had come over him. He had become surprisingly voluble.

"Is his ex back home?"

"Let's forget about her," he continued. "Crazy woman. My point is that back home you don't meet beautiful Bulgarian women who take you for a ride and offer to give you mushroom cookies. Did you bring them?"

"Yes," I said. "They're in the back seat."

"I thought you were joking on the phone, but you're for real, right?"

"I am for real," I said meeting his eyes.

I felt a burst of euphoria, then the tingle of arousal.

The sky above the highway was obscured by shape-shifting clouds of pale gray with darker bellies. Once we exited the highway, the clouds tore open. The patch of sky now gave a faint but stunning glow. Naked trees surrounded us like silent witnesses. In the crotch of some of their branches, caterpillars had set up silken white tents. They were devious, those caterpillars. I had read about them; they weakened the trees gradually, eating all the leaves and shoots.

We stopped at a red light. I was tired of the music. I was turning off the Bob Marley CD when he started kissing and licking my neck.

"I've got to focus," I told him. "Or we'll crash."

"God forbid, no."

He moved away.

"Try the cookies if you want."

"Do you want some?" he said, opening the plastic bag.

"Later," I said. "At the park. Have to drive now."

He took a couple of big bites.

"Pace yourself," I cautioned.

"Those are good," he grinned, tapping me on the arm again. "Did you make them?"

"A friend of mine makes them."

"Is she Bulgarian?"

"You're funny," I said.

He chuckled. "And so are you," he said. "But not funny *ha ha*, funny mysterious."

"Oh, yeah?"

"Yeah."

We drove in silence the rest of the way. He leaned his head on the window. He looked like he was taking a nap. Then we arrived. As I parked, he stirred, then rubbed his eyes. He glanced out. The view was more spectacular than I remembered it. The Manhattan skyscrapers reflected various strips of light on the water's surface, some golden, some white, some auburn. Beams of lights shone upward also, erasing the stars. I felt like opening the car door and walking out, away from the glitter we had traveled so far to see, toward the pure, black sky.

A strong smell of coconut and cigarettes filled my nostrils. He brought my face closer to his and kissed me, teasing my mouth with his tongue. The idea of his yellow teeth, so close to my mouth, was disgusting, but I yielded, extending my tongue to meet his as our mouths came together. He put my hand on his groin. It was a half-hearted gesture; his erection was gone. After our kiss, he closed his eyes again. He seemed preoccupied; something was happening behind his eyelids, new, exciting visuals that demanded his attention. When he opened his eyes, he appeared bewildered.

"Let's go outside," I said, opening his side of the car.

He walked out. He didn't go far and loitered close to the door. A strong gust of wind entered the car. A cold chill ran down my back.

"It's so beautiful," he said, his eyes shut again. "And complicated."

"Look at the buildings. Go," I said. "Such a nice view."

He moved a bit farther, toward the water. His steps were uncertain, but something about the distant lights attracted him. He'd left his phone on the seat, forgetting all about it. I shut and locked both car doors, but I could still hear his voice. I lowered the window.

"You okay?" I asked.

"Do you know who put all those buildings there?" he was saying. "A giant lady. She's over there. But she's coming."

"The giant lady?"

"Yeah, she's on her way here."

"All right," I said. "We'll wait for her. We'll wait for her together."

"Come out here," he said. "Let's wait for her here."

When he heard the car's engine, he turned around. He didn't rush toward the car to prevent me from driving away. He had no reason to trust me, but he did. He sat on some rocks and waited, imagining perhaps that I was going for a short ride and would come back for him. Something about that scene, the troubled clouds, the gleaming city, the still trees, reminded me of those landscape oil paintings that took up entire walls in museums, where lone, motionless men by the water were nothing but a quick brushstroke. Driving away, I felt calm. A sudden angst overwhelmed me minutes later, while going through a dark road, lit up only by my headlights. In the silence that followed I felt afraid, not only of Rakan or his potential retribution but also that it was possible to interfere in someone's life in such an intense way, and that a vague, half-baked plan could work out so flawlessly in the end.

I thought I heard his voice. My hands gripped the wheel. Of course, it couldn't have been his voice. He was miles away. Had he realized by now I wouldn't return for him? In my confusion, I took a wrong turn. *Recalculating*, said the voice from the navigation screen. I waited for further direction and kept driving. A deer was sitting on the side of the road. He seemed unable to move. He must have been injured. Startled by the lights, he blinked and turned his head toward me. There was nothing to be done. Getting close to him wasn't an option. He might try to run and make his injury worse. Tranquilizing him and treating his wound were both beyond my knowledge. "I can't help you," I kept telling him, even when he was long behind me. "Do you understand? I can't find a way."

I could still feel Rakan's jabs on my ribs. Behind my ear, where he'd licked me, my skin felt wet and cold. Instead of going straight, I took a right, toward a patch of grass inside the forest, the kind drivers use to turn around when they are going the wrong way. I stopped driving. The trees were tall and steady. Occasionally the wind howled, swaying the skeletal branches and the surrounding shrubs. I reached into my underwear. What came to mind at once was Rakan, unzipping my jeans, then his head between my legs, his insistent tongue. I feared being loud, which was absurd. There was no one around me now, besides shadows and the howling of the wind. During my drive back, I tried not to think about what had happened. I played music loud. The sound slowly erased that image of Rakan waiting by the side of the road, the dying deer, and even those few seconds afterward, when I'd been alone in the woods.

AN HOUR LATER, I was home. Leyla was in the living room working on her computer. She didn't even notice I had come in. She was writing poetry. Lost in a dreamy, distracted mood, she was staring at the Manhattan lights through the window. Since she'd come over, she hadn't left the apartment. She'd move room to room, reading, writing, listening to music, talking to her family on the phone. Our radiator was finally fixed. She wasn't used to the intense heat and always wore shorts and tank tops inside, her bare feet pattering on our wooden floor.

"Oh, I didn't see you," she said smiling. "I finally started writing again. It's actually not bad."

"Here it is," I said, showing her Rakan's phone. "I got it from him. You can do what you want with it."

Maybe I spoke too abruptly. She was startled. I placed the phone on the coffee table. She didn't touch it. She must have dimly felt that showing no excitement wasn't the appropriate reaction, so she smiled cautiously.

"How did you get it?"

"It doesn't matter," I said. "Does it?"

She thought about it for a while.

"What happened?"

"Nothing. He's okay. I think."

"Okay. But since I tried to grab it from his hands that last time," she said, "I'm wondering if he'll know it was me."

"It wasn't you," I said, picturing him sitting on those rocks in the park, waiting for the lady giant. "It was me."

"I hope he doesn't start looking for us both," she said.

"He won't," I said, sounding surer than I was.

THE NEXT DAY I took the subway to Manhattan to see Anna, who, after the accident, was staying at her parents' apartment. They lived in a duplex condo, part of a redbrick townhouse in the West Village.

It was Mrs. Cruz who opened the door. She was tall, with a big mouth that resembled Anna's, and small piercing eyes that did not. She didn't recognize me. Like her daughter, she gave the impression of a busy socialite who was bad with faces. Her aging showed only on her neck and hands; she had managed to banish it from her face. Her clothes were simple, comfortable, and expensive-looking. The only exotic aspect of Mrs. Cruz's appearance was two strands of purple amid her silver hair.

"Anna took me to her hairdresser before she left for South Korea," she said self-consciously. "I'm so glad you came to visit her."

While listening to Billy and Miles's conversation, the accident had seemed abstract, a fictional twist in a story. But seeing Mrs. Cruz's pained face brought home the fact that Anna's accident had shaken her world. I handed her a Mason jar with lemon chicken soup.

"I made this for Anna," I said. "I'm sorry about what happened."

"Oh, how nice," she said and placed it on the table. "Yes, we told her not to go. A year is a long time, isn't it? But Anna has inherited my stubbornness."

"Fortunately, she's alive."

"Of course. But she will miss playing her violin. It was her life, since when she was five."

Anna had told me she was tired of playing violin the last time we had talked. It was hardly the occasion to mention it.

"My husband and I have always been music lovers. She started playing the piano when she was three, tottering over to it and banging at the keys. The first time she saw someone playing the violin, she fell in love."

Mrs. Cruz was lonely, I realized. She reminded me of those people who squeezed a conversation out of everyone they encountered—cab drivers, grocery clerks, doormen, waiters, delivery people. Billy had once hinted that Mr. Cruz, her husband, had many affairs, even in his old age. Apparently, he had mistresses in different cities, like a sailor.

"Where is Anna?"

"Sleeping, last time I checked. She sleeps a lot. She needs it. Please take a seat. Make yourself comfortable."

I'd been to the apartment before, for Anna's parents' thirty-fifth-anniversary party.

I looked around the hallway, which years ago I had mistaken for a living room. There was a grand piano in the corner. A dozen upholstered chairs in orange tapestry lined up against the wall. During the party, a pianist had been playing Frank Sinatra while everyone danced on the thick Turkish carpet. Flushed waiters in black vests and bow ties had brought around trays of appetizers.

"Come." She veered me toward the living room, which was next door. It was a lovely room with a blue Moroccan rug, hanging plants, and velvet sofas. It opened into a library, whose four walls were covered by bookshelves that surrounded two leather chairs. To the left of the library, gliding French doors revealed an outdoor patio with furniture of a nautical theme.

"The tea in the pot should still be warm," Mrs. Cruz said. "It's black tea with a splash of peach. Do you want some? Let me get you a cup."

"Do you think we can check on Anna?"

Her phone rang. She asked me to excuse her but returned in no time.

"It was Anna's father on the phone," she said. "He had to go to Singapore for business. He was checking in."

"Do you think Anna is awake?" I asked.

"Let's go look. Come with me."

We walked to Anna's room. I waited outside. Mrs. Cruz left the door ajar. The amount of medicine bottles on the nightstand alarmed me. I could see Anna's face, thin and pale. She was wearing an oddly old-fashioned nightgown with floral embroidery. It seemed like she had been bedridden for years. Mrs. Cruz fixed the blankets around her and poured her more water. These were mechanical gestures whose purpose was less to bring comfort—there was already water in Anna's glass and she was tucked in like a mummy—than to make herself feel useful. I felt some sadness witnessing that mother-daughter scene. I wanted someone to make a fuss about me, although I felt fine.

Anna opened her eyes. Mrs. Cruz whispered something in her ear. Upon hearing my name, she pulled the blanket up around her and nodded. Mrs. Cruz motioned me to go in and left the room.

Anna was lying with her back resting on a pillow and her fingers braided above her belly. There was a lumpy shape under the sheet—her left leg was in a cast. She turned her drawn face toward me. Her long dark hair had spread on her silk pillow. She pushed aside some of the strands. She didn't react at first, although there was a moment, soon after my entry, when she tried to smile. I was late to encourage it, so it died quickly. She closed her eyes. Her muscles relaxed. I stood there looking at her. The windows faced the street, but a deep silence had suffused the room. Seconds later, the groveling and growling of car brakes startled us both. She opened her eyes.

*I should say something*, I thought, about the accident, or her recovery, but the words wouldn't come.

"I always imagined," she said in a surprisingly strong voice. "That I'd end up with Billy someday. It wasn't a conscious effort on my part, it was just an idea. Unreasonable, of course."

I pulled a chair and sat by her side.

"He was in a bad way that night," she continued. "We were sitting next to each other, and it felt natural to kiss him. He went along for a second and then pulled away. He got agitated, pacing around the apartment, calling hotels to get out of there. I told him that nothing happened—it was a silly, childish kiss, but it was no use. The two hotels he called were booked. Then he kept saying he wanted to go home to tell you about it, but he didn't know how because you had a fight that night and you were withdrawing. And this idea I've had all along that your marriage wouldn't last, that you two were too different, that he had married you for the papers and didn't know how to get out of it, seemed so absurd that I felt ashamed. But I had to tell him. I told him everything. It's like when you're falling, you know, and let yourself go, go, go. I told him that your marriage wasn't going to work, that maybe we should give it a shot after all these years. He got sort of sad and sat by the window. 'But neither will we,' he said. 'You should know that. We will never work out either.' We didn't talk again after that. I went to my bedroom. In the morning, he was gone."

Anna appeared to have run out of breath. She had likely poured all the energy she had into that monologue. I pulled my chair forward but couldn't manage to touch her hand, as my intention had been. I did feel relief, for Anna and myself, and maybe even some satisfaction. After all these years, we had scraped below the surface of our friendship. She had finally told me something true. Jealousy escaped me now. He had told her the truth, I suddenly knew. Her hands looked dry. Her nails no longer had the fake tips on. Were we to hold hands, it would be difficult to distinguish my fingers from hers.

I lowered my head on her side of her bed. Since Billy left, my sleep had been terrible, two or three hours at the most, followed by hours of insomnia. But now my body felt light; a flood of relaxation doused my shoulders and turned every muscle into slush. Was Anna falling asleep also? Maybe days later her mother would come and wake us up. We'd be healed, walk out of that room together, hand in hand. My thoughts were surrendering, giving in to visuals. Anna put her hand on my head; it felt warm and heavy. Her touch brought me back to the present, to the sound of the cars and the trembling windows.

Mrs. Cruz knocked, reminding Anna to take her medicine.

I sat up and looked at her.

"Can you?" she said, pointing to the nightstand.

I handed her the glass. She swallowed two white pills.

"I should take a nap," she said. "This makes me drowsy."

I stood up and squeezed her hand. "Get well, Anna, okay?"

Her face looked even paler now. When she said goodbye, lifting one arm in my direction, her voice sounded meek, nothing like what she had managed earlier.

Saying goodbye to Mrs. Cruz proved more complicated.

"Your tea," she said. "I just warmed it up for you."

"I'm sorry, I can't stay."

"Why not?" she said. "Sit and relax. When Anna wakes up, you can go in again. Give Billy a call, too. Tell him to come."

I felt an urge to be outside, away from that atmosphere of illness, away from Mrs. Cruz's prying and needy eyes. I wanted to go for a long walk, for the discomfort of my joints to distract from the unease I felt inside. Throughout that morning, I had tried to forget that Billy, since he'd left for Europe, hadn't called, but now that fact was weighing on me.

"Anna and I are done," I said. She seemed puzzled. "For today," I added.

Mrs. Cruz accompanied me to the door. After I kissed her cheek and left the apartment, I regretted I didn't stay for tea.

What was she doing in that living room all alone while waiting for her daughter to wake up? Maybe she was reading those *New Yorker* magazines on her coffee table or preparing Anna some food. Maybe she was calling her husband, and he was telling her he'd call her back, when the meeting was over.

When I first moved to America, I often wondered what my mother was doing at various times of the day. I would see her moving from room to room, cooking, cleaning, ironing the sheets and all the clothes, until every surface around her was warm to the touch. Then the bricks around my house would transform to glass, as would all the walls in the neighborhood. I'd see all mothers inside their houses and apartments, alone, lost in thought, moving around their small spaces in a repetitive movement, like in some synchronized domestic performance. Then the mothers would throw a sweater over their shoulders and stroll to the grocery store. They'd roam through the intricate streets of my city without an apparent purpose.

To my mother, after staying inside for so long, the people would seem harsh and vulgar. Those in a good mood would be too happy for her taste. She'd crave the comfort and silence of her home.

I called her. She picked up at once.

"Mother," I said. "I'm coming home."

"When?"

"I leave tomorrow."

Then I hung up, knowing the next question would be about Billy.

# 9.

TIRANA WAS OVERWHELMING AS USUAL. SOON AFTER landing, I was convinced that the only life that mattered was the one here: unpredictable, complicated, but truer than anything else. The conversations in the passport line, the border officer saying *welcome* in Albanian, the eager faces of relatives waiting behind the sliding doors tightened my throat. It was an emotion I was used to hiding, wondering if it was familiar to all those who returned home once a year, or less. Did the others also find it expedient to put on another face—tired, nonchalant, the face of a foreigner? My uncle's fedora hat peeped above the crowd. It was unsettling at first to see him there waiting for me, where my father used to stand. He was wearing a three-piece suit he was fond of, and was glancing at his Volna watch, which used to belong to my grandfather. Before retiring, my uncle worked as a general practitioner, the wrong profession for him. He had the soul of a poet, the tendency to lose himself in his own interpretation of reality.

His round glasses slid down his nose as he peered at my face. "You're much too pale." He still carried with him an aura of authority, and that grave expression that doctors employed before delivering a diagnosis.

"I felt sick on the plane," I said. "It was a small plane."

"Welcome home."

He hugged me with his right arm since the left one was carrying a frame enclosed in brown paper. He would uncover it minutes later, as we sat on the bus that drove us to Tirana's city center. I had a vague idea of what it could be. My uncle was preoccupied (or obsessed, depending on whom you asked) with our family's role and position in Albanian history. He'd spend weeks down south, where our family was from, researching our relatives' contribution to World War II. His dedication to the past, the pride he took in his family and the country were admirable. But he could also be selective, opting for the most palatable story. My father, his brother, had been the opposite, always zeroing in on the truth, no matter how disastrous, but privately and without a fuss.

"This is your great-grandfather," he said, showing me an oil painting of a man with handlebar whiskers sprouting from his nose. His hand was clasping a felt skullcap that was sliding down his head. "I've declared him a hero, you know?"

I wasn't sure what it took to officially declare someone a hero in Albania, but my uncle had done it twice before. Perhaps some bored and underpaid clerks in a government office had come to realize there was money to be made from his vanity. Assuming an official posture, they'd urge each other to knock it off and be serious whenever my uncle walked into their office presenting the evidence he'd collected.

"I had this portrait commissioned," he went on. "She didn't do a bad job. He was tough. It comes through, right?"

I studied the painting. My great-grandfather had a glint in his eye and looked like someone you shouldn't mess with, a mountain lion behind a cage that could break anyone's neck with a swipe of his paw. A beak nose ruled over his severe features, a well-defined chin and glistening blue eyes. An embroidered waistcoat with a foliate pattern and golden braids distracted from the artist's only failing—a neck much too thin for the enormous head.

"As far as I am concerned," I said, thinking aloud, "anyone who fought the fascists should be declared a hero."

"He also got wounded," said my uncle. "They want to place his portrait in a museum, of course, now that he's officially a hero, but the paperwork hasn't gone through yet. You can keep him at your mother's house until he gets approved."

He phrased it as if he was doing me a favor by letting me keep the portrait, but the real reason was likely that his wife wouldn't allow it into their apartment. She was less amused than the rest of us by his patriotic endeavors. *He throws money down the drain*, she always complained.

"Sure," I said, feeling a surge of affection for my uncle, who had such little regard for his own money and time, who persisted with his fixations despite everyone's discouragement. "We'll keep him in our home."

Charging through a tangled mess of cars, the bus barely managed to exit a roundabout. In Tirana, the number of lanes could be ambiguous and left up to anyone's interpretation. The only rule people obeyed was that the biggest vehicle had the right of way.

In front of us, someone was saying to their relative, "You know who causes most of the traffic problems? Foreigners or returning immigrants like you. You stop when you're supposed to, give the other cars the right-of-way, allow crowds of pedestrians to cross the street."

"We follow the rules, you mean?"

"Exactly. It causes confusion."

The visiting immigrant became silent. He was finally home, he realized.

A row of buildings striped in blue and yellow flashed by. We had entered the city center.

In Tirana, bright, eye-catching designs were painted diligently over the drab communist-era apartment buildings. This compulsory artistic experience wasn't everyone's cup of tea. *Why not let the ugliness show?* some locals said. *It's there, isn't it? It lacks dignity, this city, dressed up like a candy cane.* But to me, Tirana's colorful façade recalled the advice therapists often offered to depressed patients. *Go ahead and smile, fake it if you must, you'll feel better eventually.* Tirana was a city appearing to be fine, a city on the lookout for happier days. Those blotches of paint were a makeshift declaration of hope.

The bus dropped us off at the vast and shiny Skanderbeg Square, surrounded by buildings and monuments that loomed large in my childhood memories. Hotel Tirana, fifteen stories high, how proud we had been of that building in the old days—our only skyscraper. It looked diminutive, embarrassed almost, next to the new, glassy constructions. A large banner at the Palace of Culture, where Alma and I would sneak into operas and concerts during the intermissions, was advertising an upcoming recital. Across the square was the puppet theater, where my father used to take me on Sundays. I'd pop in every year to check that everything had remained the same, the ticket box office with the oval doors and the marionettes hanging on the walls of the lobby. I had seen them last May, dusty, lifelike, still in their velvet clothes, awaiting their next performance.

My mother's house was a fifteen-minute walk from the center, behind the New Bazaar, an open market that the locals deemed too expensive. My uncle had insisted on helping me with the suitcase, but instead of rolling it along, he kept lifting it.

"What did you put inside here?"

"I've got it," I said, handing the painting back to him.

Navigating Tirana's narrow sidewalks required focus. The bicycles of a sports goods store had spilled outside, blocking our path. We had to step into the traffic to go on. My uncle asked if I wanted blackberries; a man by the side of the road sold them in paper funnels. I told him no, but he bought them anyway. A woman in her eighties sat behind a scale, charging to read the weight of passersby. A small crowd had gathered in front of her. A portly man climbed on top of the scale and made jokes about his own weight.

"Did it crack?" he shouted, looking down.

"He used to be one of my patients," my uncle exclaimed.

This was something he said frequently. Sometimes it was true, sometimes not. My mother had been right, I should have told my uncle I'd take a taxi from the airport. I should have refused his offer to pick me up. *It's like having Don Quixote pick you up from a long trip*, she had said. *He gets distracted.*

"Doctor!" the man shouted and climbed down from the scale. He ran toward us and gave my uncle a hug.

"I haven't seen you in years," my uncle exclaimed. "I just picked up my niece from the airport. She works for the UN, you know, in New York." He knew that was no longer the case, but he enjoyed showing me off. It wasn't the right time and place to contradict him. I wanted to get home. My uncle went on chatting with the man. The crowd scattered. A new street vendor was setting up next to the woman, arranging a perplexing combination of goods on a blanket—an assortment of electrical plugs and two plays by Molière.

I tugged my uncle's sleeve. "Can we go?"

We were finally in front of my house. My mother had left the gate open. Ours was a small traditional house that had belonged to her side of the family for two hundred years. There was a garden big enough for two lemon trees and some rosebushes. A paved path from the gate to the main door divided the garden in half. Random garments were hanging over the trees and the bushes: a green woolen skirt, three white undershirts. Beige nylon stockings lay on some of the shrubs that lined the walls. My mother had done laundry. Although I had often asked her to set up an additional clothesline in the back, she never did, opting to put some clothes out to dry on various branches and shrubs. My objection was only partially aesthetic. There was something distressing about that tableau of empty clothes. It was as if the bodies inside had vanished unexpectedly, and the outfits had collapsed in despair.

She came to open the door, followed by Neta. They stood on the doorstep, one behind the other, full of smiles. They were sizing me up, evaluating my weight. Albanians always thought their children were too skinny. I squeezed them both, squashing my face into their shoulders. They emitted a medley of aromas—chamomile tea, lavender detergent, burnt cooking oil, a sweetish scent of sweat.

"She's lost weight," said my mother.

"Yes," said Neta, looking me up and down. "Definitely."

I evaluated them also, but silently, the polite American way. Neta had gained weight. My mother looked thinner than the last time we'd met. She had let her hair grow all the way to her elbows. It reminded me of rain, impossibly straight and fragmented, the way the white strands stood out among the purple dye. There was a nervous energy about her. Her hands were restless, always finding something to do—fixing the artificial flowers in the table vase, taking off one apron and putting on another, rolling the suitcase into my bedroom.

They both looked behind me, past my uncle.

"Where is Billy?"

"He isn't coming," I said. "He's in Hungary."

"What's he doing there?"

It occurred to me they might either laugh or be confused by the real purpose of Billy's trip. What could I say? *He's watching a bridge from a distance and taking notes? Counting the people who walk on it? Pretending, for six months straight, to protect it from the devastation of human beings?*

"He's working at a university there for a few months."

My answer seemed to satisfy them, as would any sentence that contained the word *university*. That Billy was a university professor had always impressed them. My uncle came in carrying the painting. My mother laid an old blanket on the sofa, a preemptive measure to keep the sofa clean. Since she'd seen my uncle sit on a dusty step once, she'd bring out the blanket whenever he came over. *His pants are filthy*, she'd say. *He'll sit wherever.* My uncle uncovered the portrait and took pictures of it from different angles. Maybe he was sending the photos to other relatives. *Here he is, our hero, on his museum journey.*

Neta handed me a pair of woolen socks she had knitted for Billy. "I made those for him," she said. "He likes blue. I know that."

"Thank you."

"I'll leave. I'll let you eat."

The table was full of dishes my mother had cooked earlier that day—a tomato and cucumber salad, roasted red peppers marinated in vinegar and garlic, rice pilaf and chicken, French fries, a spinach byrek. She'd left two bottles of cold beer next to two empty plates. I picked up one of the beers and Billy's plate and took them to the kitchen. My phone, having picked up the Wi-Fi signal, squealed. A response came to mind at once—*Funny you just texted. They've been asking about you. Neta has made you a pair of socks.* But the text wasn't from Billy. How many days had it been since we had last talked? He didn't even know I was in Albania. It was Leyla who had written to me, asking how my trip was. Fragments of that night with Rakan flashed in my memory. The Bob Marley music. His narrow eyes. His thick tongue wrestling mine. The mushroom cookies that brought his lustful advances to an end. He had stumbled toward the water, talking about the lights beyond. The naked trees. The torn sky. That dark craving.

"Something wrong?" said my mother. "Does the chicken feel too rubbery? Did I boil it too much?"

"It's perfect."

Only ten hours away from New York, and my American life had already slipped into peripheral awareness. Now it all came back. It was always like this. One life would seem like the true one, the other distant, almost imaginary. Then they would switch. A Polish film Billy and I had seen years ago came to mind. After a dramatic scene, the actors would stop acting and the camera would follow them through their supposedly actual lives. The audience had to keep track of two storylines, one that was fictional and one that purported not to be. By the end of the movie, it was impossible to distinguish one from the other. Since moving to America, my life had been like that movie, two parallel highways with regular exits into each other.

I would text Leyla back later. I wrote a quick email to Billy letting him know I was in Tirana. It was the first time one of us had reached out since he'd left for his fellowship. *Can we talk on the phone?* I wrote.

My mother's voice distracted me.

"You know what your problem is?" she was saying to my uncle. "You dream with your eyes open."

Her lips had thinned, a common side effect of having anyone on my father's side of the family visit. A universal condition, my father called it, that irritation people typically felt toward their in-laws. How long had they been arguing for? How had I missed the beginning? My uncle was holding the painting in his lap. Had he been showing it to her?

"You go on about the wonderful past," she was saying. "Anyone with brains knows we were miserable. And we were the lucky ones."

"You weren't miserable," my uncle retorted. "You were working as a gymnast, traveling to different countries for performances. My brother worked as a journalist. You had a house with a garden in the middle of Tirana."

"We lived in fear for years."

"What fear? There was no fear."

"That they'd fire your brother. That they might arrest us all."

My mother was arguing with my uncle while pouring me beer and water. She wasn't too emotionally involved in the argument, treating it as a side gig while examining my facial reactions to her cooking. It was an old disagreement, after all. My relatives sometimes got into arguments about how good or bad it had been in the old days. My uncle belonged to that group of Albanians who were nostalgic for the old regime. He'd go on about the merits of Hoxha's rule, mentioning education reforms and women's equality, omitting poverty, isolation, internments, and executions.

"Do you think it was right that they wanted to make us pay because my cousin tried to escape the country?" she asked him.

"They said he was a thief."

"He wasn't a thief. It was something they invented after they hanged him. But even if he was a thief. Do you think I should pay with my life because my cousin stole four light bulbs from a factory?"

"Mistakes were made, of course," my uncle conceded, leaning his head to the left.

My mother made a heroic attempt to restrain herself, but she didn't succeed.

"Your daughter Alma cleans houses in Greece all day long," she said. "And sends you money. What do you do with that money? You commission silly paintings."

My uncle stood up. "My wife is making me lunch," he said. "I better go."

He didn't know what to do about the painting. He didn't want to take it with him but was too afraid of my mother to leave it with us. I made a hand motion, indicating he could leave it behind the door of my bedroom. He nodded and went inside the room.

"Have a good day," he said to my mother, then turned to me. "I'll call you. Let's go get lunch one day."

"Okay."

"How did it start?" I asked her once he was gone.

"He said that even Enver Hoxha had mentioned the great-grandfather in one of his memoirs. What an honor. Anyway, forget him. My soap opera is about to start."

She picked up the blanket on which my uncle had sat and tossed it into the washing machine.

"You will not call Alma, will you?" I asked her. "It's none of our business what he does with his money."

"Of course I will. He wastes all the money she sends him. She should know."

She turned on the TV. She was fond of Turkish soap operas, popular in the Middle East and most Balkan countries. Two brunettes, dressed distinctly but played by the same actor, were amid a heated discussion.

"They're twins," my mother said, as if it wasn't obvious.

They were hatching a plan to save the life of a man who was kidnapped. The sequence jumped back and forth between their conversation and shots of a handsome bearded man in handcuffs staring out at a basement window.

I decided to call Leyla. She answered after the first ring, as if she'd been waiting by the phone.

"How was your trip?"

"Fine. Everything okay in the apartment?"

A pause followed. A sense of dread sneaked into my chest.

"You there?" I asked. "Leyla?"

"I thought I saw him today."

"Where?"

"Outside your building."

"That's ridiculous. How could he know where you are already?"

"That's what I was wondering. I guess he wasn't tracking my phone."

"Have you gone out?"

"Just to buy groceries."

"Did you share my address with anyone?"

"Just one of my roommates."

"Why did you do that?"

"My lawyer had mailed me something about my asylum application. He asked if I had read it. I asked her to bring it to me here."

"How sure are you that you saw him?"

"I don't know. Sometimes I worry it's all in my mind. Today I was thinking that maybe one of my roommates was ratting me out. Maybe I'm just paranoid."

"Keep an eye out," I said. "Please let me know if you see him again."

"I will. Have a good time, okay?"

"Okay."

After our conversation, I felt afraid. But Rakan didn't know where I lived. Leyla had tried to wrestle the phone from his hands, the same phone I'd stolen from him, but besides that, there was nothing to connect her to me. But say he knew she was in my apartment. Our car was parked in front of our building.

What if he remembered its make and model and realized that Leyla was my friend? While gathering up the dishes, my hands trembled. I dropped a glass. It didn't break.

"Don't worry about the dishes," said my mother. "I'll take care of it. You look tired. You go rest."

On the other hand, Leyla wasn't even sure she'd seen him. And what were the chances he'd remember my car? He was on the lookout for giants as I drove away from the park.

My pallid face stared back at me from the immaculate mirror in my mother's bathroom. She was right, I was exhausted. I washed my face with soap and cold water. While looking for a towel, a stubborn glare caught my eye. I let out a small scream. My great-grandfather's portrait was hanging on the back of the bathroom door, where the towels used to hang. My mother must have picked it up from my bedroom and brought it to the bathroom out of spite.

*Here he is, our hero, on his museum journey.*

Upon lying on my childhood bed, sleep came over me at once. The woman with an oval red mark on her cheek appeared behind my eyelids. I had no idea who she was, but she always made an appearance on my first night back home. Right before I fell asleep, her wrinkled, pudgy face stared at me silently, protectively. Perhaps she was the ghost of a great-grandmother, intent on dispatching a welcome whenever I returned.

MY MOTHER WOULD HAVE PREFERRED a family-style eatery that served the same dishes she cooked at home. But after eating every meal at home for two days, I wanted something new. The restaurant I chose was located near Tirana's old castle, now a bustling district of cobblestone streets, full of souvenir shops and a movie theater. It was normally only a ten-minute walk from our house, but my mother walked leisurely. Mentioning our reservation twice didn't make her refrain from chatting up random street vendors. First it was the woman operating a popcorn machine, then the man selling roasted chestnuts. She ended up buying chestnuts (for later, she said) and a fly swatter she inserted headfirst into her purse. Lastly, she deliberated at length over a flashlight, before announcing, much to the seller's objections, that they were defective.

Halfway there, we ran into an acquaintance, with whom she carried on a cryptic conversation.

"She pays for nothing around the house," the woman said. "Nothing."

"Nothing at all?"

"Nothing."

"Excuse me," I said to the woman, "But we're on our way to a restaurant."

"Which restaurant?" the woman said. "I know a good one around the corner. The best kofte around. There is one right here also—good lamb."

"Really?" said my mother. "This corner here? What else do they have?"

"I've already found a restaurant," I reminded them both, exasperated. "The one we're going to."

The woman was skeptical.

"Where is your restaurant?"

My mother told her.

"Why walk that far? There's a good one right here."

For some reason, she was determined to sway our lunch plans.

"It's not far," I said. "It's a ten-minute walk."

My mother sighed, while holding on to the woman's arm.

"My daughter is taking me out," she said in a voice that was mostly proud. "She lives in America." But there was a hint of something else in her voice also, an obvious attempt to concur with the woman. If up to her, my mother was implying, she would have preferred the restaurant around the corner, and not have to bother with that ten-minute walk. Why did taking her to lunch, a simple undertaking for anyone, feel so complicated for me? Why didn't this stranger mind her own business?

Seconds later we were finally on our way. That my mother was out of the house at all was astonishing. How many times had I been waiting for her to get ready, only for her to change her mind? We arrived at the restaurant thirty minutes late. The lunch crowd had died down. They found us a table right away, which vindicated her. "See? There was no need to rush."

A young, skinny waiter with closely cropped hair handed us the menus. He was friendly, polite, and spoke with a northern accent. The local boys usually found waiting tables beneath them. Who knew what he put up with every day—low wages, the locals' condescension, the long commute.

My mother eyed the menu with suspicion, not finding any of the dishes she knew.

"They have tapas," I said. "Small dishes. You order as many as you want."

"So why don't you order for me?" she said. "It's easier that way."

I ordered a few dishes, two glasses of wine. They were playing Andean music; it was all flutes and panpipes. The room was bright, warm, decorated in a minimalistic Scandinavian style, unusual for Albania. The ambiance was serene, first world. Two other women entered the restaurant. To them, we were a typical mother-daughter pair enjoying lunch together. They must have thought we did this all the time.

"I love this music," my mother said. I felt a sense of victory, the taste of accomplishment, as if our lunch was a celebration after an arduous project that had finally turned out well. It was better not to talk about it, to let it be, but I couldn't help myself.

"When you told me over the phone that you're going out, I almost didn't believe you."

"A small neurosis," she said. "It comes and goes."

"I was interpreting for a Kosovar Albanian. His mother went through the same thing."

"Oh, poor woman."

"It wasn't that small. We'd always cancel things."

"Not that many. We went on plenty of vacations."

My mother's apparent frankness was deceiving. Our struggles to get her to leave the house towered over those times she had left on her own. Still, her self-assurance and tone made me doubt my own version of events. I longed for Zinovia's voice, comforting and clever, arranging memories until they didn't sting. Picturing her pinkish hands under the Cetaphil nozzle made me queasy.

"Are you okay?" asked my mother.

"Alfred and I became friends," I went on. "But he was my client, so it wasn't such a good idea to be friends with him."

A sudden compulsion to discuss Alfred's situation nagged at me. She sensed that something was required of her but wasn't sure what to say.

"Have you talked to Billy recently?" she said, implying that was a conversation to be had with him. "Is everything okay between you two?"

The waiter brought out a wooden plate with slices of bread, honey, feta cheese, and prosciutto, then another wooden plate with a variety of pastries.

"Those are my favorites," the waiter said, pointing to a tiny croissant. "They're filled with chestnut cream."

"You ordered us *Moltos*?" my mother inquired, leaning toward me. Albanians frequently referred to products by their brand name. Molto was the leading brand of croissants in the Middle East, Africa, and, for some reason, Albania. Grocery stores carried them in bright plastic bags and parents bought them for their children.

"No. Those croissants are made here," I said. "In the kitchen. By a chef."

"I like the presentation," she said, folding a piece of prosciutto over a slice of bread and taking a bite. "They make it look nice."

Then she pulled out her phone.

"You know," she said. "We got here late. My soap opera already started."

"You're watching it now?"

"It's just one scene. I need to know what will happen and then I'll turn it off."

Outside, a pregnant mother handed her toddler a tablet. He grabbed it excitedly, as if he'd been waiting for it all day. The mother sat on a bench and turned her face toward the sun. She seemed exhausted, enjoying the break, letting the sun caress her shoulders and her distended stomach. We were the same, that woman and me. I was also taking a break while waiting for my child, the older woman sitting across from me, to finish watching her TV show. My mother had always preferred little children to grownups. She took pleasure in all the practical things, preparing the food and buying the clothes, but what was she to do with an adult looking to her for emotional comfort, she, who needed so much of it herself?

The waiter brought over another wooden plate. It held a green salad, some anchovies, and crackers. She put the phone to the side but left it on. I could still hear the dialogue in Turkish. Someone said *aşkım* again—*my love*. It was a word I had picked up the previous day.

I tried one of the anchovies, soft, moist, lemony. To my surprise, a cooked white breast of chicken appeared on the plate next to the crackers. Where had it come from?

"I brought it with me," my mother said, her eyes glinting. "I had an idea of what kind of place this might be. Have some. It goes well with the white sauce."

She seemed proud of herself. She picked some chicken with the fork and tried to feed it to me. "Try it." I glanced at the waiter, who looked away. Had he noticed the chicken piece she had brought from home?

"Did you and Billy fight?" she said. "Tell me the truth."

"He thinks I should see a therapist."

"You don't need a therapist," she said. "You just need to let things go. You're like a dog with a bone sometimes."

"What do you mean?"

"Do you remember Tasha across the street? The one with the two boys? They moved away many years ago."

I only remembered them vaguely.

"She came knocking on our door one night," my mother continued. "She was unemployed for a bit. Couldn't feed her kids. She asked for some bread. From that day on, you'd always take food over to their house."

"How old was I?"

"Six? Seven? Even after she found a job. It embarrassed her."

"Did she tell you that? That it embarrassed her?"

"She asked me to tell you to stop. Yes, because it embarrassed her."

It had happened years ago. Perhaps even Tasha no longer remembered it. Still, my cheeks burned. My mother had often bragged about me to others, calling me generous and good-hearted. Had she, all along, thought of me as foolishly single-minded, a half-wit do-gooder? The pipe music recalled vast yellow fields at the mercy of a burning sun. The waiter hovered around us as faithfully as a bodyguard. The women in the corner were taking pictures of their food from various angles and arguing over the best one. Nothing had changed inside the restaurant, but the atmosphere had lost its coziness. I felt restless, uneasy. A draft from the back of the room didn't help; it was blowing on my left shoulder.

"This place is good," my mother said, looking around the restaurant. "I think Billy would like it here. You should have brought him here instead of me. Why don't you ask him to come over for a weekend? I'm sure he doesn't teach on weekends."

She glanced stealthily at her phone, then at me.

"Go ahead and watch," I said. "It's fine."

"Just this one scene."

"Do you want any dessert?"

"You decide."

I checked my email again. Billy had not replied. I sent him another email, asking if he was okay.

# 10.

SOMEWHERE ON THE LOWER EAST SIDE, AN ARTIST HAD once handed me a map she'd designed. Instead of landmark buildings or venues, the map contained references to important events that had happened to her at certain cross streets, coffee shops, parks. The map had guided me through that stranger's breakups, memorable encounters, unforgettable parties, exquisite dinners. The map also revealed the exact locations of a haunting confession, a betrayal, and a promise that would soon be forgotten. A map of emotions was perhaps closer to anyone's perception of reality. While walking through a familiar city, wasn't spatial awareness always linked to old memories and regrets?

In Tirana, a city where new construction and urban development happened at an astonishing rate, navigating through instinct and feeling was inevitable. Old ghosts were everywhere and proved more helpful than the rare street signs. That morning I walked on Qemal Stafa street, then took a right on Rruga e Barrikadave before a pit stop at Mulliri i Vjetër Café. I drank a cappuccino alone; an old friend wrote to say she was on her way to Athens for work and couldn't meet. Still, an aura of excitement suffused the bar, the tables, the people. I was glad to be home.

I took a stroll on Boulevard of the Martyrs, Tirana's main thoroughfare. In the communist times, all young people, lacking other entertainment, used to parade there in their best clothes, gawking at each other. The avenue stretched for miles, expansive and lively, surrounded by pine and poplar trees. Tirana's Polytechnic University stood as a barricade at the end of the street. It was an example of fascist architecture, built by the Italians after they invaded Albania just before World War II. At nighttime, every window gleamed blue, illuminating the square even from a distance.

At Rinia Park, an elderly man carrying a film camera asked if I wanted my picture taken. Those ambulant photographers roaming public squares and parks were a relic from another era. In the distant past, we'd dress up and stroll to Skanderbeg Square for a family portrait. The photographers would always hang out there, their heavy Russian cameras tied around their necks.

"What's the meaning of this?" a woman asked the photographer. "Now everyone has cameras in their phone. Why do you keep pestering people like this?"

The photographer looked perplexed by the woman's unexpected attack.

"If you don't want a picture, just say no," he said. "What's your problem?"

"I'm letting you know that *nobody* wants a picture."

She spoke with excessive authority, assuming the elderly photographer needed lecturing, convinced he was oblivious to all technological advancements. But maybe he carried the camera in spite of his profession becoming obsolete. Having nothing else to do, he brought it on the off chance that someone might take pity on him, or that he might run into a nostalgic or eccentric person, willing to pay him for the experience.

I went on with my walk. I passed by the Pyramid, built as an homage to Enver Hoxha after his death. In the late eighties, we'd gone there for a school trip. The enormous chandelier was the most gorgeous thing, its crystals breaking the light a million ways.

The dead leader's statue, in gleaming white, loomed tall above us. He was sitting on a throne, like Zeus, staring above our heads.

In the entrance hall of the prime minister's office, an art show was taking place, exhibiting sculptures and installations by women artists. I went in. The exhibit focused on embroidery, sewing, and knitting, which the artists had used in surprising ways. A set of three white sweaters with the sleeves knitted together gave the impression of three women holding hands. Were they conspiring? Taking comfort in each other? Trapped in an endless dependency?

Tolstoy's *War and Peace* was placed on a pedestal with red threads hanging loose from its opened pages. An artist had embroidered some of the pages. Across the room draped a lengthy nightgown fit for the body of a giant mermaid. A plaque on the wall said that before the women's movement of the sixties and seventies, embroidery was denied the title of fine art. I remembered my grandmother always knitting, making sweaters and socks for everyone in the family.

My phone beeped. Another friend had written to say she was busy that week. Perhaps next week, she said. What did my friends and relatives, those who had stayed, feel toward us, who had left? The mutual affection had to fade, replaced by a faint curiosity. Did our brief yearly visits make them second-guess their choice to stay or confirm it? At least, unlike the departed, they didn't have to carry two lives in one body. The way my grandmother's needle had maneuvered across the linen with a double strand of thread came to mind.

"Më i fort kështu," she'd say. *It's stronger this way.*

As I passed by Kinema Millennium, I saw two preteen girls buying tickets to a matinee.

My first thought: *Were they skipping school?*

IT TOOK A LOT of effort to convince Alma to skip school, and when she finally agreed, she didn't enjoy the freedom the day promised or the taste of spring. She obsessed, for longer than was reasonable, over some professor realizing that both of us getting sick on the same day was suspicious. *They'll call our parents*, she cried. *We'll get in trouble.* Indulging in possible scenarios so ahead of time was futile. Most school staff were distracted and inattentive at that time of year. Random transgressions were punished and used as examples so infrequently that to fear them, as Alma did, was foolish.

We skipped down the sun-dappled pavements. The air was moist from the earlier rain and fragrant with the honey scent of linden trees. A green foliage had grown rapidly and draped over an adobe brick wall, hiding its scratches and ruin. Our beloved honeysuckles, scattered among the damp leaves, had reared their yellow faces. It only took a second to pick one up and drag out its pistil, for the drop of its translucent nectar to emerge. Eleven. Twelve. Thirteen. How many honeysuckles did we drink that morning? Alma came alive during our count, but deep down she regretted not being in school. She had probably spent hours the night before solving one of those wild math equations the teacher reserved for the brightest students. Then I'd shown up with my spontaneous plan of skipping school. I'd robbed her of the chance to prove that she'd done her best, once again. She hated disappointing her parents, or anyone really, even those she didn't care for. Her inability to be judicious about things like that used to annoy me. It was only later, when we grew older, that her easy compliance seemed worrisome.

We wandered the city all morning. It must have been March, for the acacia abounded the city, their blotches of bright yellow ornamenting the trees and staining the sidewalks. We took a momentary refuge at the Theater of Opera and Ballet, where a rehearsal of *Madama Butterfly* was taking place. Oversized Japanese fans served as a backdrop to the stage. A director was blocking two geishas wearing purple kimonos with tiny pillows on their backs. The sash was called an obi. It was used to tie the garments, a guard explained. Once the geishas started singing, we left. We found a movie theater. We had no money, but my older cousins had taught me a trick. If you showed up fifteen minutes late and marched in with confidence, pretending you had a ticket, the ushers didn't bother to leave their cozy booth. It worked every time. Come to think of it, they caught me only once, that time with Alma. She hesitated at the last minute, refusing to enter, which brought attention to us.

"Why are you just standing there?" asked my mother, breaking my reverie. "Come in."

The memory of Alma and me skipping school had tumbled out. I was already in front of my house, standing in our garden, the past quickly evaporating and out of reach.

The living room smelled like cooked cabbage.

"Why did you cook today?" I asked my mother. "I thought we'd go out to lunch. Neta is coming also, remember?"

The lunch from the day before had left behind a touch of guilt. She hadn't enjoyed it. She preferred simpler, no-fuss places.

"We'll have the byrek for dinner then."

"Are you ready to go to the restaurant?" I asked.

"I told Alma we'd call her back."

She called Alma. My cousin's voice filled our living room. It took some effort to update the old image of her with what she had become. She was telling my mother that she no longer cleaned houses; she had started working as a maid at an American hotel. She got Saturdays and Sundays off, which meant she had more time to spend with her children. And she got paid vacation. It was an easy job. She listened to music or talked on the phone as she made the beds.

"I got a raise, too," she added.

"Sweetheart," my mother said, "are you aware that your father squanders all the money you send him on useless paintings?"

A long silence followed. I crossed my arms and looked at my mother.

"We've talked to him about it," Alma said. "Often, in fact."

"Don't send him any more money," said my mother. "You work so hard for it."

Alma's daughter grabbed her phone and started tapping on it. Alma didn't reclaim it. She was incapable of telling people to leave her alone. Her children were her buffer against the world, the soft cocoon she crawled inside to keep everyone at bay.

My mother said hi to Alma's daughter, a precocious redhead, then handed the phone to me.

The child brought her green eye close to the camera.

"Do you have a penis or a vagina?"

Alma grabbed the phone from her. She wasn't amused. "Go watch TV, please," she said. "How many times have I told you not to ask people that question?"

Alma was used to the chaos around her. Problems washed over her, never leaving behind that residue of cruelty that flickered in most people with the passing of years. The only time she raised her voice was when she was around her children. She had little patience with them.

Had my mother's words upset her? Of course she didn't like to think of her father as an object of ridicule.

"How is Billy?" she asked. "When are you coming to visit me in Greece?"

My mother's body tensed up. She still suspected that something wasn't right. Neta turned toward me as well.

"Billy is doing fine," I said. "He's in Europe at the moment. We'll come visit, of course."

"I'll show you around," she said. "I have Saturday and Sunday off now."

Alma had wide, big eyes, which seemed expressionless at times. Some called her naïve. Some, considering what she did for a living, called her stupid. Having sat at the same school desk with her for years, I knew that wasn't the case. But listening to her talk so excitedly about her job as a maid made it hard to remember that her intelligence had once been intimidating.

Her daughter grabbed the phone again.

"Let's talk another day," I managed to tell her. "When we're both alone."

"How's school?" I asked her daughter. "You like it?"

"It's good. We learned about frogs today."

"What did you learn? Tell me."

"Baby frogs aren't poisonous until they grow up."

The other two kids exclaimed that their father was home. She dropped the phone.

"I better go," Alma said and hung up.

"There are some rumors," my mother said at once, "that Alma and Fatos might get divorced."

"I feel sorry for her," said Neta. "What will she do alone, with three children?"

"He hasn't worked in a long time," said my mother. "She's supporting them all. First it was the Greeks. Now she's cleaning the shit of the American tourists."

Years ago, everyone in the family had insisted on Alma getting married. Some relatives had seen her with Fatos and her parents had jumped the gun, worried about her reputation, as if it were possible to appease people for whom judgment was as frequent as appetite. I never knew if she had loved him or not.

She hadn't seemed particularly happy on her wedding day, but not sad either.

"I'm happy you're with a good man like Billy," said Neta. "From a good family. A university professor."

A queasy sensation crawled inside me as Neta went on about Billy. He still hadn't written, not even to tell me he was okay. Maybe he needed a complete break from our relationship. Had he made up his mind? Would he serve me the divorce papers as soon as I landed at JFK?

"Are we going to lunch?" I asked them both.

"Let me measure my blood pressure," said my mother. "I'm feeling a bit dizzy."

She went to the other room. Neta went on telling me about the last time she had been at that same restaurant, with her brother, an abstract painter who lived in Toronto. Focusing on her voice was difficult. The swishing sounds coming from the bedroom distracted me. It was a familiar sound, a steady companion to those long minutes and hours my father and I used to wait for her.

"You're fine, Merita," Neta called out. "Come, let's go."

"My blood pressure is a bit low," my mother said, coming into the room. "Perhaps I'll make myself some coffee to get myself together."

Standing in front of the stove, she poured water into a copper cezve.

"I know you're hungry," she told me. "Why don't you eat some byrek?"

If years of waiting around for my mother to leave the house had taught me anything, it was that all hope should be abandoned at the first sign of her resistance.

"Let's go to the restaurant. You'll like it. And Neta would like to go. Wouldn't you, Neta?"

That I had uttered such words was unbelievable. Having said them so frequently in the past, they now simply slipped out.

"Maybe for dinner. Could we go out for dinner?" she said, putting some slices of byrek on a plate for us. "Try it."

She made her coffee and headed to the bedroom to lie down.

"You can't push her," said Neta. "She has to take her time."

"But she said yes to lunch."

"She changed her mind. That's okay. Let's eat together."

Neta and I ate in silence. My mother had left her bedroom door open. She appeared to be sleeping.

"Did you tell Billy that I made those socks for him?" Neta said.

"I did. Thank you."

"Maybe we can Skype him now and show them to him?"

I wanted to tell Neta the truth. *Billy and I haven't talked in days. He isn't even replying to me.* But she always talked about him with such affection. She'd never married or had children of her own. She always took such interest and joy in my life.

"He told me he'd be out this afternoon with some of his students."

"At the university?"

"Yes. At the university."

"Another time then."

"Another time."

"Don't worry about your mother. We'll go to the restaurant tomorrow."

"Okay, tomorrow."


WE DIDN'T GO to the restaurant the next day. In fact, my mother didn't leave the house for days.

"Do you want to go out for a walk?"

"One of my soap operas is about to start. Maybe in the evening?"

Then the evening would roll around. She'd say nothing. She'd watch television for hours. She'd take long naps. I'd pick up groceries. She'd cook. The days were long and empty like the summer days of childhood. It didn't help that a spell of rain fell over the city for two days. I'd sit next to her and watch soap operas. The only people in the universe, it seemed, were pre-ternaturally attractive Brazilians and Turks whose interests were remarkably limited. Typically scions of wealthy families, they only became aware of the socioeconomic conditions in their country if they lusted after someone poor. The only other face I saw was my great-grandfather's, which stared at me whenever I sat on the toilet. His expression changed often. He'd seem furious, anxious, gloomy, depending on my mood. When his gaze became invasive, I covered the painting with a towel. One late night, on an Italian channel, *An Affair to Remember*, dubbed in Italian, was showing. The title was changed to *Un Amore Splendido, A Splendid Love*. The voice of the Italian actor standing in for Deborah Kerr's voice suited her image fine. The polished slickness of Cary Grant's voice was inimitable. Later that evening, I played the last scene again on YouTube, then played the same scene in the black-and-white version. I sent an email to Billy telling him the movie had been shown on an Italian channel—*What a coincidence, can you believe it, you were right the ending in the black-and-white version is amazing. There's magic to it, a real feeling shines through*. He didn't respond. An hour or so later, I called him. His phone rang and rang, but no one answered. I was getting worried.

Then the sun came out. The breeze felt nice on the skin. We spent time in the garden, sitting under the lemon tree that had cautiously started to bloom. She was listening to some songs on her phone, while I picked up all the clothes she had forgotten on the bushes.

A conversation my parents once had in the garden came to mind.

"You no longer take care of the roses," he was saying. "They would die if I didn't water them."

"Someone told me they're cancerous."

"What? Who? But you've lost interest in everything. We're in the same room, but you don't see or listen to me at all."

I was about to ask my mother about the roses. Who had told her they were cancerous?

Her phone rang. It was my uncle's wife. In no uncertain terms, she advised my mother that what her husband spent money on was none of her business. The argument energized my mother. Indignant, she wanted to talk about it all the time. She had only tried to help. Surely someone had to do something about my uncle's nonsense. Didn't I agree? she kept asking. But if there was one thing that bothered me about my uncle, it wasn't his vanity projects, but his steadfast belief in the old regime. Alma, his older daughter, had left Albania in the nineties, immigrating to Greece. Lina, his younger daughter, had applied for the American green card lottery ten years in a row before she finally got it. How could my uncle sustain such reverence for the communists if they'd left the country in such a state that forced its children to flee? *People should be able to live wherever*, said some. *It's a new world*. Yes, but you could jump out of a plane with a parachute or jump out with nothing, counting on the benevolence of trees. For most of my compatriots, it had been the latter.

"Don't go out to lunch with him," my mother kept saying about my uncle, passionate as she was about trivial retaliations. "Do you hear?" Staying inside all day long made her inclined to replay old slights and arguments in her mind, engaging in blame and self-righteous opinions. The soap opera plots were also to blame. They bolstered her natural fondness for holding grudges. A walk outside might have cleared her head, offered a new perspective, clued her in on how meaningless these old arguments were, but she refused.

There was comfort in repetitiveness, in shunning all adversities, in letting life drift by, as if it wasn't even yours. My father used to be fond of going places. He admired the blue of the Ionian Sea, savored the clean air of Dajti Mountain, from which you could see Tirana as if were on the palm of your hand. But since she couldn't meet him in his wonderment, he met her in her detachment. He retreated to books, to long, solitary walks. His reality, like hers, became a cornucopia of small matters, the items on sale at the local grocery store, the neighborhood gossip, a series of indoor exercises and stretching routines.

I did leave the house when the rain stopped. Staying inside, alone with my thoughts, became terrifying. I spent time at a museum, then had dinner with my uncle. Upon returning home, an imaginary, unhinged hand clasped my neck. I felt guilty for being away all day, yet I wanted to leave. On Saturday morning, a friend mentioned that her brother, who worked as a delivery driver, was about to leave for Berat. I asked her if he could take me there. Escaping somewhere for the weekend sounded good. Berat, two hours south of Tirana, was a familiar town. I'd been there years ago, while accompanying and interpreting for a group of Italian tourists. Finding a hotel for a couple of nights would be easy.

"I'm meeting up with an American friend there," I lied to my mother. "She's visiting Berat and needs a translator."

There was regret but also relief in her eyes when I mentioned leaving town for the weekend. Maybe she wanted the house to herself, without my prying eyes, always asking for more than she could give. I packed some clothes in my backpack and said goodbye. Halfway through our trip, my friend's brother got out of the car to get gas. My mother texted, saying I had forgotten the sandwich she had prepared for me. My friend's brother got back in the car complaining about the price of gas. A flood of tears blurred my eyes. I opened the window to prevent them from streaming. The crisp air dried my eyes at once. As the car drifted through vast brown fields, the frustration of that past week turned once again to guilt.

THE LEGEND WENT LIKE THIS: Tomorr and Shpirag are two brave and handsome brothers. They're inseparable, always looking out for each other. One sunny day, while roaming the wild forests of Berat, or whatever it was young boys did in those faraway days, without cafés, video games, or even newspapers, Tomorr spots a dizzying beauty, Osumi, and falls madly in love. He loses appetite and sleep, and thinks only of her. Soon after that, the same thing happens to Shpirag. After meeting Osumi, he realizes he wants to marry her. Osumi shares the brothers' affection, which is to say she falls in love with them both. She dates each of them in secret. When Tomorr finds out his brother is also dating Osumi, his pain is so great that his screams reach the sky. He pleads with Shpirag to break off his romance, but Shpirag refuses and calls Osumi his own. In a fit of passion, Tomorr pulls out his sword. Shpirag throws rocks at him. Tomorr launches forward, cutting his brother into pieces.

A tour guide next to me was telling this legend to a group of British tourists who were visiting Berat. We were all standing on the right bank of the Osum River, looking over the white houses at the base of a hill. To our left rose Shpirag Mountain.

"Notice the pattern of craters on the surface of Shpirag Mountain?" said the tour guide. "The legend says it's because of Tomorr's sword. The Tomorr Mountain, on the other hand, is full of holes and pits due to Shpirag's rocks."

"And Osumi?" asked one the tourists.

"She is still between them," the tour guide said, pointing to the gurgling river. "Forever drowning in her tears."

I kept strolling alongside the Osum River, distancing myself from the tourists. A fisherman standing on the lip of a quarry flung his fishing pole toward the grayish waters, which sparkled whenever the clouds moved. The night before, the clouds had been dense and heavy, hovering close to the ground. That a thick fog would soon infuse the valley had seemed likely. Berat had always struck me as confining, as if its hills and mountains were hatching some secret plan to cave in. But today the clouds had scattered, and strips of blue sky had come through, making way for the sun. One side of the valley lit up in a warm golden hue.

The Gorica and Mangalem districts occupied opposite sides of the river, so the houses gaped at each other from across the two shores. Gorica Bridge, one of the oldest Ottoman bridges in Albania, was popular with tourists. A tall and blond German couple, with a young daughter, asked me to take a picture of them. They insisted that the Albanian tour guide join them in the photo. The guide's narrow face peeped through the long arms enfolding him, his smile on cue with their confident grins.

I thought of Billy. The last time we had been in Albania, he had wanted to visit Berat. We had even looked at some pictures online of the same hotel I was staying in now. It crossed my mind to call the organization that had awarded him the bridge fellowship. They would know if he was okay. But maybe the only reason he wasn't responding was that he needed time alone, away from me.

I wished the Germans a good trip and headed toward the Mangalem neighborhood, where my hotel was. The voice of the tour guide boomed from behind me, regaling the crowds with another gruesome story.

"According to an ancient legend, there used to be a secret dungeon under this bridge. They would incinerate young girls to appease the spirits responsible for the safety of the bridge."

I waited to cross the street. The traffic wasn't as busy as in Tirana. A man riding a bicycle had tied a rope from its seat to a horse's bridle. As he glided forward on his bike, the horse, white, dirty, emaciated, trotted behind him at a steady pace. I stopped briefly by the art museum. The timetable on the door said that it was open every day except Monday, but it had been closed yesterday, Saturday, and it was closed again today.

Opening the iron-wrought door of my hotel required some effort. The hotel comprised several small cottages. A cobblestone pathway flanked by flower beds and vases extended to the building where my room was. The room was small. There was nothing to do inside except watch TV, so I headed for the hotel lobby. Cookie, the owner's dog, ran toward me wagging his tail. He was fond of untying shoelaces. I sat by the bar and ordered an espresso. By the time the bartender placed the coffee in front of me, Cookie had untied both my shoes.

The lobby was charming, resembling the interior of a castle, with its arched entryways and dark wooden panels. There was a vintage clock that chimed on the hour, freestanding shelves with copper pitchers and vases. A large oil painting of another dog, Cookie's predecessor, Candy, occupied one of the walls. The rest of the walls exhibited the work of a local artist who painted traditional Albanian costumes and scenes onto flat rocks. The exchange library, in the corner, displayed a variety of books in different languages—a Croatia travel guide in Russian, a Kosovo history book in French, a Greek cookbook in Portuguese. I could find only one book in Albanian, a book of poetry by Teodor Keko. In one of the poems the narrator was contemplating leaving his country without looking back. Everything there reminded him of one bitter story or another. He was ready to move on, to search for another land, a peaceful one, where people didn't aggravate each other as a hobby.

A nearby conversation in Albanian distracted me.

"You understand English better than me," one of the men told the other. "Was that man saying he spent two weeks watching a bridge?"

"Watching the bridge and taking notes. About the people who walked on the bridge."

The other man roared with laughter.

"Are you sure he wasn't working as a guard?" he managed to say. "Or maybe he was a spy? Never mind, he was pulling our leg, most likely."

"He was some kind of artist, I think. They had him looking at the bridge from a window."

"Not even in person, eh? Americans are fantastic, aren't they?"

"They were actually paying him for that."

The other man turned serious. He took a sip of raki and mulled over this information for a second.

"Who was paying him? For watching the bridge?"

"For watching the bridge. How do I know who was paying him?"

"How much?"

"I pried it out of him. A thousand a month."

The man whistled. "Dollars? To look at a bridge from a window? We were born in the wrong country, weren't we?"

"I was only making two hundred as a guard before those bastards fired me."

"Before they caught you sleeping, you mean."

"I had just closed my eyes. I wasn't sleeping."

"You were snoring."

"I wasn't. I had just closed my eyes. Can't a man close his eyes?"

"Not if you're an overnight guard, you can't."

"All overnight guards sleep."

"Get out of here."

The man picked up the raki bottle and topped both their glasses. I approached their table.

"Excuse me. I overheard you speaking. Where did he go?"

"Who? The bridge guy?"

"Yeah. The American."

"I don't know. Outside. You know him?"

"I think so."

"Is he here to watch our bridges?"

I shook my head.

"Two nice bridges right down the street. Two thousand a month!"

They were both in a ripple of laughter.

"Lucky bastard."

"Those Americans are fantastic, aren't they?"

THE TOURISTS WERE WALKING off their lunches on the boardwalk along the river and the main boulevard in town. Billy wouldn't be with a crowd. He must be alone. Had he left his fellowship for good and come to Albania? Had he remembered, a year later, us having scrolled through the online pictures of Mangalemi Hotel? I wandered the city for a couple of hours, but my efforts seemed futile. Would I be able to find him? Then doubt crept in. Was it possible that, by some bizarre turn of fate, the man they were talking about was another American who had been fawning over a bridge? I called Billy. The voicemail came on. Disheartened, I sat on a bench. Two stray dogs trotted across the sidewalk. Those pitiful, filthy, gaunt, withered dogs, drifting through cities, were a common and unfortunate sight in Albania. Some had missing limbs. Some had scars. All were hungry, lonely. One of the dogs, a gray-and-white mutt, scrunched up in a corner, his snout flat on the gravel. After a few seconds he lifted his head, craving attention. His thoughtful eyes stirred a desire to pet his head and rub his body. I hesitated. They were full of ticks and diseases.

I headed back, passing by the art museum, a habit by now. Cookie, the hotel dog, came to mind. He had everything a dog could ask for, often refusing food like a spoilt toddler, while the dogs outside were dying, or even being killed. There were reports, frequently denied by the government, of municipal vans rounding up strays to execute them. The art museum was still closed. A puppy was wandering outside the museum. Nearby, a man was crouching over, pouring water from a plastic bottle into a discarded yoghurt container. He placed it in front of the dog. When he straightened his back, I recognized the yellow windbreaker slung over his shoulders.

"It is you!" I shouted. "You're here!"

Billy looked disheveled. His wavy hair had grown in all directions. That slightly unkempt look made him seem younger, the Billy of the earlier days. A smile broke onto his face, but he didn't walk toward me. His sunglasses were clasped over his shirt. He put them on. Maybe he didn't want me to look at his eyes.

My initial inclination had been to run toward him. Now I found myself mulling over what to say. A few seconds passed as we stood at some distance from each other.

"What are you doing here?" I called out.

"I wanted to check out this art museum," he said. "It's closed. It's supposed to be closed on Monday. But it's Sunday today, isn't it? And then I saw the puppy. I stopped to give him some water."

We both turned toward the puppy. He had been hesitant to drink but was now lapping up the water.

"Why are you in Berat?"

"I got bored looking at the bridge," he said. "Went to Tirana first. Your mother said you were here, so I rented a car. Who are you interpreting for?"

"Nobody. I made up something."

"I can't believe we ran into each other," he said. "I was worried I wouldn't find you."

"I heard two guys talking about you in my hotel lobby."

"Those guys were funny."

"They called you the bridge man."

"I guess I am the bridge man."

"Are you hungry?"

"Starving."

We walked to a nearby restaurant located on a terrace, enclosed in glass walls, spiffed up with vines and plants that basked in the sun. The staff all looked alike with their ruddy complexions and dark hair. It must have been a family business.

"You didn't respond to my emails," I said. "I was worried."

"You were?" He fumbled with the plastic menu, pretending he was reading it although it was in Albanian. His movements were fretful, his expression abstracted. "Sorry. I was making plans to leave the fellowship. And come here. I thought we'd talk once I arrived."

I remembered that dream he'd told me about, the boat, the shore in the distance. Then I thought about the emptiness of our apartment after he left, and of how for days I had secretly believed he would come back.

"Did you ask any of our neighbors to water our plants?" he asked.

"Leyla is staying in our apartment. She's watering them."

"The Kurdish woman?"

"Yes. Shall we order?"

I explained what some of the items on the menu were. He checked with the waiter if the stuffed eggplant was vegetarian. They had both, the waiter answered in perfect English, a vegetarian one and one with ground beef. While he ordered, I thought about Leyla. She had written to me a few days ago. She had gone out of the apartment a few times for groceries but hadn't seen Rakan. Maybe she had imagined it after all, she said, seeing him in front of our building and at the bodega around the corner. *You must have*, I had told her. *It's possible your fears are making you see things.* Looking back now, I wasn't so sure. It was more likely that she had seen Rakan and convinced herself that she hadn't. The idea of his vengeance had been nebulous, the distance rendering it almost abstract, but now the haze lifted. Rakan's impending retribution webbed across the upcoming days and our return home.

"White looks great on you," Billy said, as we waited for the food.

I leaned toward him. He brought me closer, kissing the top of my head. It was a casually affectionate gesture, but it seemed like a breakthrough. I wrapped my arms around him, feeling at ease for the first time since we'd met.

The waiter brought us lunch. The succulent eggplant, filled with garlic, onions, and tomatoes and garnished with parsley, mint, and oregano, was cooked to perfection.

"How was your fellowship?" I asked.

"I spent two weeks completely alone. In a tiny village. I'd get excited if I saw someone walking on the bridge."

"It sounds peaceful."

"I was too lonely to think."

He was taking in the view. The clouds scattered again. Sunlight spread over the stone houses and the riverbanks. The bridges suddenly seemed freshly painted.

"I'm sorry for how I behaved in front of the Kurdish women," he said, lowering his eyes. "I embarrassed you. I was such a jerk that night."

There was a touching shyness in his apology. I reached for his hand.

"I've also been wanting to tell you something else," he added.

"What is it?" I asked, although I knew the answer.

"Shall we go up to the castle? Before it gets too late. I'll tell you there, just don't push me off, okay?"

I asked for the check. He was about to confess about Anna. I would come clean also, I decided, and tell him what had happened with Rakan.

The steep cobbled road up to the castle was about two hundred meters long. Although it was late in the afternoon, the tourist shops were all open. Artists sold paintings and drawings with local themes. Housewives peddled homespun linens, rugs, doilies. Billy was impatient to see the castle, so we decided to wander the stores on our way down. But a crocheted purse hanging on an outside rack caught my eye. It was a cabernet color, with a pink flower embroidered on the front. Unique and artisan-made, it reminded me of something Anna might like. I bought it right away, forgetting all that had transpired. The curious thing about any friendship was that its weight was impossible to gauge.

"For Anna," I told Billy. "I went and visited her after the accident."

"How was she?" he said somberly.

"She's doing much better."

"That's good."

"Yeah."

He hastened his step up the hill.

"Take it easy," I said. "We have a while to go."

A group of teenagers coming down the hill teased us about our small water bottles.

"You'll need more than that to go all the way to the top."

A local man, walking behind us, proposed another route to the castle grounds.

"Why pay the admission fee? We can go this way." He pointed to a dense wooded area to our left bursting with thorny bushes behind a low wall. "Come on. It's a shorter walk."

"We're good here," I said. "Thank you."

I explained what the man was saying to Billy.

"Faleminderit," Billy said in Albanian, which meant *thank you* and was one of the few words he knew.

The man then proposed his alternate route to two American women in front of us. Since he barely spoke English, he flung his arms toward the bushes, motioning for them to follow him.

"Come," he kept saying. "No dollar. Free."

The women took one glance at him and scurried up the road. Billy burst into laughter.

"Why is he laughing?" the man said to me in Albanian. "It's thievery to charge a fee for entering a castle that has been there for centuries. Explain that to him."

Frustrated, he then climbed the wall on his own, before disappearing into the woods.

Despite the arduous climb and various distractions, the quiet atmosphere between Billy and me felt peculiar. The unfinished conversation about Anna hovered in the air, like the pause between a question and an answer.

We entered the fortress. Various vendors were scattered around the castle's courtyard. They crouched behind their items spread out over blankets. Used clothes. Dried figs. Rugs purporting to be handwoven but imported from Turkey. Copper bracelets. Silver necklaces. Some of the vendors sold their wares from their doorsteps. All the stone houses within the castle grounds were still inhabited. The castle was like a town of its own, composed mostly of retired people. Most of the young people had immigrated to other countries.

Restaurant owners, dressed in white shirts and black slacks, extended their arms toward their entries, inviting us inside to sample their menus. We steered away from the crowds. Stumbling through narrow alleyways, stone steps, hiking along thick rocks, we marched on, hoping to find one of the twenty-four watchtowers overlooking the town.

A sweeping panorama of the valley unfolded before us. Shifting gray clouds had gathered above the undulating line of the horizon, where Shpirag met the sky. The mountain then gave way to green rolling hills at the end of which a small village nestled by the olive orchards. To our left stood the Holy Trinity Church, considered to be one of the most beautiful Orthodox churches in Albania.

"Shall we go and see it from up close?" I asked.

"What?"

"The church."

But Billy, who had seemed eager to see the castle, now showed little interest in our surroundings.

"That night I went to her apartment, Anna was there. She wasn't in Zagreb."

"She told me," I said. "About the kiss."

"She did?"

He sighed and sat on one of the stones. He kept his eyes on the view, but his hand reached behind him to hold on to my leg, as if to prevent me from walking away.

"I sent you flowers. But whenever you'd get them, I couldn't tell you the truth. And you never guessed."

"You used to send me roses."

"The hyacinths were pretty. Did you like them?"

The relief he felt showed in his face. His openness inspired me to do the same. It was important to start from the beginning. Leyla's bruises. Her panicked eyes. The flickering lights above the water. The missing stars from the sky. The tall, dark woods. That silent and long drive home. But the words were slippery. I couldn't grasp and rearrange them into a sentence.

"I don't see Anna that way," he said. "I never have."

"I'm going to see Zinovia," I said. "When we get back."

"Really?"

"Something is wrong with me," I said.

"With us all," he said. "But, yeah, seeing Zinovia is probably a good idea."

He saw something in the distance.

"What's that?"

"The mountain. Shpirag."

"No, something is written there," he said. "On the mountain's surface."

The afternoon haze obstructed the letters, but eventually N-E-V-E-R came into view. An online article came to mind about how, in the sixties, zealous villagers had written E-N-V-E-R on that side of the mountain, a typical undertaking at the time for Albanians, who frequently spent their weekends painting the leader's name and various party slogans onto buildings and mountains. In the nineties, after the fall of communism, the new democratic government had tried to remove the inscription by the use of explosives. The letters had faded but remained visible. Diehard communists had used the opportunity to restore them three years later. Later still, an Albanian artist had modified the letters to say N-E-V-E-R.

I told Billy about the article. He photographed the mountain, but the letters wouldn't show up in the picture no matter how much he zoomed.

"This place is amazing, isn't it?" he said, raising his arms. "Founded in antiquity. Conquered by the Romans. The Ottomans. Survived the communists. Still here."

The church was a picturesque and well-preserved building, a combination of Byzantine and Western architecture, made of limestone rocks, terra-cotta tiles, bricks. Old frescos, lit up by candles, covered the inside walls. Billy wandered around excitedly, chatting up some of the remaining foreigners. Would he still have that spring in his step once I told him about Rakan?

On our way down the hill and toward our hotel, we looked inside some stores. One of the vendors turned out to be American, from Missouri.

"Do you live here?" I asked.

"Yes. For many years." The man was vague about his past. "Had random jobs in the States. Here and there, you know? Came here to visit. Liked it. Stayed."

*There's nothing in Berat but rocks*, my mother often said. Why had the American moved halfway around the world? What if he was on *America's Most Wanted*? Fugitive or not, the American turned out to be a skilled salesman, regaling us with stories of a local family he knew, whose grandmother, her three daughters, and four nieces labored day and night over handwoven bags— their only source of income. Billy ate it up.

"Young kids like you love them," the Missouri man said, even though he was about the same age as Billy. "Aren't they hip?"

We both left the store wearing crossbody bags. I had on the cabernet purse I'd bought earlier for Anna, while he wore the brown one the Missouri man had hypnotized him into purchasing. Outside the store he appeared uncertain.

"Why did I buy this?"

"Narrative marketing."

"Well, it was only twenty dollars," he said, comforting himself.

"Looks great," I lied.

I was feeling sluggish. I wanted to go back to the hotel. Billy's delight in the fridge magnets and other trinkets was a reminder of my earlier cowardice. His excitement was putting me in a sulking mood.

He went inside another shop. A wiry and watchful woman dressed in black stood up to greet us.

"It's a Jewish museum," she said. "Berat's Jewish museum."

We looked around at two empty rooms painted in white. Large frames with clusters of photographs covered the walls. The woman went on to explain that the museum had been the passion of her late husband, a retired teacher who had wanted to celebrate the religious harmony in Albania and the Jewish history in Berat. They had opened the museum with their savings, barely managing to pay rent, month after month. Later on, an Albanian businessman had invested, helping to keep it open.

I interpreted everything to Billy.

"Is she Jewish?" he asked.

The woman understood.

"No," she told me in Albanian. "I'm Orthodox. And so was my husband."

The laminated printed papers next to the framed photographs were awkwardly translated, as if by a student. Some detailed the history of a Sephardic branch of Jews from Spain who had arrived in Berat in 1520. Over six hundred Jews coming from Germany, Austria, and Spain had been sheltered and protected in Berat during World War II. After the communists came to power, those same Jews had helped some Albanians, who, fearing persecution, had escaped to Italy.

"Can you ask her," Billy said, "what got her husband interested in opening a museum?"

"He had many Jewish friends," she answered. "He did it in their honor. We'd gather around evenings and tell stories. It seemed a pity that nobody would know the stories after we were gone."

Billy had more questions. I didn't feel well. I excused myself and sat on a bench outside. He followed me.

"You feel hot," he said, touching my forehead with his lips.

Fortunately, the hotel was only a few steps away. We picked up a thermometer from the lobby. I had a high fever. He ordered chamomile tea from the restaurant. He went to a pharmacy around the corner for medication. In the oil painting in front of me, a grandmother sat inside a room with two young children. They were looking out the window, at a parade of soldiers. The young boy was saluting the soldiers by raising his fist. Behind my closed eyelids, the soldiers' parade appeared animated. They were young, wearing crisp green uniforms that were knitted to one another, as if a great big cloth with openings for their heads and arms kept them in place. They moved forward in unison.

Billy tapped my shoulder.

"Take one," he said, handing me a round pill.

He lay next to me. He had to turn sideways so we could both fit in the single bed. My body ached. The strain of the past few days, dealing with my mother, leaving Tirana, Billy's unexpected arrival, had finally gotten to me.

"Can you tell me about the bridge?" I asked. "Why did you leave the fellowship?"

He spoke in a low voice, the same voice he used to read me books before bed. Every sentence bore shadows, faces, colors. He had enjoyed the silence at first, the yellow lush expanse beyond the windows, the no-frills, two-room apartment without Wi-Fi. Up close, the bridge straddling both villages was a letdown, its wood rotting, its metal rusting. He'd crossed it only once or twice, his eyes taking in the river below, gushing and surging. From his window, the bridge, a crucial part of that peaceful pastoral landscape, had seemed so much more charming than in person. In the early mornings the bridge was a passage for livestock. Random pedestrians and bicyclists crossed it throughout the day, going from one village to the next. He never saw any cars; they weren't allowed.

Each day after noon, there were no people on the bridge, until about three, when children from a nearby school raced to the other side. At night the bridge was a sad sight. Dense trees obscured the lights from the village across the river. A sole lamppost throbbed with a faint light above the empty fields.

But the absolute silence was only interesting that first week. He soon found himself incapable of doing anything except brooding and sulking as he moved between the two rooms of his spartan apartment. He'd go for long bike rides at times, but some days the wind made that difficult. Spending a weekend in a big city was necessary for his mental health, he realized.

One Friday night, the fellowship's coordinator drove him to the nearest train station. Hours later he found himself wandering alone through a swarming city, having exhausted two bookstores and two cafés. The window of a psychic parlor caught his attention. Neon lights wrote *psychic* and *welcome* in italics. The aroma of incense sticks curled into his nostrils. It was dark inside, cozy, a room adorned with candles, spheres, Egyptian masks. A woman wearing a headscarf and speaking in mangled English welcomed him. That she was surprised to have a customer wasn't lost on him. Maybe she could tell that he had gone in not hoping for revelations but company. She had been delightful, with all her mystic rituals, silly pretentions at clairvoyance, the stiletto nails that had nearly speared through his hand as she held it. It was an experience worth the admission fee.

Her tarot reading reminded him of a therapy session. Of course, he'd been careful not to reveal much about his life, but he had offered her a few crumbs to go on.

"Your relationship will not work out," she had said. "You'll marry soon after the breakup and get what you want—a child."

"What did you say to that?" I asked. "That's not true, is it?"

"I laughed at her predictions, of course. Still, I was sorry when it was over."

After the reading, he'd gone into the bar next door. It was during his drinking binge that her prediction had stung. What he wanted was for his relationship to work out. He didn't want a new relationship. Thinking back to our old arguments, his own behavior had puzzled him. In his lonely state a dinner party sounded thrilling, other people's attention and needs more a gift than a burden. He'd been different years ago, hadn't he? Every new person had seemed exciting, a whole new world. As he ordered drinks in that bar full of foreigners, he felt like a foreigner to his own self.

At some point Billy must have stopped speaking, but the images continued fusing with my earlier dream. Without much fanfare, the green soldiers picked us up from the bar. They would take Billy back to his apartment. My destination was a roaring fire under the Gorica Bridge. We marched in front of a crowd. Then one emotion took charge. The soldiers morphed into Rakan. The green cloth that kept them together turned into his bomber jacket. Two things occurred to me. One, the crowd was waiting to see my incineration. Two, Billy was watching everything from a window.

I followed Rakan obediently to the fire.

"But this is ridiculous," I said, realizing that even though Billy was far away, he could still hear me. "They're about to burn me. I should tell you the truth before that."

Rakan pushed me toward the flames.

I was drenched in sweat when I woke up. Billy was in the next bed. He handed me a cup of water and touched my forehead. The early morning sun flickered through the shutters, drawing lines of light on an unfamiliar dresser. My clothes were no longer scattered about the room. He'd already packed. Our two suitcases were by the door. My shoes were by my bed.

"I packed all our stuff," he said. "And got the address of a hospital in case you got sicker overnight. But your fever is down."

"Did I speak in my sleep?"

"A lot."

"What did I say?"

"It was in Albanian. *Mos?*"

"It means *don't.*"

"Just a bad dream. How are you feeling?"

"Much better. We should go home."

Soon after breakfast, we loaded the rental car. On our way out of town, we drove by Berat's contemporary art museum. To my surprise, the door was open. It was Monday, the only day it was supposed to be closed.

• • •

AFTER TRAVELING THROUGH OTHER major European airports like Malpensa, Frankfurt, or de Gaulle, Tirana's international airport, named after Mother Teresa, appeared modest, despite recent improvements. The other airports loomed larger, brilliant, percolating in a cosmopolitan sophistication ours was emulating. It was only on the way out, once a visitor had grown accustomed to the shoddy buildings of Tirana, that the spacious airport, with its slanted white beams, fern-colored glass walls, and gleaming, marble floors made an impression.

My mother, together with Neta, was accompanying Billy and me to the airport. They hardly ever went there. While praising the new airport building, they recalled the rambling, white-framed edifice that had stood there decades ago. Except for those departing, nobody else was allowed inside. Pressed against the glass like geckos toasting in the sun, people would gaze at their traveling relatives from the windows. It was the first taste of separation, a sampling of what it meant to have your family look at you through a screen.

Reassured that Billy and I had reconciled, my mother's demeanor had changed. He was one of the few houseguests whose presence didn't irritate her. She was livelier with him around. His high-ranking behind enjoyed the sofa without the blanket underneath. She let him treat her to that restaurant near our house. She went on extensive grocery shopping trips on his behalf. Still, traveling to the airport was unprecedented, an impulsive reaction, I suspected, to my uncle's earlier announcement that he was coming along. If she and Neta came in the car with us, my mother had calculated, there would be no room for my uncle. The hatchback Fiat Billy had rented could accommodate only three passengers. Of course, she had underestimated my uncle, who took her deliberate sabotaging of his plans in stride.

"I'll take the bus to the airport," he declared. "And meet you there."

There he was now, waiting for us in the check-in area, undaunted by my mother's moods, strutting around in his suit and fedora hat, holding two white felt hats with black eagles, which he had purchased as souvenirs. He put one hat on Billy and kissed him on the forehead, then did the same to me.

"Wait, I have more," he said, rummaging through a plastic bag. He had framed a photograph of the great-grandfather painting, which by now I associated with the toilet. He gave it to me. This time the great-grandfather looked brave, almost to the point of madness. But he must have been scared on that fateful day, I thought. Why did no one ever depict war heroes as they truly were, terrified, at least some of the time? For Billy, my uncle had brought a small poster with the Albanian flag and the words *Life Is Better with an Albanian* underneath.

Billy was a good sport about it. He thanked my uncle, gave him a hug.

In the check-in line, a man opened a suitcase and tried to squeeze an entire round hunk of kaçkavall cheese between jars of jam and branches of herbs.

"And don't forget this," the woman next to him said, pulling out of her fake Coach purse a lengthy sausage link.

"See, you should have taken that kaçkavall cheese with you," said Neta, who had shown up that morning with a large piece for me to carry. "Other people are bringing stuff."

"They sell it in Brooklyn," I said, not wanting to carry it in my suitcase.

"I'm sure it's not as good as the one I brought."

As we strolled toward the security line, we engaged in random chitchat, pretending we weren't about to say goodbye. Those last minutes were usually fraught with anxiety for me, but it was a temporary discomfort. We said goodbye. I hugged them all and gave my mother a kiss. I glanced back only when we were in line. They were still there, fixing me with their stares, my mother and Neta, in grays and blacks, and my uncle, in the middle, his arms around them both.

"I'm kind of sad to leave," said Billy, a note of surprise sneaking into his voice.

"I know," I said.

I'd heard that sentiment before from some of the foreigners I used to interpret for. Albania was a country that made you uneasy and tense, but alert and alive. It infuriated, exasperated, without apology or retribution, and yet one felt seen here, often even loved. The urge to escape its stifling confinement was tinged with unexpected melancholy—for foreigners and natives alike.

They stamped our passports. The visitors' hallway gleamed from a distance. Where my relatives had been just seconds ago, now stood a cleaning woman in uniform. Stone-faced and somber, she was mopping the shining floor.

# 11.

AS THE TAXI APPROACHED OUR BUILDING, I LOOKED UP at the lighted row of our windows. A gust of wind was swaying our basil back and forth. One of the living room windows was open. The window was next to the fire escape on the side of our building. I had told Leyla not to leave it open when she left for the day. Did that mean she was home?

"Did you text her from the airport?" Billy asked, while we were unlocking the door.

"Of course. She didn't write back."

We called her name. Silence.

"She might be asleep," Billy said. We looked around. On the dining table, she had left behind a cup of rooibos tea and half of a Milano cookie. The teacup was nearly full. The door to Billy's study was closed. I pushed it open. The blankets and pillows she had used were folded on the futon. She had taken her backpack with her, but not her suitcase, which was open on the floor.

I gave her a call. It went straight to voicemail. Another blast of wind nearly flattened the basil tendrils. The incoming coldness made me shiver. It was a double-hung window, typical for Brooklyn. The bottom sash took serious effort to slide up and down. Leyla had often complained about the heat, but she wouldn't have opened it that wide only to get some air. The opening was big enough for her to have climbed out. What was the purpose of fire escapes, anyway? Did anyone ever go down those stairs to run away from a fire? It was only an accessory, a makeshift patio, rusted and rickety, an eye blink away from an accident. I pictured her standing on the square landing in her shorts and tank top. She was laughing, holding a cigarette between her fingers. She lit it, then put it up to her lips. She sucked the smoke with a long intake while looking straight into my eyes through the thick glass.

*Where are you, Leyla?* I thought. I imagined her flinging the cigarette against the wall, leaning her head back. The wind was blowing through her hair, spreading it all around.

"Can you shut the window?" Billy asked. "It's freezing in this room. Why did she leave it open like that?"

Billy had taken a quick shower and changed into his lounge-wear, a crewneck sweatshirt and shorts. It startled me that enough time had passed for him to do all that. I could have sworn I'd been standing there for only a few seconds.

"Did she get back to you?" he asked.

"Not yet."

"Odd that she left this cookie half eaten and the teacup full like this."

The scattered food didn't suggest to Billy that she had left in a hurry. She'd been careless, he was implying.

"I'm sure she'll get back to you," he said, as I tried her again. "Her stuff is still here."

Instead of the voicemail, another message came on. *This mailbox is full.*

"Why don't you take a shower?" Billy said. "It will relax you. Take off your coat. And shoes."

I did what he said. In the bathroom, Leyla's Suave conditioner and shampoo were still on the bathroom rack. She had gone and bought her own, although I had told her repeatedly she could use mine. The hair dryer was still plugged in, hanging by the cord. She had forgotten to put it back inside the drawer, as she'd always done before.

The warm shower, the smell of my peppermint shampoo, restored a sense of well-being. The steam covered the glass shower walls and blurred the rest of the bathroom. The dark line of the hair dryer's cord was barely visible now. A streak of Billy's shaving cream on the shower's floor dissipated under water.

I had just gotten out of the shower when he called me from the living room.

"I found this letter," he said. "Inside the flower vase."

She had ripped a page out of Billy's notebook, which he often forgot on the dining table, and had scrawled on it with a black marker. I didn't dare touch the letter. Billy read it for me.

"*I'll be okay, L.* Does she have other friends or relatives in the US?" he asked. "Maybe she went to stay with them."

"Not that I know of."

*I'll be okay.* Future tense. Not reassuring in the least. What kind of plan could she have come up with, with no money and connections? Where did one go to report the disappearance of an undocumented immigrant? Of course, she might not even want me to. They might deport her the moment she was found.

"Strange, isn't it?" said Billy. "That we can't get hold of her."

I mirrored his baffled expression, but that bit of acting made me feel embarrassed. I had no control over Leyla's situation, nor could I manage to tell the truth. I suddenly found myself sitting on his lap, straddling my legs around his thighs. Only a second ago we'd been standing at some distance from each other—me, in a bath towel wrapped tightly around my body, and he, in that loungy outfit. But now the towel was on the floor. He was aroused, but his movements were slow; he was proceeding with caution. I moved with more resolve. I sneaked my fingers under and up his T-shirt. His skin, like mine, was still warm and slightly moist from the shower. Silky curls started above his belly and extended to his chest. I lowered his shorts. He brought his face close to mine and we kissed. He was relaxing now, but something about our closeness made me feel an unexpected terror. He was signing on to be hurt. Although we'd been together for years, I felt sure we were sinking into an unknown. He lifted his hips and pushed himself inside me. His movements were swift, his rhythm faster than usual. He came quickly. He wrapped me tightly in his arms. He nuzzled my neck. Beneath the sensations that surged inside, there was a warm, brief undercurrent. I focused on it, like at a focal point while trying to maintain balance in a one-legged yoga pose, or on every single step while climbing a mountain. The uncertainty over that compulsion to make love urgently—had I wanted him or a distraction?—seemed less important now. That feeling was sturdy and offered stability. I closed my eyes and wished for us to stay like that, but he looked around for Kleenex, then tried to meet my eyes, and my earlier anxieties crept forward.

Sentences that had sunk under now resurfaced. Someone had followed her for months. She climbed out of our window, dragging her backpack behind her. She went down the fire escape. He was after her. But also, after me.

"It had been a while," Billy said. "Since that blizzard."

Was that really the last time? I tried to recall the particulars of that evening. The blizzard had happened shortly before my introduction to Alfred and our visit at the dentist. The first image that came to mind was the piles of snow gathered on the windowsills. They'd blocked the view from all the windows, except the kitchen window, which had an awning above it. I'd stood there for a long time, looking outside. The snow had caught the blue tint of the LED light from the bodega across the street. It had been falling, softly, incessantly, hypnotically, against the backdrop of a redbrick wall bathed in the glow of streetlights.

"You really don't remember?" he said.

More details came to me now. He had bought a good bottle of wine, an Argentinian Merlot Anna had recommended. We had made dinner, a spicy Mexican soup of some sort. We had watched a long Swedish movie. The title of the movie escaped me. The wine, the after-dinner sex under the duvet in his study, snippets of conversation all seemed nebulous. A quick scene from the movie came to mind. The husband was telling his wife about his affair. She turned away for a moment. A sudden ache folded her body in half. *I'll be fine*, she said. *I'll be fine.* He glanced at his watch and went to pick up his coat. *Billy would never do that*, I had thought. He would never glance at his watch, had my body folded in pain in front of his eyes.

"I remember the movie," I said, caressing his cheek. "A Swedish movie."

His posture changed. I had the impression that the same old weariness had caught up with him. He let go of his grasp on me. Had my words disappointed him? Was he upset because I didn't remember that night? It didn't make sense. Still, something was happening. There were lines in his face I hadn't noticed before.

"Okay," he said in a whisper and caressed my cheek also. "Right. The Swedish movie."

Maybe my anxiety about Leyla was seeping into my other perceptions. I glanced at him again, trying to study his expression. I could no longer see the lines I'd noticed seconds ago. When he smiled, I felt a jolt of surprise. His beaming face was startling, reminding me of those Prospect Park Zoo peacocks who strutted among visitors unnoticed, until they opened their feathers and brandished all their colors. We had been apart for a while, maybe such startling observations were to be expected. He kissed me softly on the cheek, and I thought I had worried for nothing.

That weekend, we reverted to that earlier phase of our relationship, when we were swept up by the euphoria of attraction, like that night we'd sneaked into a bathroom on the Lower East Side to make out. I still remembered the walls, the sink, even the toilet graffitied with genitalia art and Nietzsche quotes. Still jet-lagged, we slept and awoke at odd hours, ordered takeout, ate leftovers, spooned, cuddled, watched movies. We set up new patterns of lovemaking. There was a pattern to my emotional states also. We'd lie in bed for long periods of time, laughing at Will Ferrell in *Elf*, one of Billy's rare commercial indulgences, when a sense of terror would burst into the room. It had been there all along, behind the door, waiting. Then I'd come up with an excuse to go to another room, where I paced around until I ran out of breath. Then I went back to bed and crawled in next to Billy. Intimacy became a go-to distraction.

Sometimes my phone would beep. *Is it Leyla?* he'd ask. *It isn't*, I'd say, pretending to be on the lookout for a message from her. But I no longer expected her to reach out. If she had run for her life, she wasn't thinking about me.

One evening, passing by Billy's office, I noticed her suitcase in the corner. It was unzipped, barely shut, with a shirtsleeve sneaking out. Something about that image struck me as eerie, as if a person, crumpled inside, was attempting an escape. I folded all her clothes, zipped the suitcase, and rolled it into a closet. A bee kept buzzing in my ear, *tell him, tell him, tell him*. I came up with the first sentences. *I'm more worried about Leyla than I've let on. There's this guy who had been following her, and I followed him one night.* But instead of uttering those words, I rushed to another room of the apartment and tried her phone again. It had become a compulsion. I knew she wouldn't pick up, yet I kept calling. The same message came on. *This mailbox is full.*

I WAS RELIEVED to return to work on Monday. The distance made me see the situation more clearly. From my silent office, our weekend looked like a land of sunshine at the mercy of upcoming storms. Keeping Rakan a secret had kept me from fully taking part in our reunion. Billy had been happy but only because he didn't know. Deliberating about whether to tell him or not was exhausting. As I sat in my office, I knew I wouldn't tell him, and I no longer even felt the need to.

Fortunately, new work had come my way. Since interpreting was no longer an option, I was relying on various translating assignments for money. An entrepreneur in Connecticut had developed a financial services website and was looking for someone to translate a few pages into Albanian and Russian. A pediatric hospital in the Bronx wanted their phone recordings done in Albanian and Italian. A friend had forwarded me a list of new appliance manual translation opportunities, which were monotonous but paid well.

In the common area where the freelancers gathered in the afternoons for lunch or coffee, I had left a box of Turkish delight, a gelatin confection made with starch and sugar. In Albania, and many other Eastern European countries, we called that dessert llokum, originating from the Turkish word *lokum*. Most of my coworkers had tried llokum before, in some sweet-shop in Queens or the Lower East Side or during their travels. The dessert was part of my earliest memories, when our relatives, dressed to the nines, would pay a visit to our house, bringing a box of llokum as a gift and, depending on the occasion, some cash. My mother would serve the llokum in an elaborate glass dish, the dusty cubes arranged in a tall pyramid shape. Relatives would pick one up and hold it between their fingers as they gave a speech, referring to the occasion and wishing everyone in the family good health and fortune. The formality emphasized the weight of the obligation and signaled its completion. Only after my parents thanked them, did the guests feel free to bite the suspended llokum. For the rest of the conversation, everyone would be sucking gelatin out of their teeth.

One of the freelancers, a computer programmer whose great-grandmother had left Albania with an Italian fiancé long before the communists came to power, asked me about my trip. He called himself Albanian although his name was Trevor Rossi and nobody in his family spoke the language.

"Someone asked for you," Trevor said before heading back to his office, shaking sugar off his fingers.

"When?"

"While you were in Albania. A man. I told him you were out of the country."

"Was he young?"

"Sort of. In his forties?"

Had it been Alfred?

"Did he smile in a funny way?"

"Nice smile, actually. Super-bright white teeth."

It didn't sound like Alfred, but at least it hadn't been Rakan.

"Did he say what he wanted?"

"It sounded like a translating thing."

Upon returning to my office, Leyla came to mind again. I looked through various social media accounts. Her last name wasn't too common. Nothing showed up. Perhaps she had deleted her online accounts. There was an email from Alfred. He had included me in a group announcement. Vilma had given birth to a baby girl. They had named her Roza, his mother's name, as he'd once told me. He had attached a picture of the baby, who, although only a few days old, looked like she was smiling. I sent him a congratulatory email and asked if he had come looking for me during my absence.

I worked for a few hours, then returned home. Billy had promised to cook dinner that night.

BILLY WAS THE KIND OF cook who didn't limit the amount of cookware and utensils he used while making a dish. He'd spread out in the kitchen like he was preparing a last meal. Piles of dirty cookware would always accumulate on counters, tables, even the kitchen stools. When I entered the apartment, he had just started. Although he was only making a stir-fry, two casserole dishes were already out, as was a bevy of forks and spoons on a clean plate.

"I bought all the ingredients," he said. "I just have to put it together."

"And here I thought that dinner would be ready," I said, teasing him. "Do you need help?"

"I've got it. Listen, some Albanian guy is waiting for you in the living room. At least, I think he's Albanian."

"Is it Zani?"

"No, a younger guy. Miles called soon after he came in, so I didn't talk to him. He's been waiting for a while."

I thought about the man who had come to my office. A translation matter, Trevor had said. But how would the man know where I lived?

"Is it Alfred?" I asked Billy, attempting to dispel my fear. "Did he have a funny smile?"

Billy had cut all the vegetables and was now preparing a soy sauce. He was eager to return to grating the garlic and ginger.

"I didn't notice his smile," he said. "Go look for yourself. Come to think of it, he might have said he was a friend of Leyla's. Maybe he knows where she is?"

The garlic aroma, the citrusy, spicy ginger, the vinegar, which moments ago had seemed mild, now struck me as pungent.

"Did he tell you his name?"

"Yes, and I forgot it."

Billy put aside a pudgy hand with some fingers missing. I blinked. It was a bulbous gingerroot. "You okay? You look pale."

"I'm okay."

A wellspring of unexpected courage made me leave the kitchen and cross the hallway to the living room. From one of the glass doors, I glimpsed inside. Rakan was pacing around our living room, his eyes toward the Manhattan skyscrapers. The red bordello light was on; it made the orange flames of his shoes appear bright. Billy always asked our guests to take off their shoes. Either he must have forgotten, or Rakan had ignored his suggestion. He lowered his bomber jacket below his shoulders, revealing an Adidas logo on his sweatshirt. The idea of leaving the apartment altogether, of running away, seemed tempting, if only for a second. A portrait of Billy and me on our wedding day stared back at me from one of the walls. Even if Rakan had happened upon our apartment by chance, while he was look-ing for Leyla, he must have realized soon after entering that it belonged to me. In a deluge of primitive thoughts, I visualized pushing him out of the window without a fire escape attached to it. In only a few seconds he'd be flat on the asphalt. We'd be free of him.

A light in our hallway turned on. I felt eyes on me. Billy was watching me from the kitchen door. He couldn't have known how things were. But he didn't ask, *Why are you standing there like that? Are you afraid to enter your own living room?* His expres-sion was more somber than curious. For how long had I been standing there? Minutes? Years?

I pushed open the glass doors.

"Nice view," Rakan said, turning around at once, as if he were a bloodhound who could smell my presence. "Why would you drive us so far to see the lights? You should have invited me over to your apartment."

His beanie was pushed down, covering his eyebrows. His eyes were restless, shifting from my body to the rest of the living room and back to me. He looked different; an impersonal expression had replaced his earlier lustful glance. He had already drunk half of the wine bottle that Billy had placed on the table. His tongue ran over his darkened teeth.

"Why are you here?" I said.

"Or did you want these lights here?" he said, grabbing his crotch.

He giggled heartily, leaning his head backward. His throat made the sound of a prolonged hiccup.

I glanced at the door.

"You afraid, huh? Wanna call him?"

He moved his hand away from his crotch.

"What?"

"Your husband, wanna call him? You don't, do you?"

He was right. I didn't want to call Billy.

"So, you're still married after all?"

"Listen, Leyla isn't here. I don't know where she is."

"Where's my fucking phone, bitch?"

"What phone? What are you talking about?"

"You stole my fucking phone. What did you do that for?"

"I don't have your phone. You must have lost it."

"You left me stranded, you cunt."

"She isn't here," I said again. "She's gone away."

"I know she isn't here. I checked your bedroom already. And the bathroom."

He was silent for a while. He pulled out one of the dining chairs and sat. His expression seemed surprisingly calm. Perhaps he had processed his anger and was now deciding about the punishment. The vision of shoving him out of the window came back to me. It was during that silence that Billy walked in. Our eyes met. His apprehension squeezed my heart and wouldn't let go. That dream I'd had in Albania came to mind. Rakan was walking me toward the fire, as Billy watched us from a window.

He smiled at us both as he glanced nervously around the living room.

"Any news about Leyla?" he said.

"No," I said. "Nobody knows where she is. Not even him."

I tried to see Rakan through Billy's eyes. A handsome face that never managed to be pleasing. An aura of suspicion weighed down his features. A twentysomething fond of sportswear and brand-name shoes, yet he didn't look rich. He was pursuing Leyla, not because he felt personally offended by what she had done. He was hounding her because his rich relative was paying him. Perhaps Rakan's entire family depended on the rich cousin. But there was no way Billy would see all that. What did he see? It was impossible to tell. His demeanor defaulted to friendliness. He kept smiling like a fool.

"Nice apartment," Rakan said. "You all rich or something?"

Billy tried to diffuse the momentary discomfort of the question with a small laughter.

"How do you know Leyla?" he asked Rakan.

"She was married to my cousin back home. We're friends."

"We have been worried about her," Billy continued. "She wasn't here when we got home from our trip. And now we can't get ahold of her."

"Oh, I'll find her," Rakan said. "I'm good at that kind of thing."

Billy nodded, pretending to be reassured. Or maybe he really was reassured. Rakan took one more sip of wine and glanced around the room, appraising each piece of furniture.

"Good wine," he told Billy. "Where did you get it?"

"At the bodega around the corner."

"How much was it?"

"Eighteen ninety-nine," Billy said quickly, meeting Rakan's glance.

"Maybe I should buy one on my way out," Rakan said. But he didn't stand up. He moved toward the edge of the chair and opened his legs wider.

"Maybe you can help me with something," he said.

"Sure!"

"I've been wanting to buy a car. How do you like your Subaru Forester?"

"You've seen my car?" Billy said.

"Yeah, I was in it."

"When?"

"Your wife took me out for a drive last month. We went to see the lights from Hamilton Park, in New Jersey. It's nice out there, yeah? Did some mushrooms. Have you been?"

Billy darted a glance at me, then at Rakan.

"Mushrooms?"

"You should have her hook you up," Rakan continued. "She's got connections. Anyway, I like that kind of car. Roomy. You want cars to be roomy, right? Who knows what can happen inside?"

He laughed again, throwing his head backward.

"Roomy cars are good, man. Real good." He pulled up his jacket. "Don't worry about it. You can tell me about your car another time. I'll come back. Now that I know where you are."

He stomped on the carpet with heavy steps before scuttling out of the room. We heard the apartment door shut. I looked at the floor, hoping to avoid Billy's eyes for a few more seconds. The footsteps were visible on the carpet. Had he stepped on a pile of dust before entering our place? On purpose? Billy wasn't saying anything. *I should start with Leyla*, I thought, *with Rakan following her, then with me following him.* The sound of the door opening again jolted us both. We heard footsteps again, loud, thoughtless. Our eyes met briefly. A flick of worry showed in Billy's eyes.

Rakan held a package in his hand.

"This was for you, Billy," Rakan said, handing it to him. "The doorman left it outside."

He winked at me playfully, but his jaw sharpened soon after.

"See you both later."

He started to whistle as he headed toward the hallway. We heard the door slam behind him.

Billy's face appeared distorted, a Picasso painting. A sinking feeling swept over me. The silence seemed to last forever.

"So, that's the park we went to together that one time?" he finally said. "Is that where you and he went?"

"That's the one."

"He asked you out?"

"Yes. At a shoe store."

I told him about that night I had followed Rakan. He had been taking pictures of Leyla, I explained, I'd seen him myself. It wasn't fair that he was frightening her like that, and nobody did anything. Most people, even her friends, even I, at first, didn't believe her. He'd beaten her. That day she came to stay at the apartment, her face was bruised. Yes, I'd given him my number. I had wanted to steal his phone. Teach him a lesson.

"It wasn't a real date, I swear it wasn't," I said.

"And the mushrooms?"

"I bought them from a friend."

"What friend?"

"A friend I met while you were in Europe. Everything worked out flawlessly, exactly as I imagined it, the way things that are supposed to happen sometimes do."

"He knows where we live," he said. "He's threatening us. What do you mean it worked out flawlessly?"

"I'm talking about our date. Of course, as I said, it wasn't a real date."

He turned toward the windows. He seemed in a daze.

"That night," he said slowly. "When we were snowed in, I talked to you about something. Then I asked you a question. You didn't answer. You hadn't been listening at all. You were staring out the window at the snow."

Nothing made any sense at all. Why was he talking about an evening that happened so long ago? Especially now? What had I missed?

"What did you talk to me about?"

"I'm not sure it matters," he said and mumbled something about needing to go to the kitchen to finish the dinner he had started.

"Wait a minute," I said.

I followed him to the kitchen. In the hallway, the ghost of Leyla was running back and forth. I could even hear her bare feet pattering on the wood floor. I knew her fear, as if it were my own.

"Billy," I called out. "Wait."

Nobody responded. In the kitchen, the counters were covered with casserole dishes, pans, wooden spoons, ladles, tongs. In a bowl, shredded garlic and ginger swam on the surface of soy sauce.

He wasn't there. He had left the apartment.

I felt too weak to stand, so I sat on the floor.

# 12.

WHEN ALFRED SHOWED UP AT MY OFFICE THE NEXT DAY, he carried with him a new bag of chamomile tea. He handed the tea to me while kissing me on the cheek. I had missed his brown eyes and wounded smile. But when he pulled back, something struck me as odd. His old smile was gone. It had transformed into the kind of grin they advertised on dentist posters and TV commercials. He found my discomfort amusing. His smile widened even more, revealing a row of perfectly shaped, spellbindingly white teeth. His new mouth, apparently, could expand like an accordion.

"What happened to your mouth?"

"Complete transformation of your smile, remember? We chose it together. The last option."

"You don't look like yourself though."

"Is that such a bad thing?"

I studied his face. Alfred's cheekbones and chin had lost their prior distinctions. His mouth demanded so much attention; one couldn't help but stare at his teeth. Even focusing on his eyes had become complicated. As is often the case with cosmetic surgeries, the slightest alteration of a single feature had triggered a transformation of his entire face.

"Congratulations on the birth of your daughter," I said. "How is being a father?"

"Where in the world did she come from?" he said. "She's amazing."

He pulled out his phone to show me pictures. Roza was sleeping peacefully, one of her tiny hands by her round cheek.

"She is so lovely," I said.

"I didn't think it was possible," he said. "To love someone that much."

He handed me his phone, assuming I wanted to see even more photos. But Roza looked the same in every photo. What caught my attention were the interiors of Alfred's house. The furniture Vilma had chosen was hefty, ornate, and a dark mahogany. The living room was carpeted corner to corner. Fake flowers cropped up in almost every photo. There was a bouquet of silk burgundy roses on a living room coffee table. White eucalyptus branches inside a porcelain floor vase in the corner. Vilma's plump toes, tucked cozily inside flip-flops, also made a cameo, and so did the red purse she'd used to hit us both. I gave him back his phone, irked by a sense of guilt.

"The red purse," Alfred said, his mouth expanding. "Remember?"

"How could I forget? Anyway, you all look happy."

"No. Things are not so good at home," he said. "After Roza's birth, Vilma and I were sleep deprived. Working as an overnight security guard didn't help. Vilma was often alone at night. I was exhausted."

"What about the creatures?"

"They multiplied. As I held Roza, I'd be surrounded by harpies, dragons, winged lions. A lot of whispers. Everywhere. Sometimes I'd talk back. It frightened Vilma. In the end she decided that it was for the best if she and Roza moved in with her parents and younger sister."

"I'm sorry, Alfred."

"She's only forty-five minutes away. I go and see them on

weekends. I'm going to move there also, at some point. I can have a garden there. Plant flowers and vegetables."

"Are you taking medications?"

"Yes, Zinovia prescribed some. They really help."

"I'm glad."

"How was your trip?" he asked. "How was your mother?"

"Sometimes she's fine. Sometimes not."

He tucked his bright teeth away as he listened.

"Did you tell her about me?"

"I mentioned your mother, yes."

He seemed disappointed. He had hoped for more.

"I told her we were friends," I said. "That we connected right away."

"That sort of thing is inexplicable. Like when you listen to a song and it speaks to you."

"Exactly."

He then went on to tell me that a few months ago, before Roza's birth, Vilma had dragged him to a New Age store. She had wanted a tarot card reading. The store also sold crystals and rocks that purported to act as guardians and shields, attracting prosperity and positive energy from the universe. He pulled out of his pocket a lime-green stone with darker stripes. He held it up to show it to me.

"I don't believe in any of that," he said. "But then I saw this inside one of the baskets. It's a kambaba jasper. I had to have it. I don't know why."

His smiling mouth was bright as a flashlight, and just as hard to look at. I missed his old face, that unreliable, struggling grin. His brown eyes had remained the same, at least, warm, enticing.

He handed the stone to me. I ran my finger over its smooth surface.

"It helps with feelings of anxiety," he said.

"It feels nice."

"Doesn't it? Keep it."

"No, it's yours."

"I got two. I thought that maybe you needed one also. Among all the other stones, this caught my eye."

I put the stone inside my pocket.

"I really need it right now," I said. "You have no idea."

"What's wrong?"

"Did you come to my office while I was gone?"

"Yes. I wanted to ask you something. I have a writer friend who wants to put together a book about the massacres in Kosovo in the nineties. Stories of those who lived through it. I will write down my story. Could you edit and translate it for me?"

"Of course."

"Thank you. I can't believe my story will be in a book."

"That's great, Alfred."

"Is someone else looking for you?" he said, searing me with his glance. "What's wrong?"

A flush started up my face.

It wasn't my intention to tell him about Rakan, but the words came out. I shared only a rough outline of the story, omitting some of the details. I told him about Rakan's visit to my home the night before, about his threats in front of my husband. Alfred crossed his arms and stared at the floor as he listened. He was taking in my every word, like a priest might a confession. He didn't ask about Billy, but I told him of his silence, of how he had left the apartment soon after.

"I don't have anything to do until tonight," Alfred said. "Can I walk you home?"

"I drove today. I didn't dare take the subway."

"I'll go for a drive with you. I'll see you home and take the subway back."

We drove home together, Alfred and me. After parking the car, he walked me to my apartment.

"You shouldn't go out alone right now," he said. "Your husband should come with you."

"He'll be coming home soon," I said, wondering if that was true.

"Be careful," Alfred said, giving me a hug. "Don't go places alone."

"Your stone will protect me."

"Call me if you need something, okay?"

"Okay."

On the fifth floor, Helen's apartment door was open. Two salespeople perked up and asked me to sign my name on a form.

"I live in the building," I said. "Just taking a look."

But there wasn't much to see. Her apartment was empty. Our voices echoed from room to room. On a narrow wall by the kitchen cabinets something caught my eye. It was a framed photograph, or rather a framed hair-dye box cutout. It took me a second to realize that the hair model was Helen. The intensity of her gaze gave her away, even though her eyes had an unfamiliar sultry vitality. Strawberry blonde locks (*terracotta blonde*, the box said) fell softly over her shoulders. That the framed hair dye box was still on the wall must have been an oversight, or maybe someone found it amusing. Nobody knew that it was the prior tenant, in her past glory.

I went home. Our apartment was silent. Billy had forgotten his pajamas on the living room sofa. A text from him showed up on my phone.

*Lock the fire escape window, please. And use the deadbolt on the door.*

THE FOLLOWING DAY I mustered enough courage to get on the subway. An impending meeting and a translation deadline occupied my attention. The entrepreneur who needed an

Albanian translator insisted on meeting me in person for the interview. An insurance company I had interpreted for before had a check ready for pick up. Running around Manhattan, among the crowds thronging the streets and the stores, Rakan retreated to the back of my mind.

But on my way back home, a glimpse of someone's bomber jacket, similar to what he wore, gave me a jolt. The flurry of activity all day had made his threats seem hazy, one of the many things the future held in store. Now they appeared genuine and looming. He would show up at any second; I felt it in my bones. The subway car was crowded at first, then people scattered. The doors in between cars would open occasionally while the train was in motion. Someone would be swaggering car to car, selling candy and chocolates for some dubious charity, begging, preaching, or with no apparent goal at all, just taking an aimless, unbroken stroll through a moving train. I was constantly on guard. It was only a question of time until he'd show up, I knew it. I imagined him bouncing toward me, swearing, grabbing his crotch. The other people would ignore us, bringing their phones even closer to their noses. If I ran, would he follow me through the crowds? Would we duel on the platform, grapple like mad, with blood on our faces?

But here was the stop for my apartment. Where was he? He had to be close. I scanned the platform, the stairs, the second-floor landing. The phrase Çdo gjë është e shkruar—*Everything is already written*—came to mind. Albanians usually offered it to an anxious person for comfort, as a reminder that the cogs of some future event had been spinning since the beginning of time. There was no point in trying to control anything. It was already written. Whatever Rakan would do, was already decided. Then I wondered if that pepper spray I'd ordered on Amazon had been delivered.

I stopped by the bodega near my house. It was just after 6:00 PM, when everyone picked up the odd grocery item to finish dinner. Craving comfort food, I selected potatoes, onions, and tomatoes from the small produce aisle for a chicken stew, the kind my mother often made in winter. The store was packed. The checkout line long. The sensation that someone was looking at me persisted, even though Rakan wasn't in the store.

"Tap on the credit card machine," said the woman behind the counter, reminding me it was my turn. She was the wife of the bodega owner, and she'd scanned all my items already. Someone in the long line behind me, eager to go home, sighed at my inattentiveness. Even a momentary delay grated on their nerves. I gathered my grocery bag and headed for the door. A man bumped into my left shoulder, against my side. It seemed innocent, that bump, the kind of encounter New Yorkers regularly ignored in a busy bodega or subway car. I felt a tug at my shopping bag. A flash of a beanie. The dull yellow of his upper teeth. *Here we go. Now. Go ahead.* He didn't pull hard on the shopping bag; I was able to hold on to it with little effort. Maybe his intention had only been to shove me aside, before opening the door and running out. I lost my balance, but only for a second.

"Watch where you're going!" a woman behind me shouted and came toward me to help. "Are you okay?"

Holding on to one of the aisles, I stood up.

"I'm fine," I told her.

"Where did that jerk go?" she asked. "Was he trying to steal your bag?"

"I don't know."

I looked around the store. He was nowhere to be seen. Was that all? A small shove in the bodega? I'd been expecting worse. What else did he have in store for me? I'd barely seen him. Everything had happened so quickly that my recollections were nebulous. Leyla must have felt that way—perplexed, doubtful, always wondering if something had happened or if she had imagined it. I stood outside the bodega for a few more seconds. The main door of my building was only a few steps away. The LED lights flashed OPEN 24 HOURS and basked the entire street in a bright cool blue. Farther up the street, a minor bike accident had happened. A police car had pulled over. The bicyclist was showing his ID.

At home, I pulled the vegetables out of my shopping bag. Rakan's shove had crushed the three tomatoes, turning them into a wet, soft texture. My fingers dug into their flesh, and red juice dripped down my hands and wrists. I grabbed a bowl and dropped them inside. A pink mouse pushed its way through the tomato skins and the pool of seeded juice.

I screamed. The mouse climbed up and traversed the lip of the bowl. It dashed across the kitchen counter at the speed of light, then down the wall and across the floor. In the span of a few seconds, it disappeared from view. Was it under one of the kitchen counters? Under the refrigerator? A new movement distracted me. Another mouse sprinted out of my purse. This one was grayish, and with a tail, which made me realize that the first mouse, the pink one, didn't have a tail. Were there mice with no tails? It didn't have one, so there had to be. The second one dashed away also, hiding somewhere in my kitchen. My encounter with the mice was just as fleeting and perplexing as my earlier confrontation with Rakan.

I was certain now that he had put the mice inside my shopping bag as he shoved me. I grabbed a broom, but why? It was useless; the mice were gone, at least it seemed that way. I emptied my shopping bag, sank it under hot water and soap. No other mice were inside. I found a ziplocked bag. Was that where the mice had been?

Feeling dizzy suddenly, I sat on the floor. Had Leyla sat on the floor like me upon seeing him? Had she felt threatened, exposed, alone, before deciding to escape from the window?

I thought of calling Billy but couldn't do it. I called Lina instead.

She didn't pick up but texted me soon after.

*On my way to Puerto Rico with Ben. How was Albania?*

I called my mother, not even knowing what I would tell her. She sounded cheerful, no longer suspecting that Billy and I were having problems. Some exciting developments had happened in the soap opera we had watched together. She gave me a quick update of the episodes I had missed.

"Your voice sounds odd," she said at some point. "Do you have a cold?"

"A friend of mine is being followed," I said. "By her ex-husband. He's angry at me also."

"Does he know your address?"

"Yes."

"Is Billy there?"

"Yes, he's here."

"Just stay inside then."

"I will."

"Now I'm worried about you. I have to check on my blood pressure. Why did you get involved with that woman? Were you trying to help her?"

"Yes."

"Why would you do that if her husband is dangerous?"

Someone was knocking on my door.

"I've got to go," I said, trying to ignore that feeling of guilt for having raised her blood pressure.

It wasn't Billy. The peephole revealed it was my neighbor next door, the one who spent half the year in Florida. Of course, it wouldn't have been Billy. He had his keys with him.

"How are you?" the neighbor said in her typically upbeat tone. She was in a white tank top and cerulean shorts, as if about to go for a walk on the beach. "I remembered that you asked for Helen's number. Bertie down the hall, the one who went to her drawing party and was traumatized—poor man, can you imagine?—had it. I got it for you. You still want it?"

What in the world had I wanted Helen's number for? Even if she slept under a bridge, how could I help her?

"I no longer want it."

"Okay," she said, smiling again, her sunny disposition undisturbed.

"How is Helen? Has Bertie talked to her?"

"Apparently, she's living in the basement of her cousin, somewhere in Staten Island. The cousin is married, with three children. I predict it will not end well."

"Okay," I said. "Thank you."

"Have a good night."

She returned to her apartment. Her tanned, muscular legs looked as if they belonged to a twenty-year-old.

THE FIRST TIME I saw a grown man's private parts, I must have been around seven. Alma and I had just left school and were walking home, taking a shortcut by a new construction site. A few meters away, a man (he appeared old back then, but was perhaps only in his thirties) was peeing in a corner, under a scaffold. Upon noticing us, he turned in our direction. He did not move his hips suggestively or even say anything; he simply exposed himself, staring us in the face. We didn't know what he was doing at first. He held his penis in his hands nonchalantly. But we were scared, and we ran.

When I was about twelve, parents in the neighborhood were alerting their children about a teenage boy with mental problems. He roamed the streets all day long, occasionally attacking people without provocation. The boy's name now escaped me, but whatever it was, everyone would add *mad* to it. My parents had pointed out the boy to me before, so when I spotted his large head and V-shaped bangs a couple of blocks away, I took a right turn to avoid him. A few minutes later, a burning sensation on my back, which rapidly turned to pain, stunned me. I had fallen face forward on the ground. A voice behind me said, "Don't you dare walk away from me again."

A passerby who helped me up told me the boy had run into me with all his might, as if I were air or invisible. It seemed strange that, from such a distance, he had realized what I had been doing. Had everyone else been avoiding him like that?

When I was about fifteen, men in their twenties, even thirties, disheveled, unkempt, wearing sports jackets and smoking cheap cigarettes, would hang outside our high school for hours. They referred to this pastime, in direct translation from Albanian, as *hunting*. It was a common word in their vocabulary and we'd often hear them say, *I'm hunting so and so*, or *Who's hunting that beauty, you know?* Afterward I'd even hear my boy cousins use it much the same way. Those boys were grown up, after all. They had to be hunting.

My hunter turned out to be a man twice my age who would follow me home, in the streets and the bus, much like Rakan had Leyla. It was strange that this story hadn't come to mind earlier, when she first told me about Rakan. In fact, it didn't come to mind until the morning following the bodega incident, while I was deciding whether to go out or not. It had been decades since leaving the house represented a tangible danger. But the internal anguish came to me at once, as did images from bygone years. My hunter must have been unemployed because he trailed me in the mornings and afternoons, before and after school. Even during lunchtime, he was there, amid that group of men who looked like they could all use a shower. What did they talk about while waiting for us to finish school? Future plans? They'd joke and jeer at every girl passing by. The girls' fear made them laugh, put them in a good mood. At last, my hunter talked to me, saying that if I didn't stop for a conversation, he would pull my hair or slap me in the middle of the street. *You don't want to be embarrassed, do you?* he asked, feigning concern. *Everyone will be looking.* With that heavy-looking head and thick legs, my hunter didn't look like a runner. Once he finished talking, I busted out of there. The next day my hunter got a bike. As I ran, he biked alongside me, muttering whatever threats came to his mind. With much trepidation, I eventually told my parents. My father had to walk me to school every morning and pick me up from then on.

From my kitchen in Brooklyn, those memories appeared fragmented, like a damaged film reel. Had they really happened? Was my current situation helping to embellish them? Maybe the hunter had been someone else's. The faces of the other girls now appeared in front of me, especially that of Nora, a pale child-woman with glossy eyes whose hunter owned or had borrowed a white van. Nora hadn't come to school for days at some point. Nobody knew why. When she returned, she was sleepy, ignored our questions. Still, I had never truly feared the hunters, not properly, deeply, not how it counted. I had always known I would survive them.

Would I go out? Stay home? Still early for a decision. The sun was shining over the brownstones across the street. My mother's advice was to stay inside, but there was nothing I wanted more than to go for a walk in that crisp air, through the tree-lined sidewalks, to lose myself inside a store or conversation. Even back then, in all those weeks that the hunter had waited for me, hoping that his insane threats would bloom into romance, I had always gone out.

While driving to my coworking space, I wondered if it was due to some genetic trickery that fear had never paralyzed my curiosity for the world. Wrestling the unknown had always held excitement for me. Or maybe, at some point, I had promised myself that staying inside would never be my choice.

It turned out to be an uneventful day. The translating assignments went smoothly. They were mindless and kept me from thinking. I had a few brief conversations with coworkers while making the tea that Alfred had left with me. Billy still didn't call, but he texted. He asked me to turn my phone's tracking on. And I did. I wanted to call him, but I couldn't manage to.

When evening rolled around, I hoped he'd be at home. But as I circled the neighborhood on a lookout for a parking spot, the living room light in our fifth-floor apartment was off. The only available parking space was a few blocks away. I scanned the street up and down before leaving the car. The pepper spray was in my right pocket. The idea for purchasing that particular pepper spray had come from one of my translating assignments. The Russian company that produced it had included pamphlets that needed to be translated to English. The history of pepper spray had held little interest at the time, but now forgotten facts popped up in my mind. The Chinese, apparently, used to wrap ground cayenne in rice paper so they could fling it at their enemies. In Japan, pepper spray was used by ninjas and samurais, who'd blow cayenne and dirt into their opponents' eyes. I held the spray in my hand during my walk home. Would it be easy to spray it into Rakan's eyes? The nozzle had to be put into the *on* position and aimed the right way, so I wouldn't spray it toward myself. Imagining him bending over in pain was gratifying.

A wan moon was struggling to come out. The sky was gray and heavy. The night before, while everyone slept, it had snowed. A thin layer had covered the streets and dirty piles had accumulated to the sides and in between cars after the plows had passed. A portly man was taking his two poodles out for their evening walk. With their long, slim limbs and pink booties, they minced about in the snow, reminding me of ballerinas. A group of teenagers, oblivious to the cold and wearing short-sleeve T-shirts, sat on a stoop, teasing one another, laughing, smoking pot. They paused their conversation as I walked by and said good evening.

It might have been a pleasant walk, but the next block was badly lit. It was also quieter. Aware of the deep silence, my steps faltered. I thought I saw a fantastic creature, the kind Alfred saw all the time, crouching behind a car. It was a beast with Rakan's upper body, but with the long tail and ears of a horse. A few steps down loomed a creature with horns, a pointed snout, and the hind legs of a goat. They were just piles of snow, I reminded myself, yet they still looked like creatures.

The steady footsteps behind me stopped me in my tracks.

"Good evening," said a voice. I turned around. It belonged to a man holding a baby in a carrier. He smiled at me in a reassuring manner. At the next brownstone, he went up the stairs. All that could be heard now were my own footsteps. Or were they the footsteps of someone else? Leaving the house had been foolish. My mother was right. I suddenly wished to be home, lost in a soap opera. I tried the pepper spray's flip-top just in case; it was easy to open. I sped up.

Behind me, the long, empty street stretched for several blocks. Why did I look back? It was a voice, someone calling my name. On the dark sidewalks, the streetlights formed large circles of lights. The next street over, a man was standing under one of those circles. He kept one hand on his beanie hat, the other held what from a distance seemed like a massive silver fish with jagged horizontal stripes across its flanks. Its mouth wide open, the fish appeared freshly caught. Upon noticing me, Rakan started waving and pointing at the fish. I ran fast. A car was crossing the intersection. I took a right instead of going straight.

"Prit, moj. Prit."

What was he saying? What did he want? It dawned on me the voice was speaking in Albanian. It was asking me to wait. While still running, I looked back.

Zani appeared behind me, holding a bottle of wine.

"Did I scare you?" he said, running out of breath. "What's wrong?"

Had that image of Rakan been a hallucination? Was I becoming mad? Or it had been him, and he had run away the moment he'd seen Zani?

Zani touched me on the shoulder.

"What's going on?"

"What are you doing here?"

"That lawyer accepted my case," he said. "So I brought you a bottle of wine. Wanted to thank you. I remembered that your husband likes red wine."

"He does?"

"Why were you running like that? Was someone following you?"

The words felt distant, hard to grasp. A sudden flood of tears gushed out. I was wiping them silently, as Zani looked on.

"Someone is after me, yes."

"Who? It's not your husband, is it?"

"No, it's not my husband. Someone else. Were you under the light before?"

"Under the light?" He looked behind us. "What do you mean? I came from that direction."

He pointed toward the direction where Rakan had appeared earlier. I told him the story. About Leyla. About Rakan. About the night before at the bodega. About the baby mice, peeping out of the tomato slush. It all poured out. Zani listened carefully, sometimes looking at my face, sometimes turning around and staring out into the night. I was fifteen again, telling my father about the hunter, asking him to walk me to school.

Zani was squinting so much that his eyes looked closed.

"Are you talking about that bodega on the corner? Is that where he bumped into you?"

"Yeah."

"Let's go over there."

I hesitated.

"Don't worry. Let's go get a drink. I know the owners."

The bodega was only a few minutes away. The after-work rush was gone. The owner, an affable man in his early sixties, was behind the counter.

"What do you want? Coffee?" Zani asked.

"No. A tea."

"Peppermint? Black?"

"Nothing with caffeine."

"Okay, peppermint."

He went toward the counter as I waited outside. He talked to the owner for a while. It didn't seem like an important discussion. They were in a good mood, laughing and high-fiving each other. When Zani was about to pay, the guy didn't let him. He placed one hand on his heart, then made a motion for him to put his money away.

Zani came outside with two cups.

"Nice people, the owners," he said, handing me a cup. "Egyptians. They're building two houses for their families and need my help."

I remembered then that Zani worked in construction.

"How long have you known them?"

"A couple of years. Since when I was fixing bathrooms at a fancy building around here. We started talking about history. Egyptian and Albanian history are connected, you know?"

He was looking at me, expecting me to agree and elaborate. My mind went blank. Nothing would rise to the surface. Zani was disappointed at my silence.

"You must know about Mehmet Ali, the Egyptians' Albanian King? They called him the founder of modern Egypt."

"I know," I said, suddenly remembering. "He built a dam across the Nile or something."

"There you go."

The bodega's light suffused the sidewalk with a luminous haze. Our silhouettes were outlined in blue sapphire. Zani went on about the two houses the bodega owner and his brother wanted to build in Jersey. Their expectations surpassed their budget, but he didn't mind doing favors.

"We're like brothers," he said. "It's a no-brainer."

It did seem odd that Zani wasn't mentioning Rakan at all, as if he had forgotten the reason we had come to the bodega. On the other hand, something about his voice, talking about unrelated things that meant nothing to me, was comforting. I had no sense of how long he talked before taking a break. He finally took a sip of his drink.

"You see," he said, lowering his voice. "I can't get involved in anything. I'm in the middle of my immigration papers. It wouldn't look good."

It took me a second to realize that he was no longer talking about the owners.

"Of course," I said, matching the volume of his voice. "I'm not asking you to."

"I can't have any more brushes with the law. Plus, my wife would kill me. But maybe those owners can tell him something.

Not to come around here anymore, not to bother you. What does he look like, this man? What does he wear?"

"A beanie. A bomber jacket. Green eyes. Square jaw."

"And what's his name?"

"Rakan."

"Okay, very well. I'll tell them later. Is your husband home?"

"He's not. He's on a business trip."

"You shouldn't stay alone. Don't you have a friend you can stay with?"

At the mention of the word *friend*, it dawned on me that Anna's apartment was nearby. I had her key on my key chain. Was she still at her parents' house? I wrote her a text, asking if I could spend the night there. Anything would be better than being alone in that apartment with Leyla's ghost.

She responded at once. *Come.*

"Actually," I told Zani. "There's one place I can go to. Not too far."

"I'll walk you there."

"How old is Rakan?" Zani asked during our walk.

"In his twenties."

"Don't worry about it," he then said, tapping me on the arm. "Everything will be fine."

ANNA WAS WELCOMING. She offered me a hug and Greek food from a neighborhood restaurant that was still on her table. My text had piqued her curiosity, so she inquired at once what was the matter. Being on the verge of anxiety for days had made me loquacious. Or, maybe, our last meeting had unlocked the door to our intimacy. I was incapable of lying to Anna, omitting details as I had done earlier with Alfred and Zani. I told her the entire story of how I had followed Rakan to that shoe store, of our fake date and that drive to Jersey. I confessed about Rakan's sexual appeal, of leaving him there stranded, then of his sudden visit. I also told her about Billy's detached reaction, how he had left the apartment without saying a word. After telling her the entire story, I felt lighter. It took a second for my distrust toward her to rear its head again.

"I'll call Billy tomorrow," she said. "I don't care if I have to drag him to your house myself."

Realizing how absurd she sounded, she chuckled. One of her crutches was leaning on her knee and the other on the seat next to her. That Anna, who could barely walk, would drag anyone anywhere was ridiculous.

"But let me get this right," she said after pouring me a glass of wine. I had handed her the bottle Zani had given me, but the unfamiliar Albanian wine apparently didn't make the cut. She had opted for an Argentinian Malbec. "This guy Rakan put two mice into your shopping bag, and you still didn't call Billy?"

"Maybe he wants some time to himself," I said. "After what Rakan told him."

"Time to himself doesn't apply in this situation," she said. "Not when someone might actually kill you."

But respecting his boundaries was only part of the reason why I had delayed calling Billy.

"At least he'll kill only one of us," I said. "Not two."

Anna's eyes went wide with shock. She clutched one of the pink sofa pillows to her chest. For all her worldwide travels, she was unfamiliar with the more sordid aspects of life.

We were sitting in her spacious living room, where the furniture was either pompous Baroque or perfectly suitable for an Almodóvar movie set. She had a knack for combining outlandish colors in such a way that they seemed made for one another. Her chandelier was of a bronze finish and featured intricate cherub carvings. Its style was elaborate, but the light sparse, illuminating little besides the dining table right below it and a set of wine-glasses hanging on a rack above the kitchen counter. The corner where we were sitting—Anna on a velvet chaise lounge of bright pink, and I on a red sofa next to it—remained steeped in shadows.

"Do you have any idea," she suddenly said, "what happened to Leyla?"

"Her phone is no longer in service," I said. "Maybe she has changed her number."

"Do you think he did something to her?"

"I don't know. But that night he came to our apartment, I got the feeling he didn't know where she was either."

"He must be looking for her now."

"He does seem able to find people. Leyla was always wondering how he did that. If he was tracing her phone or something."

Anna's shoulders shivered. She grabbed a blanket and adjusted it on her lap. Despite the poor lighting, she looked as if she belonged on a magazine cover. She was wearing an indigo robe, in whose soft folds a Persian cat was napping and purring. By her feet, on a fluffy carpet, slept her second Persian cat. She had named the cats March and April, after the months she had bought them. She took a break from petting March and adjusted her hair, tucking some strands behind her small ear.

"I'm sorry for dumping all this on you," I said. "You're still recovering from your accident."

"Oh, please. I've been bored out of my mind. All I do every day is shop online for clothes. I can't manage to do anything else."

"By the way," I said. "I bought you a purse in Albania. It's handmade. I hope you'll like it."

"I'm sure I'll like it."

I then told her about the man from Missouri who lived and worked in Berat, and how he had flattered Billy. I described how bewildered Billy had been afterward, realizing the man's charm had hypnotized him into buying a purse. We laughed at that together. When the laughter died down, I thought about how odd it was that we were acting as if nothing was the matter in light of her recent confession that she was in love with my husband. She had been mentioning his name casually, as if that awkward conversation at her mother's house hadn't happened. She would call him on my behalf, she had said.

"Don't you feel strange contacting him?" I blurted.

"Who?"

"Come on. Billy."

My question didn't perturb her.

"It's different for us artists," she said shrugging, telling me things I already knew, but not answering my question. It had always been travel and performances she looked forward to. The signposts that most other women coveted—a relationship, kids—had been less significant in her journey. She had gotten used to her demanding schedule and sleeping alone, although the older she got, the more she couldn't decide if her life was empty or full. There were occasional one-night stands in various cities, short relationships that fizzled due to distance, that sharp ache of loneliness some evenings she tried to ignore, telling herself it would disappear by the morning.

"Billy was an idea, a consolation prize," she said, getting to the point. "Whenever I was disappointed that something didn't work out, I'd think that maybe we'd get together at some point. That, maybe, deep down he felt the same."

March was awake. Having had enough of Anna's petting, she jumped off her lap and onto the carpet. Tentatively, she took a few steps toward my feet. Having decided against climbing onto my lap, she sat on the floor, but still glanced back at me flirtatiously, hoping to be petted. I envied the simple lives of cats. Although restricted between walls, they had ample food and love, and no complicated, confusing emotions to disturb their peace.

"I've always avoided devoting myself to something true," she said. "One way or another."

I suddenly missed Billy. That weekend we'd spent together, before Rakan had appeared on our doorstep, seemed so far away, but it had only been days ago.

"Have you tried playing violin again?" I asked Anna.

"Today I tried it."

Before I could say anything, she picked up her violin from behind the sofa and played it. The tune transported me to that day when I'd been searching for Billy around Berat. I saw the river gurgling through the valley, the clouds threatening to close in. The dirty white horse galloping behind the bike. The two men clanking their raki glasses and laughing about the bridge man. The thirsty puppy lapping up the water. Billy's smile opening when our eyes met. The way he'd held on to my leg as he told me about their kiss, as if afraid I might run away.

Anna stopped playing abruptly. I gulped back the tears.

"Sorry," she said, oblivious to my emotion. "I'll never be what I once was. But I can always teach."

"Beautiful," I said. "You still have it."

"You don't know anything about violin, though."

"I don't. But I loved it."

"I've decided to go back to South Korea," she continued. "To resume my job at the university. Once I recover, of course."

"Why so far?" I said. "Why not stay here?"

She was quiet, as if I hadn't spoken. Once again, she hadn't answered my question. Maybe she still felt drowsy from her medications. At least she was no longer going on about things she had already told me. That last comment about me not knowing anything about violin had been snappy. *It must be stressful,*

I thought, *to lose the ability to do the thing you loved the most.* March and April were both asleep. Listening to their purring and the heater's hissing had a soporific effect. Anna also seemed asleep. I closed my eyes, half dreaming about Berat again, lying next to Billy that night I'd been sick.

Anna's voice jolted me awake.

"I know, in my mind, that he was only an idea, but I still think of him," she said. "It will take me a while to get over the habit. And yes, calling him will be hard. That's why going away to South Korea is the best option."

I sat up, startled, not knowing what to say.

"The sheets are in the cupboard in the hallway," she said. "The red sofa is a pullout. Very comfortable."

She gathered her crutches and hobbled toward the bedroom. Her cats shook their bodies and followed her like two obedient soldiers. Anna's apartment, so superior in elegance and insight, had made me nervous at first. It forced me to reflect on my own shortcomings when it came to décor and personal style. But it was also comfortable and pleasant, and the vibrant colors had a way of lifting my mood. Her declaration of love now hovered in the room, among the dark shadows. Like her furniture, it was flashy and jarring.

*But Billy doesn't love her*, I reminded myself.

While preparing my bed on her living room sofa, a short poem came to mind.

*There is nothing you can see that is not a flower.*
*There is nothing you can think that is not the moon.*

Where had I heard it before?

# 13.

AS ANNA PROMISED, THE FOLLOWING DAY BILLY CAME home. I found him sitting in the living room, reading a *National Geographic*. On its cover was an illustration of human development from ape to bionic man. He must not have heard me come in for he didn't move, focused as he was on the article. His glasses had smudges on them. It wasn't like him not to wipe them.

"I'm glad you're home," I said.

He lowered the magazine.

"I was on my way back when Anna called," he said, meeting my eyes. His curly hair was graying at the temples and up front. Even some of his chin bristles were turning white. "She told me about the mice. How are you doing?"

"I'm okay."

"Have you seen him again since that night?"

"No."

"Hopefully he'll leave us alone."

He spoke in a calming voice, giving the impression that he wanted to comfort me, but I sensed detachment. He engaged me in a quick conversation by asking questions about the apartment. When was the house cleaner coming? Had I checked the mail? Did I have time to drop off those bags of clothes at

Housing Works? Our short conversation seemed to tire him out. He picked up the magazine again.

I left him alone. Minutes later I heard him rummaging around the apartment. I found him crouching behind the dining table.

"What are you doing?" I asked.

"I bought some catch-and-release mousetraps."

"Did you put one in the kitchen?"

"Yes, I put one in every room."

He got dizzy upon standing and leaned on the table.

"Why don't you rest?" I said. "I'll go get some groceries and make dinner."

"No, we should go to the bodega together."

Something about the way he spoke made me sad. He wasn't cold, exactly. He gave the impression of a man who was doing something because he had to, even though he lacked energy and interest. It had only been three days since we'd last seen each other, but he had changed.

The bodega was mostly empty that night. It was easy to see at a glance that Rakan wasn't there. Billy was fidgety. When someone tapped him on the shoulder, asking if he could reach a can on an upper shelf, he jumped.

"So that's where he put the mice into your purse," he said outside.

"Yes. This is also where Leyla told me that she saw him before she disappeared."

The light of the bodega bathed the sidewalk in blue. He hated that light. He'd always complain about how awfully bright it was. He felt sorry, he'd tell me, for those who lived in the apartments above the bodega. *Can you imagine? Surrounded by that infernal haze, every night?* He was indifferent to the blue light now, stopping smack in the middle of the sidewalk, as if it didn't bother him at all. When the traffic light across the street turned red, the thick border around his body dissolved. Purple and red rings appeared above his head. The traffic light changed back to green. His curls materialized, each of them emitting a faint glow. He lowered the shopping bags and glanced around us. He seemed relaxed. He'd been expecting us to run into Rakan and now realized that we wouldn't.

Zani popped into my mind, and how, just the other night, we'd been standing there together. He had talked about the Egyptian owners, about the houses he was helping them build. It suddenly occurred to me that the bodega owner, who always said hello or made small talk whenever I bought things, had ignored me that evening. He usually inquired after the soups and stews I was making, the spices I used, asked jokingly why I never brought him some to try. Tonight, the owner had checked out my vegetables in complete silence as if he didn't know me at all. Maybe he felt awkward about chatting me up in front of Billy. He was used to seeing me alone. Or perhaps his mind was elsewhere, on the two houses, and the expenses that went with building them. Still, his attitude struck me as odd. Had Zani already told him to talk to Rakan on my behalf? It seemed unlikely that Rakan would have listened quietly and respectfully, that he would have agreed to whatever had been asked of him. But then perhaps he had, the same way the bravery of my old childhood hunter evaporated when he'd seen me with my father. He never approached me afterward. Zani's squinting came back to mind, and how, in the darkness, his eyes had disappeared entirely.

A little boy came out of the bodega and climbed onto a coin-operated horse positioned strategically near the exit. In the daylight, the horse was a tired yellow, with big patches of silver where the paint had peeled off. Under the light, the horse appeared enticing, enveloped in a playful sea-green color. The boy's face broke into a smile the moment he got on top of the horse. He reached into his pocket and pulled out two quarters, inserting them into the coin slot, where the owner had hand-written *.50 ¢* on a white piece of paper. The horse didn't move at all. The boy looked confused as he inspected the horse, touching its flanks and tapping on the coin box. After a second or two, as if suddenly remembering an errand, the horse jerked forward, then back. Billy, who had, so far, been staring absentmindedly toward the street, ran toward the boy, who was leaning to his left, about to fall. He was able to catch him in time.

"Hold on next time, okay?" he told him, but the boy didn't seem to be listening, delighted by the horse's rocking. Smiling, he was gazing at his mother, who exited the bodega thanking Billy.

He seemed more like his old self after that incident. He no lon-ger spoke in that monotone, low voice. I felt an urge to embrace him, to take advantage of that glimmer of joy the encounter with the boy had sparked. But he didn't want any physical con-tact, I could tell. He grabbed our shopping bags and hurried along. His body shed the tacky blue away. I had to run to catch up with him.

"How old do you think he was?" he asked.

"The boy?"

"Yeah."

I knew nothing of children's ages, often making ridiculous mistakes. Once, in Tirana, while taking the bus with Klinton, Alma's younger son, I had told someone that he was twelve, when he was only nine. He had promptly corrected me. "Don't you remember, auntie," he had said, much to my embarrass-ment, his brown eyes opening wide, "that you bought me a gift? For my ninth birthday?"

The boy riding the horse could have been six, or seven, what did I know?

"Around four," Billy said abruptly, not waiting for my answer.

At home, the mousetrap in one of the bedrooms had caught a rodent. He lifted the box to show it to me, but something about that tiny mouse jammed inside made me feel sick. The pinkish, round back of the mouse pressed against the transparent cage walls persisted in my mind's eye, even after Billy put the box inside a plastic bag.

"Shall we let it free after dinner? We can walk to the park."

"Can we please do it now?"

"All right."

We strolled to the park. Billy went into some bushes and let the mouse out. It was a badly lit area. A cold breeze moved among the leaves. As the mouse scurried toward freedom, I felt at ease. I wasn't afraid to be in that park at such a late hour. Rakan's threat, for some reason, barely registered. But the bodega owner's attitude had stayed in my mind.

"It's done," Billy said. "Let's go home."

"The other day," I blurted, "Zani came over with a bottle of wine for you."

"Who is Zani again?" he asked.

"The one who came over with his entire family."

"Oh, right. The one who wants to live in Darien."

"I told him about Rakan."

"That you went on a date with him?"

I ignored that comment.

"It turns out he knows the bodega owners. He said he'd tell them to have a talk with Rakan about harassing me."

"I don't know about Zani," Billy said, holding on to my arm. "He seems kind of shady, honestly."

"Zani wouldn't get involved," I said. "He has his immigration paperwork to think of."

"You didn't ask him to go to the bodega, did you?"

"I didn't. It was his suggestion."

"What did he say?"

"'Let's go to the bodega,' he said. He bought me peppermint tea."

Billy let go of me and crossed his arms.

"About Rakan. What did he say about Rakan?"

"He said that he didn't want to be involved. That he couldn't. But that the owners, who are like his brothers, apparently, would have a talk with him."

The more I spoke, the stranger Billy's face seemed. He pulled me toward a bench.

"Let's sit. Are you telling me everything?"

"What do you mean?"

"Why do I have the feeling that you're not?"

"The owner of the bodega didn't say hi to me today, that's all."

"What are you talking about?"

"Normally the owner chats with me, but tonight he said nothing at all."

"What am I supposed to do with that?"

"Nothing. It's just something I noticed."

"That night Zani came to our apartment," Billy said. "He said he owed his life to you."

"It didn't mean anything."

"Are you sure?"

"Yes. I was only his interpreter."

He stood up at once.

"Right. Let's go home."

The walk back to the apartment relaxed us both. My earlier fears about the bodega owner let up. There must have been other times he didn't strike up a conversation with me. Yes, of course. There must have. Mentioning his silence to Billy had been a mistake.

"I'm sorry I've got us into this," I said. "I really am."

A full moon, its surface orange and battered, loomed ahead of us in the night sky.

"That night we were snowed in," he said, "I talked about us having children. Starting to think about it, you know? You were standing by the window, looking outside. You even nodded once or twice. You don't remember any of it, do you?"

He moved up his glasses, his eyes sizing me up. All I remembered from that night was the blue snow outside the windows, the heartless husband in the movie, the two glasses of wine.

"Are you sure?" I muttered.

Our conversations about children had always been brief, unremarkable.

He didn't respond.

"I didn't know you felt like that," I said.

Another version of that night now played out in my mind, the version Billy described. It seemed peculiar, as if I hadn't been there at all. *I'm hanging out with ghosts*, he would joke whenever I found him watching old films alone. But clearly, the ghost he had been hanging out with all along was me.

I ONCE INTERPRETED for a charismatic Italian psychic who specialized in auras. She explained auras as life energy forces in various colors, surrounding each person. She said that my own color was indigo, the aura of a sensitive, empathic person. One day, she predicted, through my intuitive gifts, which, to her, were as plain as day, I'd be able to see the auras of other people. Her prediction had yet to come true. My third eye had not, so far, detected the green and red mists she had so vividly described. My only claim to the supernatural was an occasional sense of composure, a transitory calmness when things were about to work out in my favor.

After that night at the park, when Billy had let the mouse out, I'd felt serene. The prior anguish that would often choke me at the thought of Rakan had eased. The orange of his shoes and the military green of his jacket, always so vibrant in my mind, had paled. His image, for some reason, now only registered in black and white. Billy's presence in the apartment was making me feel safe, although even our interactions demanded some vigilance. After telling me something, he would study my face, wanting to check if I had been paying attention. Or he'd quiz me slyly. A remnant of guilt made me eager to prove myself even in the most mundane situations. I'd quickly confirm that yes, I was aware that the super had visited that afternoon to fix our wall, that the plates in the dishwasher were clean, that I had scheduled the grocery delivery as discussed. I didn't talk about my newfound calmness, which, after all, was an abstraction. I agreed to doing every errand together, to him walking me to my car every morning, to keeping our phones' tracking feature on.

Strolls around the neighborhood lost their appeal. The building's gym, located in the basement, became a place of refuge. Billy started lifting weights again and so did I. A possible physical confrontation with Rakan loomed in the distance, like some Olympic event we needed training for.

The mousetraps hadn't yet caught the second mouse. It was elusive and daring, that mouse, leaving droppings on the kitchen counter and cupboards. At times, while hanging out in the living room, or watching a movie, Billy would jump up, having seen a shadow flit across the wall. He'd look under the sofas and heaters, wander room to room, mumble under his breath.

"He's gone," he'd say in despair.

He bought more mousetraps, but none of them worked.

One afternoon, after spending some time at the building's gym, I found him in a state. He was pacing back and forth in the living room, cracking his knuckles. Had our situation finally gotten to him?

"Did you get my text?" he said. "Leyla called."

"She called *you*?"

"No. She called the landline."

We stared at the phone, sitting on a side table between the sofa and the chair, as if it could talk and explain why Leyla had not called my cell phone. Nobody ever used our landline, except Billy's mother and a distant, lonely uncle who would call on holidays. We had inherited it from the people who sold us the apartment. It had cost next to nothing to keep it through a cable deal a door-to-door salesman had convinced us to sign up for.

"Why does she have this number?" I asked him.

"How do I know? You should know."

"What did she say?"

"She wanted to talk to you. Said she's in Connecticut. She asked if you could go and see her."

"What is she doing in Connecticut?"

He shrugged.

"Gave me an address of a shopping center."

He put on his shoes and jacket.

"Are you coming also?" I asked.

"You're not going alone, are you?"

"Are we going now?"

"She said she had the afternoon off."

"From what?"

"I don't know."

While driving to the address she had given Billy, I realized how much Leyla's disappearance had weighed on us both. Her absence had added to our paranoia. Now that she had called, letting us know she was alive, we'd awakened from a depressive slumber. Our hushed, polite conversations, appropriate for our self-imposed house stay, gave way to lively exchanges. Billy, having once confessed how much he would hate living near a highway, found amusement in pointing to those elevated constructions with glass walls displaying, in startling proximity, flashing TV sets and families lounging around them. We drove for an hour through slow-moving traffic along gray highways before taking an exit that spit us onto an ugly road, flanked on both sides by cheap car dealerships and rickety gas stations. But the more we drove, in an almost eerie progression, the swankier the cars became and so did the buildings. We finally parked in front of a suburban shopping center, a sprawling taupe building housing a few clothing stores, an Italian restaurant, a sushi place, a Subway, and a Chinese massage parlor.

"She said we should wait over there," Billy said, pointing at the sushi place.

Even though it was lunchtime, the sushi place had no customers. A chef who looked about twenty stood behind thick cuts of red tuna, texting furiously on his phone. The waitress was wearing a cut-off top, showing off her midriff's diamond ring. She seemed surprised when we entered but recovered quickly and handed us two long leather-bound menus. The menus spanned several cuisines. That little restaurant, somehow, managed to serve food from four continents. The waitress, having nothing else to do, hovered around us. To her disappointment, Billy ordered only two green teas.

We didn't have to wait long for Leyla. Her appearance had changed considerably. She'd cut her hair short. She had gained weight. As if the coral jacket I'd given her, which she now wore, wasn't bright enough, she had on purple slacks and a pink blouse underneath. When she gave me a hug, she smelled like cotton candy. One could mistake her for a slightly off suburban mom who, having surrendered to motherhood for years, had trouble fitting in with grownups.

"I walked for half an hour to get here," she said, looking straight at me and ignoring Billy.

The waitress placed some ice water in front of her. She drank greedily. Her nails were painted purple. On top of her hands were colorful stickers and pen scribbles—a sun with a happy face, a sad moon.

"That's Pinkalicious," she said, pointing to one of the stickers. "You know, the show?"

"What show?"

"A children's show."

Billy and I both stared at her. What was she talking about?

"I've been babysitting," she said. "While I was staying at your house, one of my Kurdish friends knew this family who needed a live-in sitter. Rakan figured out where you live. He would stand outside the apartment."

"Did you use the fire escape to leave my apartment?"

"I sure did."

"Why didn't you let me know?"

"I wasn't trusting my cell phone. Maybe he had bugged it or something. It turned out he had befriended one of my roommates, the Bulgarian redhead. I couldn't believe it. How can anyone be interested in him?"

"Good question," Billy said, catching my eye for a second. "But he showed up at our home. Looking for you."

She turned to him. Their eyes met for the first time since she'd entered the restaurant.

"I'm sorry," she said, touching her head. Chunks of her hair were braided, I noticed, haphazardly, as if someone had been practicing on her.

"Do you two want a bite?" Billy asked.

The waitress drew near us at once.

"I'll have an eel and avocado roll," Leyla said. "And some tuna sashimi."

"An eel and avocado roll," the waitress called out in a surprisingly high, girlish voice. "And tuna sashimi."

The sushi chef put his phone aside and started making Leyla's roll.

"You don't have to worry about him anymore," Leyla said. "Rakan seems to have disappeared."

Under the table, Billy squeezed my hand.

"How do you know that?" he said.

"The Bulgarian redhead, my old roommate, was having a fling with him." Leyla shook her body in disgust. "She can't get ahold of him now. It has been three days apparently."

"I'm feeling a bit hot," Billy said, releasing my hand. "I'll go get some air."

He walked outside and stood near the glass door of the restaurant. The sun was glinting off the long row of cars, and his body was enveloped in a golden haze.

"What's wrong with him?" asked Leyla.

"We've been stressed out. Since Rakan came to our house."

"Anyway, she can't go to the police since she doesn't have her papers. But I'm relieved that he seems to have disappeared. Aren't you?"

A vortex was spinning fast inside me. If I were alone with Billy, it might slow down, I thought. I longed for us to be in the apartment, the same apartment we had so much wanted to escape.

"What do you think happened to him?" I asked.

"I wouldn't be surprised if they caught him for shoplifting. I always thought he might be stealing those shoes he wears. My ex gives him money, sure, but not that much."

The waitress brought her roll and sashimi. She ate ravenously.

"I'm so sick of chicken nuggets and fries. That's all those kids want to eat. Kids back home aren't like that. They eat whatever the parents eat."

Leyla went on to tell me about the family she babysat for. Three children. The oldest, a girl, was six. The father was a dermatologist. The mother, an entrepreneur and businesswoman. The mother traveled so frequently that when she came home, it felt like she was a guest.

"The older girl raids her closet," she said. "This is what she picked out for me today. She insists that I wear whatever she chooses. I've been dressing up for a week straight. She's always braiding my hair, too. She pretends I'm her doll. She wants to put me to sleep."

"Have you been able to write at all?"

Leyla poured more soy sauce into her dipping bowl and stirred in some wasabi with her chopsticks.

"I once read the interview of a European poet who had somehow ended up in a small desert town in Nevada. He said that feeling like a fish out of water inspired his writing. I don't feel like that at all."

I looked at the parking lot. The wind drove a lone shopping cart toward the sidewalk. Someone's forgotten supersize soda rattled inside it.

"It's not exactly inspiring here," I said.

"This parking lot is designed to make you feel nothing," Leyla continued. "You could never love it, of course, but hating it would be absurd. I mean, it's spacious, functional, useful. What's not to like? And yet it eats at you. Slowly."

"I'm back," Billy said, returning to the table. "So cold outside. I'm ready for this winter to be over."

He was trying to be affable, but he was worried. His attention, clearly, was absorbed by something else. When I had first told him about Zani talking to the bodega owners on my behalf, he hadn't liked it. He was now connecting the news of Rakan's disappearance, which Leyla had so casually delivered, to that conversation. The more I thought about it, the more outlandish that possibility seemed.

"I know you and I started off on the wrong foot," he told Leyla. "I want to apologize for my behavior that night you came over. I'm sorry. There was no excuse."

"Thank you," Leyla said. "I appreciate that."

"I'll wait for you in the car," he told me, tapping me on the shoulder. I wanted to go after him, give him a hug for his sake and mine, but Leyla wasn't done with her sushi.

"I'm glad things worked out," I told her.

"Not really," she said, shaking her head. "Things haven't worked out at all."

The nanny position had seemed ideal, she explained, a chance to move away from Rakan, an opportunity to live somewhere rent-free and not have to pay for food. The children were adorable. The house was comfortable and spacious; there were two swings and a sandbox in the backyard.

"In some sense, it's kind of great. All the American movies I used to watch have come to life," she said. "I'm cooking in an enormous kitchen filled with sunlight. When the mother is home, I have more free time, although there isn't much to do except go to the park or take a thirty-minute walk to this shopping center."

She was quiet for a while, mulling over what she was about to say. The young sushi chef had put his phone aside. He was cutting a slab of tuna into thin slices. The waitress was staring at the shopping cart outside, which was speeding downhill.

One evening, Leyla said, the dermatologist had suggested teaching her how to drive. It was an exciting proposition, yet another scene in the American movie that kept playing in her mind. He had sat in the passenger's seat as she drove. Wanting to be careful, she had driven up the street and turned around by a cul-de-sac. He had been charming, telling jokes, reminiscing about learning how to drive himself, while explaining to her the function of gears and turn signals.

"Sitting next to him made me uncomfortable," she said. "I told myself it was nothing, a natural reaction to being alone with a man I barely knew. But the feeling didn't go away."

"Did he do anything?"

"Not that night, no."

She asked the waitress for more water and took a few sips before continuing.

"It seemed innocent at first. Like, I'd hand him the six-month-old. His fingers would linger over my hands. *Is it because he's being careful, so we don't drop the baby?* I'd wonder."

She paused and looked at my face.

"But you don't wonder anymore, do you?" I asked.

"When the kids go to sleep, he'll ask if I want a drink. To relax. If I say no, he pouts. I had a dream that he was watching me as I slept. Then I woke up. I heard footsteps down the hall. This weekend the wife is here. But she leaves in couple of days."

"That this is happening to you right after Rakan," I said, "is terrible . . . I'm sorry."

She shrugged in response, as if to say, *Is it such a wonder?* A person tumbling down a flight of stairs couldn't stop the continuous movement. They had to bump on every step until they reached the bottom.

"Can I stay with you?" she said. "Temporarily. Until I find another arrangement."

I pictured Billy sitting in the car alone, his face tense with worry. The vortex of emotions slowed down. A feeling of guilt engulfed me.

"I'll have to check with Billy. He's upset about Rakan."

"Rakan is not around anymore."

"He might return."

She was quiet then, observing me.

"I've had a feeling," she said. "And I'm not usually wrong when I have a feeling."

"What kind of feeling?"

"That I'm free. That he won't get out of jail if that's where he is."

She reached toward me. As we held hands, I wanted to tell her about the calmness I'd felt those past few days. It had come out of nowhere. It had felt natural, like nightfall or daybreak. But saying it felt wrong, as if it might implicate me somehow.

"Give me your new number," I said. "I'll give you a call later. After I talk to Billy."

"Okay."

I paid the check. We walked out of the restaurant together.

"What happened to Rakan's phone?" I asked on my way out. "Do you still have it?"

"I threw it into a lake. What was I supposed to do with it? I didn't have his password or anything."

In her colorful outfit, she bounced along the sidewalk, turning left at the corner where the building ended. She climbed up the hilly path and disappeared quickly from view. In front of me the sea of cars looked daunting, but then I saw Billy waving from a distance.

AT FIRST, and for the duration of the ride home, we each sat alone with our own thoughts. I started to tell him about Leyla's situation once or twice, but the stillness between us was pleasant, almost hypnotic. Before leaving the car, I leaned toward him. He made a half-hearted attempt to hug me.

I'd bring it up later, I decided.

Discussing a disappearance and our possible role in it took some getting used to.

"Here is the message Zani last sent me," I said, once we arrived home. I handed him my phone.

After that night at the bodega Zani had sent me a text saying that his asylum application had moved forward. The lawyer, he wrote, did exactly what he said he would do. Worth every penny.

"Has moved forward," Billy said slowly, as if it were an ominous phrase.

"Three other lawyers had rejected his case," I said. "This one is moving the application forward."

For Billy, I realized, it wasn't entirely out of the question that Rakan's vanishing related to my conversation with Zani. That night came back to my mind—the dark sidewalks, Rakan thudding briskly behind me, then standing under a streetlight, raising the dead fish in my direction. Zani tearing across the street calling my name, trying to find out what was wrong. His voice had been comforting, hadn't it? *Don't worry about it*, he had said, his mouth tinted blue.

"It's just odd," Billy said, "that he vanished. Don't you think?"

"Maybe he got arrested. Or had other enemies."

"Zani said you saved his life."

"He would not have jumped out that window. Not Zani. Didn't you meet him?"

"What does that mean? I'm supposed to tell if he would have jumped? He might have."

"He was being dramatic."

Eventually we stopped discussing it; it was futile. Billy continued to accompany me places. He insisted on keeping up our vigilance. *He might show up*, he'd say. *When we least expect it, like an earth-shattering earthquake.* To Billy, I started to suspect, letting down our guard meant acknowledging that Rakan had disappeared. I still hadn't told him that I felt lighter. That I no longer scanned the street a million times before leaving the car.

"Let's have Zani over," Billy said one morning. "Zani and his wife."

"What for?"

"He might tell us if the Egyptians at the bodega talked to Rakan. And how he took it."

He was obviously envisioning a scenario where, over wine and appetizers, Zani would reassure us that our suspicions had no basis in reality. *I didn't touch him, happy?* Of course, that would require one of us to ask him about his involvement in the situation.

"Will you do that?" I asked Billy. "Ask him point-blank if he did something to Rakan?"

"Or maybe," Billy said, "having Zani over will make us realize how absurd these suspicions really are."

"Will make *you* realize," I said. "I'm already sure."

As we left the building so he could walk me to my car, a young woman was standing in the vestibule of our apartment building. She appeared uncertain while eyeing the buzzers. She must be a visitor, we assumed.

Outside, the sun was glaring. Our eyes hurt the moment we opened the door.

"I'll go get our sunglasses," Billy said. "I'll be right back."

I waited for him in the vestibule. The woman pressed 5C on the buzzer, which caught my attention. She was calling our apartment. She was wearing knee-high boots, a miniskirt, a biker jacket. Her hair was a fire-engine red, broken by occasional pitch-black strands. Billy, already on his way to the elevator, turned around. Something about the woman's appearance put him belatedly on guard.

While we were gawking at her, she barely glanced our way. She appeared distracted, showing little interest in her surroundings. She took off her jacket. Her top was all black lace; it revealed a red bra underneath. She was in the habit of flinging back her hair, a sort of nervous, crude tic. She pressed the button again.

Billy didn't go up. He came back into the vestibule.

"Can I help you?" he said to her. "I live in 5C."

She turned to Billy. She wore fake eyelashes, skyscraper-length. They gave her eyes a cheap and tragic quality.

"I've been looking for my boyfriend. He's disappeared," she said in a strong Eastern European accent, emphasizing her *h*'s and using a trilled *r*. "You know him?"

"Who's your boyfriend?" Billy said with the right amount of nonchalance and curiosity.

Having been anxious all along about the situation, he had acquired some mastery over it and managed to be calm. The opposite was happening to me. Rakan's disappearance had been as speculative as gossip. Although I had enjoyed my newfound freedom, the consequences had been obscure until now, when it was literally standing on my doorstep.

"His name is Rakan. I found this envelope in his house. With your address on it. Why did he have your mail? Who is Lina?"

"He must have stolen it," Billy said sharply, grabbing the envelope from her hand.

That night Rakan had come over, I remembered, before leaving our apartment, he had brought back to the living room an Amazon box. There must have been something else on top of it, some piece of mail belonging to my cousin he had pocketed.

"So he came to your house?" the girl said. "What for?"

"He had been following Leyla, a friend of ours. He came looking for her," said Billy.

For a while, she didn't speak. She was flicking what looked like pieces of hair off her arms. Brown. Blonde. C-shaped. Straight.

That careless, creepy gesture made my knees buckle.

"I'm a hairdresser. Just got off work," she explained.

Billy nodded, unperturbed.

"He wasn't doing anything to Leyla," she then said, looking up at him. "He was only following and taking pictures of her. His cousin is supporting his family. It's not like he's got a choice. Have you seen him since that night in your apartment?"

There wasn't enough air in that tiny vestibule. Not enough to breathe normally. Billy somehow knew. He opened the door and motioned me into the lobby. Only then did she become aware of my presence. She didn't bother with me. Billy assumed the responsibility of answering her questions.

"I haven't seen your boyfriend since that night," he said, before the door closed behind me.

I took a seat on the sofa in the lobby. Three deep breaths and a shallow one. It seemed to help. To my left, the doorman was nestled in his leather seat, dwarfed by towers of packages. If any of them tumbled, he'd be hurt. He might have been curious, normally, if one of the residents was talking at length to such a colorful character as the woman outside. But he was immersed in a phone conversation.

Now she was wiping off her eyes. It left behind a grayish smudge. Billy's posture was rigid. I couldn't see his face.

The doorman was talking to an insurance agent about a surgery bill.

"IV therapy, two thousand? Why so much?"

She was saying something. She moved her hands as she spoke. Billy shook his head.

"And why does anesthesia show up twice? A mistake?"

Billy shrugged. *I've got nothing else to say*, he seemed to be saying.

"What is pathology? What does that even mean?" the doorman said, raising his voice.

Billy opened the outside door for her. She wasn't ready to leave but his action was so determined and immediate; she had no choice. She shuffled her feet behind him, looking down. He walked her down the stairs, to the sidewalk. At some point, he said something else. It must have been brusque, for she flinched. He turned toward the building. She looked behind him for a few seconds, before going on her way.

"Lab hematology. Lab chemistry. What are all those labs for?"

Billy came back to the lobby. Our eyes met. *Something inside him just broke*, I thought. He sat next to me.

"She wanted to alert his family," he said. "But she didn't have their number. She had been looking for his phone in his apartment. She knew that someone had stolen his prior phone. He knew the thief, she suspected, but he wouldn't tell her who."

Of course, he wouldn't tell her who, I thought. If they were dating.

"Leyla threw his phone into a lake," I said. "She didn't know what else to do with it."

Billy leaned forward. He put his head in his hands. It occurred to me that maybe the reason why he stayed away from entangling himself in such situations was because he grasped ahead of time their danger. He'd been worried about Zani's involvement from the start. Repercussions, to me, were often an afterthought.

"I told her," he said, "that if she came back again, I'd call immigration."

He was bleak. And somewhat flattened. I wrapped my arm around him.

Our doorman had finished his conversation with the insurance agent. The outcome must not have been to his liking for he looked morose. He was pacing behind us, back and forth, his hands clasped behind his back.

"Is he okay?" he asked about Billy.

"He's all right," I said.

ZANI'S BROAD FACE APPEARED at the center of the intercom's screen. He lifted a wine bottle toward the camera and brought it close to his cheek.

"We're here," he said excitedly. "Let us in."

Billy and I rushed to put the finishing touches on the appetizers, spraying olive oil on a platter of mozzarella and sliced beefsteak tomatoes. We arranged warm sourdough around the Manchego and the imported Greek olives. Billy had also bought a surprising quantity of dry-cured salami and prosciutto for our guests, which was now on the counter.

"Do you want me to cut the salami?" I offered, considering he was a vegetarian.

"I'll do it myself."

It was the first time I'd seen Billy handle meat. He cut up everything and arranged it on the bread plate.

Our guests entered our apartment with aplomb, in a surprisingly stylish ensemble. Zani was in a gray suit and polka-dot tie matching his wife's scarf and skirt. They seemed in a good mood. Considering how awkward their last visit had been, they must have been flattered, if surprised, to be invited. Billy greeted them effusively, doling out compliments and obligatory comments.

"You two look nice. It's windy outside, isn't it? It was warm this morning, but the temperature dropped again."

"It's warm inside," said Zani, shaking my hand. "What a great idea to bring us all together." His wife kissed me on the cheek.

Her name was Lëndina, we discovered, which in Albanian meant *meadow*. It conveyed images of sunlit pastures, but it didn't suit her personality in the least.

"It's nice to be out without the baby for once," she said.

"And without your parents, for once," Zani retorted, which provoked laughter from all of us, except her.

It took effort for Lëndina to laugh; she preferred being on guard. She was so young, in her early twenties, but her past struggles were written on her face.

Already in his fifties, Zani had obviously been slow to settle down. For how long had his Albanian relatives barraged him with questions about when he was getting married and having children? *Time is passing, Zani. You won't be able to lift up your child if you wait. Your back will hurt.* Had he been tired of the pressure, at last? *Let's go see,* he must have finally exclaimed, both exasperated and excited. *Let's go meet this young woman everyone keeps talking to me about, this beautiful, neat, extraordinary woman who bleach-dyes her hair and looks like Marilyn Monroe, whose parents are such good-hearted people, as you say, fine, let's go see this woman.* On one of his travels back to Albania, his cousin had probably driven him to the city where she lived. When their eyes met, he hadn't felt that instant connection he had hoped for, nor had he thought that she resembled Marilyn Monroe in the least, yet he had realized that life, as he knew it, had come to an end. Had Zani told me that story before, or had that scenario, similar to others I'd heard, flashed in my mind the moment I'd seen them?

Something about them had always screamed *arranged marriage* to me, because he was older and considerably less attractive. But as they made themselves comfortable on my sofa, it seemed they had more in common than that first glance suggested. They had only been married for a few years but already looked alike, their expressions mirroring each other's like those of siblings. They had even opted for matching outfits, intuiting a more remarkable appearance in their joint styling than they could manage on their own.

"I'm glad I came and asked you for a lawyer," he said, pointing at me. "I knew you'd find someone good. You've always been a good omen in my life. I believe in those things. God put you on my path for a reason."

"Nobody would take his case," said Lëndina. "We thought it was a lost cause."

"He's like a movie star, that lawyer," said Zani. "You should see his office. Extraordinary. Mirrors, glass, everywhere."

"His assistants look like Miss America," said Lëndina. "Long legs. Big hair. Even the chairs smell like perfume."

"All he said was, 'Tell me about your case.' I told him. Then he said, '$50,000, yes?' I said yes. He shook my hand. Done deal." Zani rubbed his palms together and turned to his wife. "Did you give them the wine?"

"I forgot," she said, handing Billy a bag with two wine bottles.

"This wine is from my brother's vineyard in Albania. It's terrific. He's got a winery near Berat."

"We went to Berat," Billy said. "I loved it there."

"You went all the way to Berat and didn't go to my brother's winery? You should have told me. He'd have given you the grand tour. His wine won third place in a European contest."

They were kind people, Zani and his wife, generous and loyal. But clearly, there was an edge to them. When Zani focused his eyes, and she gave that cold, belittling side-glance, they didn't look like the sort of people you wanted to cross.

"I brought you a bottle last week, did you try it?" he asked.

I had left the wine bottle at Anna's apartment.

"Not yet," I said. "Things have a been a bit crazy."

"It has been hard," Billy jumped in. "A lot going on, right?"

I looked at Zani. He nodded in acknowledgment and turned toward his wife. He put his arm around her shoulder.

"Help me bring out the llokum," Billy said to me.

"Do you like llokum?" I asked.

"Love it," said Lëndina.

In the kitchen, as we whispered to each other, we discovered that we had a different read on Zani's reluctance in bringing up that night. Our perspectives had flipped. His reaction seemed suspicious to me, while Billy considered it an oversight, proof that Zani hadn't thought at all about me or Rakan.

"He's been busy with his immigration case," he said. "What if we ask him if he's talked to the Egyptians? It's possible he didn't even talk to them."

"It's odd he didn't mention it."

"His own life has been on the line."

"Let's go back, shall we?"

In the living room, Billy poured everyone wine. It was decent, although with an astringent aftertaste.

"Delicious," I said. "Third place in Europe, eh?"

"What did I tell you?" said Zani. "I'll never steer you wrong."

Lëndina was glancing outside. The setting sun demanded attention. It was squeezing itself among the cement structures, which, in spite of the bright borders, looked darker already. Billy turned on the red light. It reflected on the window glass like on a mirror, as did our table and the rest of the furniture.

"Please, get something to eat," said Billy. "Don't be shy."

Zani and Lëndina stood up. They appeared on the glass, suspended over countless windows and roofs, their silhouettes imprinted over the city.

"Gëzuar," Billy said to Zani. "Congratulations again on your paperwork."

Zani pointed at the ceiling.

"God was looking out for me."

"You must be relieved."

"I don't know if you know my story. Years ago, some scoundrels who did human trafficking hired me as a driver. I had no idea what they were doing. I found out later. Eventually, I gave their names to the American authorities. Not because I was hoping for something in return. No. The main reason was that if someone is hurting innocent people, they deserve hell, don't they? They're the devil and they deserve hell."

Lëndina nodded in agreement.

"They sure do deserve hell."

"God knows everything. God was looking down on me. He knows what's in my heart. Helping people is in my heart. She knows it," he said, pointing at me again. "Don't you?"

Billy cleared his throat and looked down at the carpet.

"I want to thank you for watching out for my wife the other night," he said. "She was frightened. And I wasn't around."

Zani sat down. While looking at his plate he squinted, as if he were peering out behind a nylon curtain.

"Ah, that night, that's right. Everything okay now?"

"We haven't seen or heard from Rakan since," said Billy.

"Good riddance. Terrorizing you and that other girl. What a scoundrel," Zani said.

"Of course," I said, studying his face. "It's odd that he used to pop up everywhere and now he's disappeared. His girlfriend, apparently, hasn't heard from him either."

"Someone like him had it coming," said Lëndina, taking a seat next to Zani. "I wouldn't worry about it."

We looked back at Zani. He was unperturbed, taking bites of bruschetta and sips of wine. The matter, you'd think, didn't concern him in the least.

"I don't even know why I got involved," I blurted, frustrated by his silence. "It has been one headache after another."

"If you're committed to helping people," Zani said, fixing me with his eyes, "you have to go all the way. Otherwise, don't start at all. You don't just keep to yourself, like most people, who mind their own business. Not you and me. We are fighters. And a bit mad, to be honest."

Lëndina kept nodding.

"There's a limit," Billy said. "Always a limit."

"We can't just let the world go by, can we?" Zani continued. "Some have to step in, get involved. *Who?* is the question. You need strength. It's not easy. Other people will take you for a fool. But someone has to deal with evil. With those who hurt the innocent. You can't just watch. Otherwise, what's the point of life?"

"There's also the authorities," Billy said.

"Of course," Zani said, making that Albanian facial expression, the one Billy said was like shrugging with the mouth. "Of course, there's them. We're not denying them."

Billy seemed dejected. I gulped more wine and went for broke. "You wouldn't have anything to do with it, would you?"

Zani's eyes widened. "With what?"

"With his disappearance."

He furrowed his brows for a second. Then he pointed at himself.

"Me?"

He tapped his knee and burst into laughter. After a short pause, Lëndina, who at first didn't understand what I was talking about, tittered also, but then she said, "Zani wouldn't get involved in anything like that. He's got enough problems as is." She turned to her husband for confirmation. He didn't offer any. He just sat there eating and enjoying his wine.

I looked at Billy, who seemed more relaxed already. When our eyes met, he touched my shoulder affectionately. Perhaps Zani's amusement at my question had been sufficient. Still, his attitude felt off to me. It was like playing a game of cards with someone and suspecting they were cheating.

"Did you mention anything to the bodega owners about Rakan?" I asked.

"I did."

"Did they say anything?"

"They said they'd talk to him, sure. But I haven't talked to them lately," Zani said shrugging. "I don't know."

"Maybe we can ask them?"

"But why?" said Zani. "If he's not bothering you anymore, you shouldn't worry about it. If he shows up again, then we'll deal with it."

Zani turned to his wife. They smiled at each other again. Arranged marriage or not, they seemed in love.

"So many people in New York City," Lëndina said, noticing the lights turning on outside. "Like ants. Eating and making nests." But we could only see buildings. It was hard for me to imagine bodies behind the walls, breathing, worrying, laughing, milling about the dinner table, conversing, obsessing. The spectacle inside my own apartment took all my attention.

I glimpsed at Zani, munching on bread, cheese, and salami, eating them separately, a bite each time, the Albanian way, not the sandwiched American way. A simple man, an open book, nothing to hide. But was he? He hadn't batted an eye at paying $50,000 to the lawyer. If he had money, he didn't show it. Zani wasn't the type to brag about money, I realized. But he did enjoy an aura of mystique and danger about him. Maybe there was no crime at the root of his opacity, only conceit. Despite his rough appearance, I suspected Zani was a bit vain.

"Way too many people," he said. "But the most important thing in the world is not to drink alone. To have someone to clink a glass with. Why did God create so many different kinds of people, do you know? To share love, and everything else."

"Gëzuar," said Lëndina.

"Gëzuar," I said.

"To friends. You are no longer alone," Zani said. "You have us."

A blinding light from a nearby balcony turned on. Our image on the glass died, replaced by that of the gray buildings.

# 14.

"I DO FEEL BETTER," BILLY SAID ONCE OUR GUESTS LEFT. "Do you?"

I started to say, "I still have doubts," but did not. Billy's earlier manic energy, his volubility and unease, had been replaced by stillness. He hadn't been that composed in days.

"I do," I said. "I feel better. Leyla was right. Rakan was probably arrested for shoplifting. He had a thing for brand-name clothes."

We were sitting in bed, in our pajamas, finishing the rest of the wine. It no longer tasted astringent. It felt thick and viscous on the tongue. The third glass made me lax, first in body, then mind. Reality appeared malleable, subject to my desires. Rakan was behind bars, serving time for robbing a store. How many months would he be inside? Or would it be only days? People did get out of jail. He might knock on our door tomorrow. Threads of possibilities stretched out in front of me again, drab, taut, like the strings of a guitar whose melody depended on me alone. Maybe Rakan wasn't in jail. He was in the back room of a bodega. Men in stocking masks took turns punching him in the stomach.

"I hope the Bulgarian never comes back," Billy said. "She didn't know about you and Rakan."

He wanted to say something else but hesitated.

"It wasn't a date," I said. "I pretended that it was. For Leyla's sake."

"It's fine. I understand."

A shadow passed across his face. *Something is broken inside him*, I thought again. *He hides it well, but it's there, a crack, an abyss. It might be there for a long time, perhaps forever. His composure is a front.*

"When are you seeing Zinovia?" he asked.

"Next week."

"Good."

I heard a woman's voice. It sounded like Leyla's at first, but it was one of our neighbors calling out to someone in the hallway. I wished Leyla were in our apartment, in Billy's office. Sleeping. Safe. It was a Friday night, almost ten o'clock. The wife must have already left. Since that day she'd told me about the dermatologist and his advances, I had tracked the hours as she must have, even though I had never managed to broach the subject with Billy. *Later*, I'd always think, *later*, unable to fight the inclination to postpone our conversation.

I pictured the suburban living room where the couple and their three children lived, expansive, bright, aspiring to be modern, although never quite managing. The pink toys scattered around the house had a way of cheapening every classy piece of furniture.

"I've been meaning to tell you something," I told Billy. "The dermatologist, Leyla's employer, has been coming on to her."

"What a bastard. Shall we invite her to stay with us for a bit?"

His quick offer took me by surprise.

"I left my phone in the other room," I said, wondering if it was too late to call her.

My head felt heavy from the wine. Upon closing my eyes, Leyla appeared in the suburban living room. She was burping the baby. The six-year-old screamed from the other room; the two-year-old had messed up her drawing. Leyla rushed to the living room while holding the infant. Sensing the commotion, the baby puckered his mouth and let out a cry.

"Give him to me," said the husband, appearing on cue. He reached for his son, allowing his hands to rest on hers. She, who didn't think twice about telling anyone off, had to exert restraint over her reactions. She couldn't shrug him off, not while holding his helpless child.

Billy put down his *National Geographic* and left the room. I picked it up. I read a short article about hermaphroditic sea slugs, which were delicate as glass but apparently stabbed each other between the eyes during sex. It was followed by an article about anti-poaching measures in India, illustrated with a photo spread of a panther heading toward a thicket while dragging a helpless fawn by its neck.

I was studying the picture when I felt Billy's eyes on me. For how long had he been looking at me like that?

"Here is your phone," he said. "Shall we call her?"

"Yes," I said. "But maybe it's better if you talk to her. She'll need to know you're on board with it."

He picked up the phone.

"Leyla," I heard him say. "It's Billy. How are you? We wanted to see how you are. Do you want to stay with us for a while, until you find another arrangement?"

Then he listened to her speak for a few seconds. What else did she need to tell him besides the address to come get her?

"Okay, are you sure?" Another pause followed. He shrugged his shoulders.

"Let us know if anything changes, okay? Take care."

He hung up.

"She said she's fine there. She said she wants to stay."

"Did she tell you anything about the man?"

"No. She said everything was fine."

"I don't understand."

"Maybe his wife noticed something and told him to knock it off?"

"The wife is on a business trip."

"Why don't you call her back?" he said. "You talk to her."

I picked up my phone, but instead of dialing I pictured the scene again.

The children were all asleep. The living room, which earlier had struck the dermatologist as unpleasant, a place to run away from, now appeared peaceful, the way it had been before they had children. He missed those childless years, as he missed his wife, as she used to be. He sat on the sofa but got up again after finding a Lego truck stuck between the cushions. He lowered the lights. He made himself a drink—a scotch, no ice. He didn't put the bottle back on the rack. He was waiting for her to emerge from the baby's bedroom. She was putting the baby to sleep, feeding him formula, singing songs in her own language.

His favorite thing about her was that twinkle in her eyes when she spoke. She was feisty, wasn't she? He imagined himself catching her unaware with a kiss while she was telling him something about the children, or during one of those strange moods of hers when she was faraway. She was a poet, she had said. She had even read him a couple of lines from her poetry. It had made no sense, as expected. Trying too hard, always comparing one thing to another. But the kiss. She might protest initially, but he'd hold her tightly, reassure her, until he'd feel her body go limp. The thought of her sighing while his tongue was inside her mouth excited him. He went to knock on the bedroom door.

She heard the knock but wasn't afraid. She had dreaded this moment but now that it was happening it was as if it had happened already and she had survived it, like she had survived everything else in her past. The devil one knew . . . Did she want a drink after such a long day? She must. He was saying what she had thought he'd say. He was right. She was exhausted, from the kids, from the lawyers who never made any progress on her immigration application but constantly asked for money. Yes, she wanted a drink.

When she entered the living room, she remembered the magazine she'd flipped through earlier, that of the panther sinking its teeth into the fawn. Wasn't killing predictable, didn't it happen in nature all the time? The dermatologist was not going to kill her. She would survive him. Years later, while trying to sort out that winter from long ago, the shame would leave her body and flow into a verse. Her future poems had all been inside her, she'd realize, even while she couldn't write a word.

*I should call her now*, I thought, staring at the phone in my hand. But I still didn't dial. It was as if the images of Leyla were playing in a separate floor of my mind, while the action of calling her was in another. One was easy to enter and hang out in. The other was high up and out of reach. It was late. My eyes did feel heavy. I'd call her tomorrow, I decided.

I must have slept for an hour or two before waking up drenched in sweat. I got up and left the bedroom. I paced around the living room. Rakan's arms still weighed on my shoulders. He had been hugging me in a dream, just to say hello, before it had turned sexual. He had breathed heavily as he came, his yellow teeth about to bite my shoulder. With each breath new wounds had spread on his skin, shoulders, neck, thighs—infected, bloody wounds. His eyes had looked at me reproachfully, as if to say, *It's all your fault.*

I opened the living room window. The cold gusts of air filled my lungs and pushed aside my doubts. My head felt clear. If Rakan's disappearance were a physical presence, it would resemble the panther I'd read about earlier, the panther with the black, shiny fur and unsettling emerald eyes. I'd been hunting the panther by stealth all along, lurking in the distant shadows, approaching it slowly. I was closing in now. All my fears were quickly slipping away. I was staring at the panther straight in the face. I was ready for a kill. The panther curved its back and leaped into the air, but instead of coming toward me, it changed direction and landed somewhere else, behind my back.

*Yes*, I said to Rakan's pitiful, wounded image. *It could be my fault. I might never know. But I can't let the world go by. Not always, anyway. I've got to fight sometimes. I've got to live.* I lingered for a while in that feeling. The circumstances weren't that perplexing after all. Zani had been right. Feeling bad over someone like Rakan was useless. I was done.

I went back to bed. Billy was sleeping with his arms crossed in front of his body, like he was protecting himself. I drew near. He opened his arms and embraced me.

"It will be fine," I whispered. "You'll see."

I fell asleep soon after, while keeping track of his breathing.

LINA HAD COME OVER that afternoon to pick up her mail. Even though she had moved out of our apartment months ago and officially changed her address at the post office, some of her mail still came to our place.

"How was your vacation?" I asked, noticing her glowing skin.

"Downtown San Juan was wonderful," she said in a surprisingly monotone voice. "It reminded me of Europe."

Billy and I had also gone to San Juan once, shortly after we started dating. We had booked a kayak tour around an island famous for its bioluminescence. A bright fish school had darted beneath the surface, accompanying our boat. Even our fingers had glowed as we trailed them through the water.

"Billy and I loved it there," I said, recalling a bouquet of blue orchids he'd left for me in the hotel lobby. "They've got beautiful orchids in Puerto Rico."

"Ben would insist," Lina said, "on buying me a rose every time those girls with flower baskets tied around their necks would sashay around us."

I was expecting some gushing about the new boyfriend, but instead her face contorted into a grimace, revealing hurt and a touch of incredulity. She was reluctant, at first, to confide in me, resorting to generic phrases. But once she started, she became generous with the details. While she had considered their trip an affirmation of their commitment, Ben had seen it as, well, a vacation. Soon after returning from their trip, he had officially informed her that someone at work was interested in getting a drink with him, a date, to be exact, although he never used the word, specifying the person in question was in publicity, not finance, where he was.

"As if I was in the human resources," she scoffed. "And he needed a permission slip."

His informative, asking-for-permission tone had baffled her. He was hoping, it had seemed to her, that she would believe he had given her a say in the matter.

"What did you say?"

"Nothing."

She had expressed her sinking feelings by gathering her things, scattered around the apartment under the earlier assumption she would spend the night there. Her impending departure had made Ben uneasy, prompted him to launch into a monologue. They had only been dating for a month and a half and had never had a conversation about being exclusive. The default was nonexclusive, everyone knew that. How did she *not* know that? he had wondered aloud. Lina had stared at him, not comprehending, trying to remember what the word *default* meant in English—realizing she'd been partaking in a callous game.

"I asked him," she said, "why was it that he didn't tell me the default earlier?"

"What did he say?"

The answer had been quick. "Because it would have ruined the mood."

"Because it would have ruined the mood," she scoffed. "That was the worst thing he said."

Too worked up to express her sadness, she went for a cheap parting shot, listing Ben's flaws and faults. She attempted to articulate that, despite his posturing, Ben had known that a conversation outlining the rules would not have resulted in a second date with her, let alone a shared-room vacation in Puerto Rico. The earlier euphoria gone, Lina was left nursing the emotional wounds of a calculated and effective seduction, her hopes ridiculed by the cold logic of biology.

"Let's not talk about it anymore. How was Albania? I heard your mother called Alma to talk about my father's spending habits."

"I tried to stop her. She wouldn't listen."

"My mother was upset after that call. We all know how my father is. He spends money for things that are superfluous, but we allow him that. It makes him happy."

"To be fair, your mother complains to everyone who'll listen about his spending habits."

Discussing our parents, under the circumstances, was foolish. Our acknowledgment of their shortcomings had little bearing on our natural tendency to stick up for them.

"It's different when other people complain," she said. "And she can't forget the blanket."

"The blanket?"

"Your mother only blankets the sofa when my dad visits. It reflects on her, my mother thinks, as if she's untidy, and doesn't wash her husband's pants."

"He'll sit wherever," I said. "Without thinking twice."

"He no longer does," she said. "We've talked to him about it."

"That's good," I said, wanting to give her the last word, but feeling unable to. "But the last time I saw him, he did have a gray circle of dirt on the back of his pants."

We both laughed.

"She knows your mother is clean," I added. "It's not that."

Lina nodded pensively. She glanced at my face, then averted her eyes. She was deliberating telling me something, the same way she had earlier, about Ben's behavior after Puerto Rico.

"My mother and yours used to be close," she said. "But after they hanged your mother's cousin, they didn't speak for years."

In the blue haze of memories, a lace curtain appeared, and behind it the shrubby garden, where my father's white tank tops lay. My parents' arguments were as familiar as the sound of TV, but I did remember my mother refusing to get on the phone with Lina's mother once or twice.

"Yes, I do remember that."

"Do you remember the cousin they hanged?" she asked.

"Barely."

A jolly bachelor in his midthirties who enjoyed swimming and droning along to polyphonic songs at family gatherings, the cousin had been a regular visitor to our house. He'd bring me a box of cookies each time, ask me about school, watch soccer with my dad. But his features had not registered in my mind. He was a faceless ghost. I remembered the whispers around the house. He'd been caught escaping the country, swimming through Lake Ohrid to Yugoslavia. No, he'd stolen light bulbs from the place where he worked. Never mind, it wasn't light bulbs, it was money, lots of money. What he was guilty of was unclear, but the authorities still hanged him at 5:15 AM one morning, without trial, in some unknown little town. A sense of apprehension permeated our house. The government punished the relatives of those who attempted to escape the country—some lost their jobs, some were denied the right to study, many were interned in purgatory. My parents would rehearse what they needed to say at work. *We'd cut ties with him already, for years. If we saw him in the street, we wouldn't say hello.*

My mother, like many, had faced an unbearable conundrum, although not the worst one, grieving a relative while denying her connection to him. How many people had shunned her back then? She'd never talked about it.

"By the way," Lina said. "Who is Rakan?"

The panther started prowling through the hallways. Its existence obliterated everything else and tweaked my heartbeat.

"Why do you ask?"

"A girl contacted me through Facebook."

"What girl?"

"What's wrong?"

"What girl?"

"A Bulgarian girl, Svetlana or something. A redheaded hairdresser, I looked her up. She had an envelope addressed to me, she said. She found the envelope in a room her boyfriend was renting."

"Billy took that envelope from her," I said. "She must have remembered your name."

"She doesn't know what happened to her boyfriend. She's looking for him."

"He was following Leyla, a friend of mine."

"Like online?"

"No, he was following her in real life. He was taking pictures of her."

"Why?"

"Her ex-husband wanted revenge."

"What?"

The panther bounded into the hallway again. It would come in sooner or later. The trick was to look it in the face. To show courage.

"If she approaches you again, don't talk to her," I said.

"She wrote me again this morning. I didn't respond."

"Just tell her," I said, "that you will call immigration on her."

Lina hesitated. "I can't tell her that."

"Why not?"

"I can't tell her I'll call immigration. I mean, how can I?"

The panther trotted into the living room. I felt the heat of its smoldering emerald eyes. "You have to. If she won't leave you alone."

The panther retreated slowly, making its way through the kitchen.

"What are you making for dinner?" Lina asked, changing the conversation.

"Ordering out," I said.

Maybe we had run out of things to say. Maybe I had made her uncomfortable. She pulled out her phone and withdrew online, into other people's photos and lives. I did the same. As usual, Anna had posted new pictures. She'd used a filter that emulated the dusty look and the cropped frame of a Super 8 camera. There she was, in a black party dress, wearing a hat embellished with peacock feathers. A distinguished-looking man in a waistcoat and bow tie nuzzled her neck. The comments revealed he was some famous film director from Korea.

An email from Alfred popped up on the screen.

*Literature used to be my favorite subject. I loved reading poems especially. Some find them cryptic, but they're keys that open invisible doors. I feel better since I started writing. The demons retreat, if only for a short while. My personal essay is finished. I've read it aloud many times, pacing around the living room. My words will be in a book, can you believe it? I want you to read my essay first, before anyone else.*

*When and where are we meeting?*

*PS: Roza has started to smile.*

The thought of Alfred, pacing around his home, reading his essay aloud, was depressing. Although Lina had put her phone away and was looking at me, I kept scrolling through meaningless photos, until his brown eyes and their earnest expression faded from my awareness.

"I should go," Lina said. "My boss is having one of those last-minute crises. We have a big presentation on Monday."

I walked her to the door.

"What happened to your friend?" she said unexpectedly, on her way out. "Is she okay now that Rakan is gone?"

"Leyla is okay," I said, realizing that I had yet to call her. "She's fine."

WHEN BILLY MENTIONED Anna's parents fortieth-anniversary party, hesitation and a slight resentment replaced my old excitement.

"She's going back to South Korea in a few days," he said. "She's dating a film director from there."

"I know. She posted some photos. Do you know him?"

"I've seen his movies. Always interesting. Low-budget indie types."

Billy left the room, implying that if we went to the party or not was up to me. It made little difference to him, he seemed to be saying. But he wanted us to go. Since Anna had been the one to call and tell him to return home, he must have thought that she and I were fine. The situation was more confusing than I let on. Distancing myself completely was complicated, maybe even out of the question. Still, going to the party felt like a chore.

An Albanian woman who had been one of my interpreting clients came to mind. Not long after her wedding to an Albanian businessman, she'd gone to see Zinovia. She struggled with various situational anxieties. Her mother-in-law, who lived in Jersey, cooked dinner for the entire family every Sunday evening. Everyone was expected to attend. Once a week, the young couple would make the drive from Manhattan to the in-laws' house. Although the new bride had a pleasant and restful time during those weekly dinners, she felt extreme unease on her way there. Later on, over dessert, her earlier fears would appear absurd. Why had she not wanted to come? Why had she worried like that? Zinovia had proposed a thought experiment. Do not engage in dilemmas about whether they like you, or you like them, or what that unsettling comment from last Sunday meant. Gloss over all your questions, for there are no answers. If someone stepped on your toes, resolve to forgive them. On your drive there, pay close attention to the other vehicles, the trees, the music, the conversation with your husband.

Perhaps the only way to preserve my friendship with Anna was to free myself from pondering her feelings for Billy. It was best not to form a judgment or arrive at a conclusion. Per Zinovia's advice to the other woman, I decided to ignore Anna's confession and her reiteration of it. We busied ourselves with finding the right outfits, for the party had a forties theme. We scouted thrift stores and found a vintage black dress for me. Billy already owned a double-breasted taupe suit and an old fedora that would do.

The night of the party, spruced up like extras in *Casablanca*, we walked the red carpet into Anna's parents' salon. Red lips, gleaming jewels, satiny dresses, laughter, effusive greetings spun around us. A Frank Sinatra impersonator with thinning silver hair swaggered through the crowd crooning "Fly Me to the Moon." Waiters in bow ties promptly refilled glasses of wine and champagne. Others meandered around the crowd holding silver trays. Women in satin opera gloves kept reaching for deviled eggs and tomato sandwiches. Men in zoot suits poured rum into cognac glasses, took long sips, and sighed with satisfaction.

Anna's mother caught my eye. She was in a buttoned-up purple dress that matched her purple hair strand, but it didn't flatter her figure. Impervious to the music, she threw greedy glances around her, checking on everything. Upon noticing Billy and me, that nervous expression on her face softened. She seemed pleased. She curled her arm around a tall man with protruding eyes and turned him toward us.

"It's Billy," she told him, smiling widely.

Anna's father, with his gentle smile, had never struck me as a Lothario, despite Billy's stories about him. He opened his arms in an embrace for us both.

"It has been so long. Why don't you drop by more often, Billy? You both should."

Anna's mother thanked me for coming to visit Anna when she was sick. She wanted to know the recipe for my chicken soup, but as I was listing the ingredients, her eyes glazed over. Someone in the crowd distracted her. She was studying Anna, I realized, and the film director, who were standing by the French doors leading to the outdoor patio. Anna had on the same peacock feather hat as in that online photo and a stunning velvet dress with a plunging neckline. The film director kissed her on the lips. A cloud of worry passed over Mrs. Cruz's face at that display of affection. Did she have the same concerns as I about her latest tryst? Would this, like the rest of Anna's affairs, be only a pit stop, at the end of which she would return to that imaginary love for Billy, or would it prove long-lasting, shaking off, eventually, that hold my husband had on her?

"It's a great party," I said. "A wonderful idea."

"It was Anna's idea," she said sheepishly. "Fred and I used to listen to all these songs growing up. We still do."

A man in a trench coat, his eyes concealed by a fedora hat, holding a retro boxy camera with a reflector flash appeared in front of us. A spark of light and a loud clack disrupted our conversation.

"Ah, the paparazzi," Anna's father laughed. "They got us again."

The Frank Sinatra impersonator introduced the next singing group as the Triplets of Bronxville. Three blondes in yellow dresses, with gardenias tucked behind their ears, sashayed into the room to enthusiastic applause. Frank Sinatra accompanied them on the piano. Their wholesome type of flirting was irresistible. With eye flutters, gentle swaying, and choreographed steps, they threw themselves into the refrain, making the most of the lyrics, which cautioned a former flame not to sit under an apple tree with another woman.

Their overexuberance appealed to everyone in the room. Many were bopping to the rhythm. Some were friends and relatives of Anna's parents, casual, affluent world travelers. Others were significantly younger, poetic-looking hipsters, the kind who were game for anything different. I assumed they were Anna's friends, or her students.

To my left, Billy was talking to Anna's father, who was explaining why he liked Paris better than London. *Paris is a woman*, he was saying, *while London is a man*. I wasn't sure what that meant, but Billy nodded, as if in agreement. The film director was now standing behind me, offering a free lecture to an obsequious young man inquiring about his process. Yes, he did the casting and found locations first, the director was saying. "Because if you start by writing a script, you have to choose from infinite stories. But if the casting is complete, and you get to know the actors, there are only about five stories to write."

Anna waved at me from across the room. I was about to excuse myself from her mother, but Mrs. Cruz held on to my arm with her purple-gloved hand.

"Before you came to visit her that day, Anna kept asking about you. 'When is she coming?' 'Why is she late?' She was drowsy, but she kept asking. Be her friend, okay?"

"I am her friend," I said, finding her grasp unsettling.

"Don't give up on her," she said, bringing her lips close to my ear. "This thing about Billy is nonsense. She doesn't care for him. She's afraid of commitment, that's all."

Her bluntness reduced my reaction to a simple nod.

"I lost a child," she said. "A two-year-old, when Anna was about six. I was depressed for years. I've been wondering if that gave her the wrong idea about family. Family can be a beautiful thing, you know?"

Without waiting for a response, she went on. "It can, trust me. But Anna doesn't believe it. Deep down she doesn't." She let go of my arm. "Do you believe it?"

"How did you lose your child?"

She had trouble saying it, then decided not to. Maybe she hadn't answered that question in a long time. A relative came up to us. I was glad for that, for I instantly regretted asking her the details. I didn't need to know. What if I said something trite in response, a compulsory consolation, a disingenuous promise, which wouldn't do justice to her revelation?

"Any travels coming up?" asked the relative.

"We're planning a Mediterranean cruise in the early summer," Mrs. Cruz said. "A friend of ours owns a yacht and he invited us."

Anna hobbled toward me on her crutch.

"What was my mother talking to you about?" she asked. "It seemed intense."

"About her upcoming cruise," I said.

Billy came over. She kissed him on the cheek. There was no awkwardness between them. The man of her fantasies was one thing. The friend she liked and saw frequently, my husband, was another. How had that boundary become vague that night? He'd showed up so late at her apartment, reticent to speak. He'd asked for a drink.

Zinovia's voice in my ear. *If someone steps on your toe, forgive them.*

"Let me introduce you to my boyfriend," she said.

"Yes, please," said Billy. "I love his work."

As soon as the director came to join us, the paparazzi materialized. A photo of the four of us, almost immediately, showed up on the wall, to our left. The projector had so far eluded me, but now the slideshow caught my attention. Pictures of Mr. and Mrs. Cruz, throughout the years, and occasionally of Anna, alternated in between the party pictures taken by the paparazzi.

In one picture, Mrs. Cruz, with poofy eighties hair, was standing by what looked like the leather seat of a private jet. She had her arm around a child Anna. There was something forced and unnatural in that embrace. The subtle ache in the young girl's eyes quickened my heartbeat. I'd rarely noticed it during our friendship, but it had always been there. Whatever mask she wore had always managed to distract me from it. It occurred to me now, although not for the first time, that our friendship wasn't as accidental as I'd convinced myself it was. That we had more in common than met the eye, even if it was only a melancholy childhood.

Billy was expressing his admiration for one of the director's films. The interesting thing, he said, was that the film's structure was bifurcated, showing the same story twice: A celebrated filmmaker visits a small town where he happens to meet a young woman, an aspiring painter. He is flirtatious, compliments her paintings, even hints that he wants to marry her. She falls for it, but her friends, who follow the filmmaker online, tell her not to trust him. He is already married, they say, with two children. The second half of the movie shows the same story with slight variations. The director meets the young woman and they hit it off. At some point he tells her that he likes her very much, maybe has even fallen in love, but, alas, he's married and has two children, so nothing can happen between them. When she shows him her paintings, he tells her she has talent, but also what he believes she might improve.

"In the first version, she felt betrayed," Billy said. "But in the second, there was a warm feeling, a budding friendship between her and the director, respect even."

One of Anna's friends took a quick break from sipping her martini, just long enough to say, "The second version is a fraud. A man on the prowl never thinks of a woman as a potential friend."

"Implying that a do-over is possible is deceiving," said Anna, a sad note sneaking into her voice. "It never is, is it?"

We all turned to the director. He put his palms together while turning her question over in his mind.

"Reality can be deceiving," he said. "Only art doesn't leave you in a lurch. It swoops in. It offers something better."

"There is always an alternative," Billy said, meeting my eyes. "One must think of the consequences." Then he turned to the director. "How long are you in New York?"

"I leave tomorrow," the director answered, reaching for Anna's hand. "I'm going to the Berlin International Film Festival. After

Berlin, I'm returning to Korea. Anna is in for a treat. I will show her my favorite places."

"Are you premiering a new film in Berlin?" asked Billy.

"Yes," said the director. "I make a film a year and usually show it there."

"Enough of shoptalk," Anna said. "How about some cocktails? The specials tonight are Missing in Action and Crimes of Passion. Any preference?"

Rakan's face appeared in my mind's eye at once. Billy adjusted his tie and wiped his sweaty forehead with a handkerchief. He took off his fedora and handed it to me. He didn't look well. He placed one hand on his stomach and leaned forward.

"I'm feeling a bit off," he told Anna. "I need to go outside for a bit."

"Why don't you two go out on the patio?" Anna said. "I'll come and check on you in a bit."

The Triplets of Bronxville were about to start a duet with Frank Sinatra, so everyone from the outside was coming in. We barely managed to edge through the crowd.

All alone, on the patio, we sat on the beach chairs, arranged around a space heater.

"I've come to terms with it," I said. "I don't regret helping Leyla and standing up to Rakan."

I was about to tell him about the panther, and how it always disappeared the moment I looked it in the face, but his body crumpled.

"You okay?"

"I've been eating meat," he blurted. "It's not agreeing with me tonight."

I was too startled to speak.

"I ate too many of those filet mignon appetizers," he continued. "There was no end to them."

"Since when have you been eating meat?"

He'd been a vegetarian for as long as I'd known him.

"Since that night Rakan came over," he said. "After I left the apartment, I went straight to a burger joint. Ordered a double cheeseburger. The first in thirty years. The next morning, I got some bacon with my eggs. I've been keeping it a secret, obviously. I've been ashamed."

I remembered now how the salami leftovers from our dinner with Zani had vanished from our refrigerator. I had thought he had thrown them away.

"When did you eat the filet mignons? We were together the whole time."

"When you weren't looking."

"Shall we call a cab and go home?"

He straightened his body. "I'll feel better soon. Transitory pain."

I put my arm around his shoulder. The patio was higher than many other buildings, affording us a glimpse of other terraces and balconies. Taking advantage of the milder weather, many people were out, huddled with bottles of wine or board games. Below us loomed the city, pulsating under the glitter, then, above us, the calm steel-gray sky.

But why did the view feel so smothering? The strangers were much too close for comfort, our movements so exposed to their judgments.

"We should talk about it," I said.

"I've come to terms with it also," he said. "You were helping your friend."

"Not that," I said. "You know what I'm talking about."

"That night he came over," he said at once. "There was a certain energy in the room. The way he looked at you. Were you interested in someone like him?"

"I hated him," I said. "But, yes, there was something. It's true."

"How could there be something?" he said, his voice shaking. Behind the glass doors, people were dancing. The room appeared seeped in yellow. Frank Sinatra was leading one of the blondes into a turn, then spun her into a dip.

"I don't know," I said. "I don't know how that happened."

He stood up to pace around. He stopped by the railing. The crescent moon was leaning on his shoulder. Under the red glare of the heater, his silhouette appeared fuzzy, as if, ever so slowly, he was slipping away. My chest tightened.

"We should probably call a cab, anyway," he said, walking back. "Not in the mood to dance."

"When you left for Europe," I said, "I slept in the bed in your office, in your sheets, in your T-shirt. Every evening I'd write an email in my head, then erase it. That day in Berat, when I heard those guys talking about the American bridge man, I promised myself that, if you were that man, we'd never be apart again. I wandered the city for hours. But when I saw you, I was afraid to get close. I thought I might do or say something wrong."

He sat next to me. I was afraid to look at his face. When we established eye contact, a gleam slipped across his face. Oddly, what came to mind was Boyer's acting in *Love Affair*. Upon seeing the painting, none of Boyer's features changed; he didn't close his eyes to take in the truth or part his lips in astonishment. A transformation happened seamlessly, as if a lighter spirit had entered his body. The same kind of spirit that now lit up Billy's face.

"Ours is a love story also," I blurted. "I think so."

He embraced me. We walked inside holding hands. A group of devotees had surrounded Anna and the director.

"That's not how I had intended the ending to come across," the director was saying. "Such interpretations surprise me."

We were sorting out the coat and hat business when a picture of Billy and me appeared on the wall. The paparazzi had snapped it just seconds ago, from the inside, while we were hugging on the terrace. It looked staged and artificial, like those stock photos with bland inscriptions. *Couple embracing in front of a New York City skyline.*

But on closer inspection, my heart slowed down. The smile Billy was trying on was passive, the Cheshire cat's. He wanted to seem happy, but something inside him was still broken.

• • •

ALTHOUGH I WAS TEN MINUTES early for my appointment with Zinovia, her office door was open. One of her colleagues, passing by in the hallway, told me to wait for her inside. I was alone in her pristine office, facing her clean and bare desk, which smelled faintly of apple cider vinegar. A simple vase with a single daisy stood on top of a round side table. A cactus plant in a miniature pot perched on the sunny windowsill. The city, humming behind the windows, with all its chaos, felt distant. A cluttered mindset wouldn't be tolerated here, Zinovia wanted her clients to know.

The books on the shelves were thick, with shiny dust jackets and titles like *Personality Disorders in Modern Life* and *Adult Attachment*. A few photos, scattered throughout the shelves, showed a different side to her—she was also someone who snorkeled in blue waters, ice-skated at the Rockefeller Center, and dined with large groups. Still, the photos seemed curated, impersonal. One of the photo frames was facedown. *Here we go,* I thought, picking it up. Zinovia was soaking up the sun on the seashore, her arm around a stocky biker type with a ragged beard. Maybe they had broken up. Or she didn't want her patients to do what I was doing, stealing a glimpse at her private life.

The sun was illuminating half her desk. I opened one of the drawers. Flawless. A tray with rubber bands, staples, and Post-it notes in designated sections. The second drawer contained two reams of printer paper. The third drawer was empty. The fourth drawer was the exception. She kept a sewing kit in there. It contained needles, spools of thread, safety pins, a box of tampons, a pair of woolen gloves. It reminded me of a drawer from home containing miscellaneous items, scissors, measuring tapes, storage bags. My mother tried to put everything where it belonged, but many things would eventually end up there.

That snippet of conversation from long ago came to mind, but this time my parents weren't in the garden, as I once remembered, but in the living room. My father's words still hovered above the kitchen table.

*We're in the same room, but you don't see or listen to me at all.*

I stood by the drawer and looked inside, rummaging through an old deck of cards and a couple of plastic dolls, the kind produced during communism in Albania, which nobody wanted. With their legs and arms stuck to the body, they were as useless as mummies.

"Only a few films are any good," my mother said suddenly. "But if they are, they end too soon. You're left bereft, in a dark room. Perhaps the roses aren't cancerous, who knows. But why take the chance? Better not to touch them at all."

The drawer creaked. I'd shut it without intending to.

I turned around. They were both looking at me.

My mother's blonde hair. Her red dress. My father's white shirt, rolled at the sleeves. His tank top underneath. *To soak up the sweat*, he'd say.

The images wouldn't hold. Their silhouettes moved farther away from me; they were steadily shrinking, until they were reduced to specks. The roses in the garden were growing at a rapid speed, their stems thick as trees, their petals vast as sailcloths. There was nothing but a daisy and a cactus in Zinovia's office, but the smell of the roses was suffocating. I had to remind myself they weren't cancerous. Then I said that to my mother. *They're lovely, Mother.*

The geography of my mother's face was complicated. Her skin now stretched for miles and miles. Her features were part of a field, a country, a universe, and it dawned on me that although her words to me would resonate forever, she was incapable of hearing mine. For mothers bathed babies in nourishment and all their emotions. For the conditions of the womb persisted and it was a one-way street. That trouble in the mothers' eyes, passed down and down and down, from their own mothers, and those before them, was there to stay. Daughters could do as little about it as about a choppy ocean, or a river that had run dry. Then Anna came to mind, traveling the world with her Coach duffel bag, only dimly aware of the fact that she was stuck back in time, in the enormous desert of her own mother's face during those earlier years. For how long had she wandered aimlessly under the open skies, at the mercy of mirages that would always disappear?

Zinovia's approaching steps brought my daydreams to an end. A wave of panic washed over me. But why? Wasn't I there to talk to her?

"Sorry to keep you waiting," she said.

She double-checked that the windows were closed before closing the blinds, which concealed all the people on their purposeful walks, and an electronic billboard, advertising the hourly parking rate of an underground garage.

She turned on a soft light that infused the room in sepia. She lathered her hands in Cetaphil. The smell wasn't bad this time.

"So," she said, sitting down and placing one hand on top of the other. "How have you been?"

"Fine," I said. The idea of getting up and leaving still lurked at the back of my mind. "The sun is finally out."

"Did you have a nice weekend? Any parties?" she said, her smile bright.

"My friend Anna's party. Was there with Billy," I blurted.

UPON LEAVING ZINOVIA'S OFFICE, sunlight flooded my vision. The glare of the street was disorienting. The sounds startling. This was a material world, made of brick, cement, flesh. A Mercedes cut into a lane, nearly causing a crash. A horn, sharp as a scream, blasted the street. A pedestrian launched into expletives toward a bicyclist, who scurried away. The streetlights commanded the flow of the traffic. The phones people's attention.

I wanted to return to Zinovia's office, resume my recline on her sofa. I longed to close my eyes and remain in a suspended state, weaving the threads of emotions she had managed to yank from my tangled pile. I wanted to be in a tidy room again, for my body to feel nothing but the sting and comfort of a voice.

What was expected of me that afternoon? One appointment came into focus. I had to meet Alfred in the park in fifteen minutes.

Someone called my name. The doorman of Zinovia's office building was running toward me.

"I look you," he said, in his Russian accent. "I look you and don't find. I feel myself anxious."

He handed me a red rose. It was bright and plump, accented in leafy ferns, and wrapped in cellophane.

"It's your husband," he said. "He drops it off. He is late teaching class."

A bead of sweat was rolling down the doorman's neck. His left eye was twitching. He knew me by name but hadn't seen me come out of the elevator. Having to find me in the crowd had made him nervous. The smallest tasks upended him. He used to be a gym teacher in Russia, he had told me once, but no longer had the strength for exercise.

"Thank you."

"It's nice," he said, before heading back. "The rose. The husband."

I walked along the sidewalk. Pops of purple and yellow sprinkled the streets. New Yorkers and tourists alike looked content as they sipped on iced drinks, their jackets tied around their waists, their sleeves rolled up. The business of enjoying life was about to be taken seriously. The rose's petals were smooth. It crossed my mind to surprise Billy, to show up at NYU after his class. He'd shuffle out of the classroom absentmindedly, adjusting the strap of his cross-body satchel. Upon seeing me standing there, in the hallway, a shadow would cross his face. But he would recover. He would manage a smile. Just then my phone beeped. *Do you want to come and meet me?* Billy wrote, as if he'd been reading my mind. *Let me know.*

But I couldn't go to NYU. Alfred was waiting for me in the park. I hurried my step.

By the Thompson Street entrance, the first cherry trees had already flowered. The garden beds were bursting with blossoms. *Subway troubles*, Alfred wrote in a text. *Be there soon.* I sat under a cherry tree. The earth was soft and moist from the sprinklers. The white and pink blooms gave off a sweet scent. To my left, a clown was blowing bubbles. Squealing, eager kids were chasing them. One of the children tripped and fell face forward, not far from me. She stayed put on the ground, about to cry. I helped her up.

"Want to pop bubbles with me?" she asked.

"Of course," I said.

Her father approached us. He thanked me and took her, but he stood nearby, talking on the phone.

"They say it could be a false spring," he said. "A temperature drop is expected this week. I hope all those flowers and buds make it. It would be a shame if they don't."

There was Alfred now, in front of the Garibaldi statue, his head jutting forward and turning side to side. He was over-dressed. The black winter coat didn't seem like something he'd own, but he looked handsome in it. He had parted his hair on the side. His deep-set eyes kept scanning the park. Two skate-boarders almost bumped into him. He didn't even notice. He continued wandering around the sculpture, indifferent to the commotion. Under his arm he held his orange folder.

He took a break from pacing to write me a message. *I'm here*, he wrote. *I'm here. Did you leave already? Where are you?* We weren't far from each other. But he couldn't see me. The grassy area was packed with children, and I was sitting down.

In the flower beds, daffodils, tulips, and irises were com-peting over their colors. Alfred resumed his pacing. Then he stopped, opened his folder. He read and read. The blossoming trees did not exist for him. He was oblivious to everything. He was far back, in those distant, shadowy years. He would soon pass his story on to me. The blue sky, the flowers, the children would disappear from me also.

A ray of sunshine fell over his face. He was staring at the flower beds. He then looked at his phone again. A striking expression crept up his face. It threatened to scuttle toward me, his sadness, like one of the more erratic squirrels. I didn't move. He was leaving the park. I stood up and hurried behind him, but not fast enough to catch up. I followed him, ensuring there was enough distance between us, assuming I'd call his name any second, or maybe just eventually.

He lengthened his stride. He didn't look back.

By the park's exit, I stopped. Alfred featured as a blot against the crowd. A street performer, his body and clothes painted gold, was staring at me. Then his posture changed. He leaned forward on a golden cane. He was pointing toward his tip bowl, positioned in front of his feet.

A woman walking by tossed in a few dollars. The golden man bowed his head. The blue velvet of the woman's jacket and the silver toggle of her shoes shimmered in the sun. She was the same woman from the dentist's office, I realized, the one who had been staring at the aquarium with the unusual creatures. The timing of her entrances into my life gave me pause. She'd appeared on the first day I met Alfred, then right after Vilma found us together, and now again, when he had just walked off. I ran my finger over the smooth surface of the kambaba jasper inside my pocket. The stone was calming, as Alfred had promised.

"Can you believe it?" the woman said, moving her blue-sleeved arm up, toward the sky. "That it's finally spring, after all that?"

She skipped along the sidewalk in the same direction as Alfred had. Once she vanished, I was certain I'd never see her or Alfred again. I turned down a tree-lined street and headed toward NYU. Scraggly branches hovered above my head. A clustering of buds, at the end of the twigs, were just about to bloom.

# ACKNOWLEDGMENTS

CLAIRE ROBERTS AND ALYSSA OGI—YOU ARE MY NORTH Stars in the publishing wilderness. This wouldn't have happened without you. Meg Storey. Lisa Dusenbery. Beth Steidle. Elizabeth Gaffney. Jennifer Croft and Idra Novey for their generous praise. Everyone attending the Public Space writing workshop. Anna Katsnelson. Coleman Bigelow. For enduring my even earlier drafts—Jeno Pineda, Megan Paonessa, Flavia Zgjani, Kledja Aliskenderaj. My dear Dorothy Mazlum. My mentor and friend Tom Grimes. Every professor and student I encountered at Texas State. Debra Monroe. My friend Richard—your infectious love for books and films kept me afloat. My beta readers: Ken, Barbara, Emily Leish. My warrior writer friends Maisy Card and Meryl Branch-McTiernan. Sage Jacobs. And Matthew, who's read more drafts than he cared to, without complaints, perspicacious and kind as ever. Thank you!

TODD ESTRIN

**LEDIA XHOGA** is an Albanian American fiction writer and playwright. Before getting an MFA in fiction from Texas State University, she worked in publishing in New York City. She has been published in *Intrepid Times*, *Hobart*, and other journals. Originally from Tirana, Albania, she lives with her family in Brooklyn and the Catskills.